NEVER EVER GETTING BACK TOGETHER

TOGETHER

PHOEBE MACLEOD

Boldwood

First published in Great Britain in 2023 by Boldwood Books Ltd.

Cover Design by Head Design Ltd

Cover Photography: Shutterstock

A CIP catalogue record for this book is available from the British Library.

Paperback ISBN 978-1-83751-430-4

Large Print ISBN 978-1-83751-426-7

Hardback ISBN 978-1-83751-425-0

Ebook ISBN 978-1-83751-423-6

Kindle ISBN 978-1-83751-424-3

Audio CD ISBN 978-1-83751-431-1

MP3 CD ISBN 978-1-83751-428-1

Digital audio download ISBN 978-1-83751-422-9

Boldwood Books Ltd
23 Bowerdean Street
London SW6 3TN
www.boldwoodbooks.com

To my sisters, Frances and Samantha

'Oh, wow! That looks even better than I'd hoped. Thank you so much, Jess, you're a miracle worker!'

Elodie crouches down to inspect the three-tiered wedding cake on its stand and sighs with delight. It's the final tasting of the menu for her wedding breakfast, and the first time she's set eyes on the cake. In some ways, I'm as amazed as her that it actually exists. I've worked with a number of brides over the years, and none have been so prone to sudden changes of mind as Elodie Waters.

'I love the little figurine of me,' she gushes. 'It looks so lifelike, and you've captured the dress perfectly. It does look a little odd without Daniel, though.'

'He'll be there on the day,' I reassure her, 'but, just as he's not allowed to see your dress in advance, he was very clear that you couldn't see what he was going to be wearing.'

'It's so exciting!' she squeaks, clapping her hands in delight. 'I can't wait.'

In truth, making accurate models of the bride and groom in sugar paste has been a massive pain in the backside, mainly because Elodie's indecisiveness has characterised pretty much every element of the wedding, not just the cake. Her dress has been through so many alterations that I suspect it would have been better for her to have started with a completely different design. The problem for me is that, every time she phoned through the latest changes, I had to replicate them on her figurine. Thankfully Daniel, her fiancé, has been much more straightforward. The dark-blue morning coat and top hat were easy. The striped trousers and intricate design on the waistcoat were slightly harder work, but at least he hasn't changed his mind on any of it.

'The top layer is a fruitcake, as you requested. We won't be serving that to the guests; as soon as you and Daniel have made your cut, we'll take it all away to portion up, and we'll put the top layer in a box, like you asked.'

'I'm a traditional girl,' she confides. 'I'm keeping the top layer for my first child's christening.'

'What a lovely idea,' I smile. I have absolutely zero interest in her plans for the top layer, if I'm honest, but it's important for every client to feel that I'm completely fascinated by them, even if they've been driving me insane, as Elodie has been. 'I've changed the bottom two layers to carrot cake, as we discussed last week.'

I can see the doubt creep into her face, and my heart sinks. *No, Elodie*, I'm silently begging. *We are only a few days away from the wedding, please don't change your mind again.*

'Are we sure that's the right thing?' she asks. 'What if some people don't like carrot cake? Should we go back to the coffee and walnut idea for the second layer?'

'Everybody will love carrot cake, darling,' Elodie's mother reassures her. 'It's just perfect as it is.'

Elodie's face clears, and I briefly want to hug her mum. 'You're right, Mum,' she says. 'It's just so hard to keep on top of everything.'

'You're doing a brilliant job, sweetheart,' her father adds. 'I guess you and I need to settle up then, Jess?'

I hand him the envelope containing the invoice and watch as he opens it and scans every line.

'Does it include the, ah, discount?' he queries after he's checked it thoroughly.

'Terry's a born haggler,' Elodie's mother interjects proudly. 'He doesn't pay full price for anything, do you, darling?'

'I know it's my daughter's wedding, but I'm a businessman at heart,' he replies, self-importantly. 'This is a transaction like every other. Jess wants to get as much money as she can out of me, and I want to pay as little as I can get away with. I prefer to call it negotiation rather than haggling. Somewhere between the two prices is a figure we can both be happy with, isn't that right, Jess?'

'Absolutely,' I reassure him. 'You'll see here that I've taken off the five per cent on food and corkage, as we agreed.' I indicate the line on the invoice.

'What about staff?'

'I can't do anything there, I'm afraid. I pay them exactly what I charge for them, so there's no fat to trim. I'm sure a businessman like you can understand that.'

The small but deliberate stroke of his ego has the desired effect, and he hands over his gold charge card with a flourish.

'I don't know about anyone else,' he remarks, 'but my bank account will certainly be glad when this wedding is over. You're bankrupting me, Elodie.'

'Thank you, Daddy,' she simpers at him, and I resist the urge to throw up.

'If you wouldn't mind just entering your PIN,' I ask him, after entering a figure just shy of sixteen thousand pounds into the card reader. He glances at the total, harrumphs and enters his number. A few seconds later, the machine spits out the receipt and the transaction is done.

'Perfect,' I tell him. 'My team and I are very much looking

forward to taking care of you on Saturday. Good luck with all the other preparations, Elodie. You're going to make a smashing bride, I'm sure.'

'Thank you!' she beams.

'Right, now that's dealt with,' her father remarks. 'I think we've earned a drink. See you on Saturday, Jess.'

Elodie hangs back as her parents make for the door.

'Is everything OK?' I ask her, praying that she hasn't thought of a last-minute amendment.

'Yes. I've been meaning to ask you something.'

'Go on.'

'Every time I see you, I can't help feeling that you look vaguely familiar. Have we met before?'

I smile as genuinely as I can. 'I don't think so.'

'Oh, OK.'

As soon as they leave, I lock the door behind them and turn to my business partner, Alice, who has been observing from the kitchen doorway.

'What do you think?' I ask her.

'She is a spectacularly irritating young woman, but you've pulled a blinder as always. Shame about the five per cent discount though.'

'Oh, I wouldn't worry too much about that,' I smile.

'Really?'

'The thing is,' I confide, 'I inflated the prices a little before I applied the discount. Call it un-mates rates if you like. In many ways, I'd have preferred it if they'd gone somewhere else.'

'Why? You love doing weddings, and they're very profitable.'

'Not this one.'

'Because?'

'She may not have recognised me, but I do know her. We were at school together. To be fair to her, I look very different now.'

'Ooh. This I have to hear. Is it going to be a *Mean Girls* type setup, where Elodie is one of the plastics who made your life a misery, and that's why you have to conceal your identity from her?'

'Not quite. She was a bit of a queen bee in our year, as much as we had one. Her father used to drop her off every day in a Mercedes with blacked out windows and a personalised number plate. That kind of thing stood out at my school. She also lived in this big, detached house out in Sturry and she threw the most amazing parties. So she was popular.'

'Was she mean?'

'No, not as far as I know. Anyway, she was my best friend Laura's friend more than she was mine, so I didn't really have much to do with her. She was very much of the "how far can I roll up my skirt before I get told off and how tight can my top be" school of thought, where I was more...'

'Let me guess,' she interrupts. 'More of a Billie Eilish vibe.'

'How did you know?'

'I remember meeting you on our first day at catering college,' she says. 'Dressed from head to toe in black, shapeless clothing. I wasn't entirely sure if you were a girl or a boy until you spoke, and that was nearly a week later.'

'I had a few body confidence issues, OK?' I remind her.

'I know. Anyway, we're getting off topic. She sounds like she was pleasant enough, so I'm not seeing any reason why you might have it in for Elodie yet,' Alice observes, 'beyond her silly name at least. Who calls their child Elodie? It's like Melody with the M missing. What are her siblings called? Imphonie and Oncerto?'

'I don't hate her,' I tell her when we've finished laughing. 'She was the ringleader of a clique, and I didn't fit in to any of the groups particularly. Her clique was also really pally with some boys who had formed a band. They were moody, gothic types, you know?'

'Incredibly pretentious, you mean?'

'Looking back on it, yeah, you're right. But you have different views of these things as a teenager, don't you? They were obviously destined for stardom, or at least that's what they thought, and I think a lot of people went along with it. They never actually played any sets anywhere as far as I know, but they were always rehearsing and only the select few were allowed to hear their stuff.'

'And this wasn't you, I'm guessing.'

'Of course not. I was Miss Invisible in my baggy clothes. But Elodie and her friends would have long conversations in the canteen about how deep the lyrics of their latest song were, you know, just to make the point that they were "in" and the rest of us were "out". It pissed me off.'

'Why? It doesn't sound like you wanted to be part of their group.'

'It's the fact that there was a group, and it was exclusive. That kind of thing just gets up my nose.'

'Let me get this straight. She was popular and hung out with a group of boys who thought they were their generation's answer to The Smiths, but probably all work in accountancy now, and this is grounds to dislike her?'

'When you say it like that, it does seem a little petty, and I didn't actively dislike her. I just didn't particularly *like* her.'

'Were you jealous of her?'

'No. Why would I be?'

'I don't know. Maybe you secretly wanted to be like her, or you wanted to be in with the band like she was.'

'Definitely not,' I say firmly. She's getting worryingly close to the truth, and I need to deflect her. 'And anyway, it's not as if I didn't have any friends. There was Laura—'

'—who was also friends with her. Was that difficult?'

'You're reading way too much into this, and you just said yourself how irritating she is.'

'That's based on my real-time observation that she appears to be a spoiled, vacuous little tart with a silly name who needs to learn how to make a decision and stick with it, rather than some imaginary secondary school slight. Much more solid evidence, I reckon. Anyway, back to the wedding. Tell me about the un-mates rates.'

'I'd barely met her father before he was telling me what a brilliant businessman he was, and that he wouldn't be taken for a ride. "Good business is all about negotiation, getting something for the right price," he kept saying. So I slapped a little markup on all the prices I gave him.'

'That's risky, isn't it?' She doesn't sound altogether pleased.

'It was a gamble, I agree. But, given how impossible she's been, I almost wish I'd charged more.'

'Fair enough.'

'Anyway, the point is that it gave me wiggle room to give him his discount without impacting our margins. He thinks he's got a good deal and we're not out of pocket. Everybody wins.'

'If you say so.'

'Look, we've both come across his type before: tin-pot entrepreneurs who like to think they've got one over on everyone else. He's the kind of guy that would buy an empty beluga caviar tin for a quid on eBay, fill it with lumpfish caviar and try to pass it off as the real deal. He was always going to try to screw me down on the price. I just made sure I left room for him to do that.'

'Fine. Shall we look at the rotas for next week, or is there somewhere you need to be?'

'Let me consult my crowded social calendar,' I joke as I mime flicking through a diary. 'Ah, here we are. I have absolutely nothing else going on this evening, or any other evening for that matter.'

'Your prince is out there, you know. How is he ever going to find you if you're always hiding away?'

'Maybe I'll trip over him at the wedding while I'm carrying a tray of canapés. It'll be the dill pancakes with salmon caviar and lemon crème fraiche. Some of the crème fraiche will get onto his jacket and I'll have to wipe it off with a napkin. As if by magic, our eyes will meet and stirring music will start playing in the background. Does that help?'

'When did you have your heart broken and become such a cynic?' she laughs.

I smile. As far as Alice knows, I've always been firmly single, apart from a few disastrous dates on the occasions that she's tried to set me up with someone. The truth is that I did have my heart profoundly broken and, although I was certain that I'd got over it and moved on, seeing Elodie again has stirred up some very unwelcome memories. *That's* why I don't want to do this wedding.

2

_____

'How many people do you think you need for Saturday?' Alice asks me, once we've finished the shop rotas, which are fairly simple.

We talk it through together, totting up the numbers as we go. As well as the chefs, who will come from our commercial kitchen, we also need waiting staff, who we employ on a casual basis, so we spend a lot of time ringing around to see who's available, and it's nearly eight o'clock in the evening by the time we're done. Alice looks at her watch and sighs.

'Another late night. I'll be getting "the talk" from Richard again soon at this rate.'

'Which talk?' I ask.

'You know, the one where he reminds me that I didn't give up a well-paid career at a top consultancy firm to work even longer hours for less money.'

'Do you ever regret changing direction?'

'God, no! Starting this business with you has been one of the best things to happen to me.'

'Apart from your husband and daughter, obviously.'

'They kind of go without saying. But one of the reasons I

changed career was that I was supposed to be around more for Mia.'

'You have been. You were there to drop her off at the school gate pretty much every morning and pick her up every afternoon when she was little. You wouldn't have been able to do that if you'd been working in London, would you? How many parent-teacher meetings have you missed?'

'None.'

'Exactly.'

'You're right. Plus, I quite often feel she doesn't need me any more. These days, I'm just the embarrassing mum that has to be kept as far as possible from school and her social life.'

'Yeah, well we can all remember what it was like to be fourteen.'

'It was more recent for some of us than others,' she smiles.

I think back to when Alice and I met for the first time, the day we both started catering college. I was incredibly nervous and I think she picked up on it. We ended up sharing a workbench and, despite the ten-year age gap, soon became firm friends. My original plan was to find a job at the end of the course, gain some experience and then set up an external catering company. Alice, on the other hand, was always going to go solo from the outset. Her view was that her experience as a consultant meant she knew how to run a business, and she obviously knew how to cook, so she was ready to go. I found her enthusiasm infectious and practically bit her hand off when she asked if I'd come and work for her. By the time we'd spent countless hours finessing the business plan together, her idea had grown from a simple tea shop to an all-day offering, and I'd been upgraded to partner.

'What are you thinking about?' she asks, interrupting my reverie. 'You've gone all vacant on me.'

'I was just thinking back to when we dreamed this all up. I was only two years older than Mia is now when we first met. Scary, isn't it?'

'And yet I couldn't have done it without you. If I'd been left to my own devices, I'd have opened a single tea shop called Alice's Wonderland that probably would have gone out of business by now.'

'It was Richard who pointed out that "Alice's Wonderland" sounded a bit like a cross between the name of a really grim theme park and a euphemism for your vagina, not me,' I laugh.

'That may be true, but it was you that came up with "The Mad Hatter" instead. And it was you who kept pushing for us to expand with more shops and the external catering.'

I grin. 'That's because it wasn't my house on the line as collateral.'

'Do you know, I still have the odd dream where it's all crashed and burned, and we're standing outside helplessly as the bailiffs change the locks on the house.'

'Really?' Given that we're both profitable and a limited company now, which means her house is safe even in the unlikely event the business collapses, the fact that she's still anxious about this comes as a bit of a surprise.

'Yup. It was just such a massive gamble at the start, wasn't it. It's probably PTSD.'

'If it's any comfort, it still terrifies me that I was a partner in a business before I was old enough to have a credit card,' I reply.

We carefully pack the cake back into its boxes and load it into my car so I can drop it back to the kitchen on my way home. Although it is a bit of a faff, we made the decision that we'd always bring clients to one of our three shops for tastings, as they're much more inviting environments than the commercial kitchen, which is on an industrial estate on the outskirts of Canterbury. Since we've branched out into external catering, I spend most of my time at the commercial kitchen, leaving Alice to handle the retail side of things. It generally works pretty well; Alice has Saturdays and Sundays off so she's still around for Mia at weekends, and I usually take Sundays and Mondays, although we're both technically 'on call' if there's a crisis in one of the shops on a Sunday.

'Do you know anything about Elodie's fiancé?' Alice asks me as we secure the final cake box on its foam mat in the boot.

'Why?'

'No reason. I figured that, since you knew her from school, you might know him as well. I was just curious to know whether he's as irritating as she is.'

'Daniel was the drummer in the band I told you about,' I tell her. 'I have no idea what he's like now, but he fitted the stereotype of a drummer pretty well at the time.'

'What do you mean?'

'Not particularly bright. Don't you know the joke about drummers?'

'No.'

'OK, so there's this drummer and he's fed up with everyone calling him stupid, so he decides to learn the guitar. He practices and practices until he's pretty good, and then he goes to a shop and reels off the list of all the cool guitar equipment he wants to buy to the assistant. Only the assistant says, "You're a drummer, aren't you?". "How did you guess?" he asks. "This is a fish and chip shop," the assistant tells him. That's Daniel.'

'Still, they're practically childhood sweethearts. If my experience is anything to go by, that's not a bad basis for a marriage,' she comments.

'Not exactly. She was going out with the lead guitarist at school, so she must have swapped band members at some point.'

'Oh. That's a bit incestuous.'

'Mm. Anyway, he might have improved. I can't see Elodie's dad letting her marry a dunce, can you?'

'You'll be able to find out at the wedding.'

'Not likely. I'm going to be keeping well out of the way, thank you. I have no desire to see any of them again.'

'Isn't there anyone from school that you kept in touch with?'

'Not really. Don't get me wrong, I did have friends, despite not fitting into any of the cliques. It's just that they all stayed on to do A-levels, and I guess we drifted apart.'

'Do you ever wish you'd done that?'

'And miss out on all of this? Not for a minute! I could have done A-Levels if I'd wanted to. I had a decent crop of GCSEs, but—'

'But you didn't see the point of analysing more of Shakespeare's plays. I know,' she interrupts. 'I'm sorry I mentioned it.'

This is a well-worn conversation that we've had many times over the years. I love Alice to bits but, despite regularly telling me how pleased she is to be working with me, she's never really understood why I chose catering college over A-Levels and a degree. The reality is that I couldn't think of a single subject that I wanted to continue with. I considered French, but only because I had this fantasy where I lived in Provence, painting incredible landscapes, smoking Gauloises (even though I practically threw up the one time I tried a cigarette) and drinking cheap red wine in rustic cafés.

It wasn't a totally impractical dream, as I was pretty good at art, but I knew studying Voltaire and writing essays about *Madame Bovary* wasn't going to either interest me or get me any closer to my dream and, if I'm honest, I wasn't actually very good at French. I was rubbish at science, especially Biology (is there anyone in the world who finds plant reproduction interesting?) and Maths bored me witless. Mum and Dad were resistant to me leaving school at first, but eventually they understood where I was coming from and agreed to let me study something vocational at college instead. We pored over the list of courses, crossing out the ones that I was either not interested in (car mechanic and plumber) or not qualified for (quite a few) until we'd narrowed it down to hairdressing or catering, both of which appealed to me by giving me the scope to launch my own business as soon as I was ready.

'Plenty of money in hairdressing, if you're good,' Mum had encouraged. 'Look at Nicky Clarke; he's got to be worth a bob or two.'

'Yeah, but using scissors all day can't be good for you,' Dad had countered. 'If there's ever a recipe for repetitive strain injury, that's got to be it, wouldn't you think?'

'You might be right,' Mum had conceded. 'Plus there's all the chemicals. What if you get the mixture wrong and turn someone's hair green, or it all falls out?'

'That's true, but what if I go into catering and give a whole load of people food poisoning?' I'd pointed out.

'Are we sure there isn't something less risky? What about bookkeeping? Why did we cross that one off?' Dad had asked.

'Because it's basically Maths, and I'd probably die of boredom before I complete the course, plus I don't want to spend the rest of my life stuck in an office adding stuff up!' I'd exclaimed.

In the end, we hadn't quite tossed a coin, but it wasn't much more scientific than that. Dad reckoned that, even if it never went anywhere, at least I'd be able to feed myself after two years on a catering course, and that had decided it.

3

The day of Elodie's wedding is here, and you couldn't wish for better weather; it's been consistently warm and dry all week and the forecast for today is more of the same, with a gentle breeze. I'm sure that will all be lovely for the guests and the photos, but my interest is more down to earth, literally. The reception is being held in an enormous marquee that's been erected in the middle of a field, and we have to get our mobile kitchen trailers, plus our vans full of food, across said field so we can unpack them in the area that's been set aside for us. No provision is ever made for vehicles at these things, so a wet and muddy field would have made life very difficult indeed, both for the guests who will all be parking in the field next door, and for us. We've had to be pulled out of locations like this by friendly farmers with tractors on more than one occasion and, not only does it make us really late getting back to base, but we then have to spend ages cleaning the vans and trailers to get all the mud off.

The trailers are my pride and joy. When I persuaded Alice to branch out into external catering, we looked at all sorts of second-hand mobile kitchens, but they were either too small or so large that you'd need a truck to tow them. These ones, which we ended up buying brand new, are like a kind of cross between a dolls' house and a jigsaw puzzle. When you get on site, all sorts of panels swing open, and there is a series of lightweight poles and canvas sections that go up in no time to make you weathertight. They're designed so that they can either be used on their own, or you can join them together to make a larger kitchen for big events, which is what we'll be doing today. As long as there is electricity, we're good to go. The vans both have small water tanks built in, so we even have our own hot water for washing up.

The only downside of the trailers is that I've never, despite plenty of attempts, managed to learn how to reverse them. It was bad enough when we first got the vans and I had to try to reverse without being able to see out of the back, but the trailers just seem completely counterintuitive in that you have to steer one way to get the trailer to go the other, so I rely on a couple of the chefs who seem to have the knack down to a fine art. Alice's husband has also been known to help out very occasionally, although it's not exactly his forte either and one of the trailers has a dent in the corner caused by a disagreement with a gatepost that he didn't see.

We all assemble at the commercial kitchen at eight, and we're ready to leave an hour or so later. When we pull up on site just after ten, I'm surprised to see that we're not the first to arrive; a van and trailer bearing the logo Bar on the Run is already parked up next to the marquee, exactly where the kitchen is supposed to go.

'Great,' I mutter under my breath as I park my car. From experience, getting other trades to move their vehicles is always a massive pain, as everyone tends to think they're more important than everyone else and they have no idea that we're actually on quite a tight schedule and need to get set up and operating. Martin, from Bar on the Run, is one of the worst. With a sigh, I get out and go in search of him. When I step inside, I have to admit that the marquee looks amazing. As well as the top table, where the bride and groom will be sitting, there are nineteen round tables with ten chairs around each one. Each table has a pristine white tablecloth, and the chairs also have white material covers. Someone is in for a large laundry bill if things get messy. The tables have all been laid with cutlery and glassware, and I can see the boxes of plates and champagne flutes stacked in the corner. Alice and I have had a fair number of discussions over the years about whether we should buy our own cutlery and crockery, but every time we've agreed that it's much less hassle for us to hire it when we need to. Of course, Elodie's dad wasn't prepared to let us do that; he was determined to source it himself and secure his magical discount from a company we'd never dealt with before, so I'm relieved to see that it's actually turned up.

'Are you all right there?' a youngish man with a beard asks me.

'I'm looking for Martin,' I explain. 'I need him to move his van so we can set up the kitchen.'

'You'll have a long search. Martin retired three months ago. I'm George, the new owner. You must be the Mad Hatter lot.' He smiles. 'You don't look mad, if you don't mind me saying.'

'I might get mad if I can't get my kitchen where it needs to be,' I reply coolly.

'Well, we don't want that, do we?' he laughs. 'Give me two seconds to grab the keys.'

To my surprise, he's as good as his word, and it's not long before the kitchen trailers have been manoeuvred into position and we're starting to set up.

'That is a serious piece of kit,' George observes when he wanders out around half an hour later. 'I thought my bar was clever, but that's something else. Let me know when you want to talk booze.'

'Will do. It'll probably take us another thirty minutes or so and then I'll come and find you, OK?' I reply.

He smiles and raises his hand. 'Whenever. I'm not going anywhere.' Unlike his predecessor, he seems genuinely chilled, and I decide I like him.

* * *

'All the wine and champagne is stacked in the van, so it'll be easier for your staff to retrieve it if I park up next to you,' he explains later as he reverses neatly into position next to us. 'Mr Waters has asked for two bottles of red and two of white on each table to begin with. I'll put the red out for you now, but you'll want to hang on and get your staff to put the white out just before the guests arrive, so it's still cool. I've brought ninety-six bottles of each. It's way more than they're going to drink, but nobody wants to be at a wedding where the wine runs out, do they? So, if your staff can keep an eye and replenish the bottles as necessary during the meal, that would be good.'

'That's fine,' I tell him. 'They're used to that, so don't worry.'

'Great. Where we do need to be careful is with the champagne. I've got sixty-four bottles of that, which should be plenty for the arrival drinks and the toasts as long as we get six glasses out of each bottle. In fact, you don't even need to fill the glasses for the toasts, so you might even get seven if you're careful. Mr Waters wants his guests to have a good time, but not too good a time, if you catch my drift.'

'Is this your first wedding since taking over Bar on the Run?'

'No, it's been really busy this season actually, although this has easily been the most difficult. Elodie's father pretty much nailed me to the floor on all the prices. Between you and me, he's a bit of a tight bastard, isn't he?'

'He's also my uncle,' I tell him.

'Oh shit, I'm so sorry. Me and my big mouth. Forget I said anything.' He looks absolutely crestfallen.

'Relax, I'm joking,' I smile. 'I had you going for a minute though, didn't I?'

'I can see I'm going to have to watch you,' he remarks when he's gathered his composure.

'Sorry, I can't help myself. It's part of the training I give to anyone who works for me and I kind of do it on autopilot. Never make remarks about the guests, because you have no idea whether the person you're talking to knows them or not.'

'Good advice; you scared the shit out of me for a moment there. Anyway, have you got any questions about the wine?'

'Nope. That all seems pretty straightforward. Thanks, George.'

'No worries. I'll be behind the bar if you need anything.'

The kitchen swings into action, and the next few hours are a blur of activity. I set the cake up on the table reserved for it, carefully arranging the figurines of Elodie and Daniel on the top. The waiting staff arrive, all dressed in black and white as I've asked, and I take some time out to brief them on the timings and the dietary restrictions. I have a copy of the table plan in the kitchen, and Elodie has marked out the vegetarians and a woman with a gluten intolerance so I know where to send the special meals, but they'll all be milling around when we're serving canapés, so it's important for the servers to know what's in each one if they're asked.

By the time the guests start to arrive at three o'clock, we're in good shape. The servers are out, offering glasses of champagne, buck's fizz and orange juice and passing around the canapés, while we focus on getting the main meal ready. I'm relieved when they all sit down on time at four thirty; it really makes life difficult if we have to start keeping things warm because the bridal party is running late. The starter, a salmon mousse served with smoked salmon garnish and Melba toast, just requires plating up and I settle into the rhythm of running the pass. As soon as the starters have gone, all focus turns to the main: a beef wellington served with roasted root vegetables and a red wine sauce. I smile as I start to send it out, remembering how hard Elodie's dad tried to persuade her to go for the chicken supreme instead as it was a fraction of the price, but Elodie was dead set on the beef. That's got to have hurt him. A quick clear down gets us ready for the dessert: a glazed lemon tart with mascarpone ice cream. Everything flows smoothly and Amelia, one of the servers, even passes a message from Elodie's dad to say how delicious it's all been.

While we're waiting for the speeches and the cutting of the cake, we clean the kitchen, washing up our own equipment and stacking the dirty plates carefully in their boxes to be collected by the suppliers. The main work, for us, is over now. We just have the light buffet to put out for the evening guests, but that's all cold food, thankfully. Despite telling Alice I wanted to keep well out of the way, curiosity gets the better of me and I take the opportunity to stand just outside the marquee and watch as the speeches begin. They're pretty standard wedding fair stuff, but my heart leaps into my mouth when the best man stands to give his speech. I haven't seen him for twelve years but, apart from his haircut, Jamie Ferguson hasn't changed a bit. I was pretty sure he'd be here – I expect all the members of the band probably are – but actually seeing him in the flesh affects me much more than I was expecting, and I'm surprised by the loathing that suddenly fills me. My good mood shattered, I turn away and return to the kitchen, determined to keep well away from Elodie and her guests for the rest of the day.

* * *

Sadly, it's not to be. Amelia comes into the kitchen a few minutes later to say that the bride is asking for me.

'Why? What does she want?' I ask crossly. Amelia is obviously caught by surprise and takes a step back.

'She didn't say,' she tells me. 'She just asked me to come and get you.'

'For goodness' sake,' I mutter as I reluctantly head back towards the marquee. 'This had better be important.'

Once inside, I skirt around the edge towards the top table, trying to be as inconspicuous as possible. I spot George behind the bar, and he gives me a smile, but I'm feeling more and more uncomfortable the closer I get to the top table and Jamie. As soon as Elodie spots me, she stands up and grabs the microphone off the table.

'Ladies and gentlemen, before we cut the cake, I just have a couple of words to say,' she begins. Immediately, the room falls silent and I'm begging for the floor to swallow me up as all eyes turn in our direction.

'I think we can all agree that we've had a wonderful meal,' Elodie continues, oblivious of my mortification, 'and I wanted to introduce you to the amazing woman behind it. This is Jess, everyone, and I'd like you to show your appreciation to her and her team.'

I try to smile as the room breaks out in thunderous applause, but I know it's a rictus grin. I hate being the centre of attention at the best of times, but this is close to being my worst nightmare. Everyone is on their feet now, but all I'm aware of is the man standing a few feet away from me, smiling and applauding along with everyone else and seemingly completely unaware of who I am. I hope he chokes on his champagne.

4

TWELVE YEARS AGO

'Remind me why I'm doing this?' I ask my best friend Laura as I stare into her bedroom mirror, trying to recreate the smoky eye effect that I've been looking at online. It's not a total disaster, but it doesn't look much like the picture I'm using for reference either.

'Because it's the end of GCSEs, because it's the first time you've been invited to a party at Elodie's house and, for you, because Jamie Ferguson is going to be there and it might be the last time you see him. Are you going to muster up the courage and actually talk to him tonight, do you think? Or will you just sit miserably in a corner pining like you usually do when he's around?' She leans in next to me and starts applying her lip gloss.

'I don't pine!'

'You totally do. You sigh wistfully sometimes as well.'

'It's torture,' I tell her, letting out exactly the type of sigh she's just described, which makes her giggle. 'Do you know how much time I've spent listening to Arcade Fire albums in the hope that I'll have something to talk to him about when he finally notices me? And, of course, he never does because he's only got eyes for bloody Sarah.'

Laura is the only person I've ever told about my crush on Jamie, and I swore her to absolute secrecy before I did. The truth is that I've been a bit obsessed with him ever since my hormones kicked in and I first started to see the opposite sex as interesting rather than just annoying. Even Laura doesn't know the full extent of it; yes, of course I've practised signing my name as Jessica Ferguson, but everyone does that when they fancy someone, don't they? What everyone definitely doesn't do is have a strand of his hair, which I plucked ever so carefully off the collar of his shirt when I was sitting behind him in Chemistry one day and stuck into my scrapbook. I've also put a lot of work into designing 'our' monogram: a richly decorated letter J with another J slightly lower and to the right, but with its top wrapped around the tail of the first J. Nobody, not even Laura, has seen that, or the countless prototype versions I discarded before I was happy.

Of course, lots of the girls in our year have a bit of a thing for him, but I know they don't feel like I do. Unlike the others, including (I suspect) his girlfriend Sarah, my love for him runs much deeper than just him being the lead singer in The Misfits. He wasn't even in the group when I first fell for him so, although I admit I waste hours daydreaming about us being snuggled up together discussing his favourite indie bands, or him asking my opinion of his latest song lyrics (which are obviously all about his love for me), there's more to it than that. I know there is, even if I can't describe it.

'What do you think he sees in her?' Laura asks. 'She's not exactly a sparkling personality, is she?'

'Besides her tits, you mean? Oh, I don't know. Maybe her slavish devotion to him?'

'Wouldn't you find that annoying though? It's probably cute for, like, the first week or so, but after that you'd want a bit of personality, wouldn't you? That's why I ended up dumping Tom in the end.'

'You broke his heart, you know that? He cornered me in the canteen after my English Lit exam last week and all he wanted to talk about was you.'

'Really? What did he say?'

'He wanted to know what he needed to do to get you back. For some reason, he thought that I'd know, being your best friend and all.'

'What did you tell him?'

'I stuck to the line: that you needed space, that you were just really confused about a lot of things right now and that kind of stuff.'

'It's true. I do need space and there are lots of things I'm confused about. Just not him. Every time I asked him what he wanted to do—'

'—he said, "Whatever you want to do." I know.'

'That gets old really quickly, I can tell you. I also got a bit bored with him pawing at me every time he thought we were alone. It was like, "Hey, do you think you could stop trying to get in my knickers for five minutes so we could actually have a conversation?"'

'I'll have to take your word for it. The boys aren't exactly queueing round the block to date me, are they.'

'You wouldn't have noticed if they were! You've only got eyes for Jamie.'

'Yeah, well, if it's tits he's after, I've got no hope.' I glance down at my depressingly flat chest.

Since hitting puberty, I've spent my life trying to hide my lack of bust with baggy tops and, on the rare occasions (like tonight) where I'm wearing something a little more fitted, I slip some padding into my bra. I'm hoping against hope that I'll turn out to be some kind of late developer in the chest department but, given that I started my periods when I was twelve, it's looking more and more unlikely. It's like my body has turned against me in some way; my mind is ready to embrace womanhood and everything that comes with it, but the most visible symbol of said womanhood is nowhere to be seen.

I remember Laura being mortified when one of the boys made a derogatory remark about her 'bee stings' in year eight, but at least she's gone on to develop a wholly acceptable B cup. I'm still stuck firmly in my AA or, as someone else put it, the 'why bother' bra. Laura does her best to cheer me up about them, and sends me countless links to online articles with titles like, *Why men secretly prefer small breasted women* and, *Why small breasted women have more fun*, but I'd still give almost anything for a reasonable set of boobs.

* * *

The party is already in full swing when Laura's mum drops us off, clutching our bottles of Coke, plus the secret half bottle of vodka in Laura's handbag that she persuaded her older brother to buy for her. We can hear the thump of the bass from the end of the driveway (yes, Elodie is posh enough to have a driveway) and I feel a mix of terror and excitement as we approach the front door. It takes a couple of goes with the knocker before anyone inside hears us over the din, and then the door is thrown open by a boy I recognise vaguely from our year group.

'Hey, girls,' he yells over the music. 'Come on in.'

'Thanks,' Laura shouts back as we cross the threshold. 'Where's Elodie?'

'No idea,' he laughs. 'She's bound to be around somewhere, though. Drinks are through there,' he points at a doorway, 'and the food's laid out in the kitchen.'

Our exploration of the ground floor reveals a sitting room off to the left, which is where the music is coming from. All the furniture has been pushed to the side, and a few people are dancing in the centre, while others watch from the edge. Laura is looking for

Elodie, I know, but I'm scanning to see if I can spot Jamie. Laura's right about one thing; this might be the last time I see him in the flesh, so I need to make the most of it. He's not in here though, and neither is Elodie.

There is an impressive array of bottles laid out in what is obviously the dining room, on the other side of the hallway. The soft drinks that were probably supplied by Elodie's parents have been handsomely supplemented with beer, cider and quite a few bottles of wine. There is also a bucket of what looks like fruit punch in the middle of the table, which Laura makes a beeline for.

'Fuck me!' she exclaims after pouring some into a glass and taking a sip. 'God only knows what's in that, but it's strong enough to stop a horse in its tracks, I reckon.' She holds the glass out to me and I take a tentative sip. She's right; I can feel the heat of the alcohol in the back of my throat as I swallow. I make a mental note to stay away from the punch; the last thing I want is to make a fool of myself in front of everyone.

'I think I'll have a cider instead,' I say to Laura, grabbing one of the bottles of Strongbow and filling a plastic pint glass. 'It's very brave of Elodie's parents to do this, isn't it? What happens if someone throws up all over the carpet, or the furniture?'

'I don't think they know. They go out before people start to arrive.'

'They must see the empty bottles, though, and realise we haven't just been sitting around drinking Fanta and discussing our homework.'

'Maybe Elodie hides them.'

We finally discover Elodie in the kitchen, where the table is groaning under a mountain of food.

'Hi, you two. Glad you could make it, Jessica,' Elodie says as she spots us.

'Thank you for inviting me. I was just saying how brave your parents are to let you do this. What happens if someone breaks something or chucks up?'

'You chuck up, you clean it up,' she laughs. 'And we hide everything valuable and fragile. Smoking strictly outside only. I guess I've been lucky so far. Thinking of which, I need to go and arrange for the fruit punch to disappear. Someone emptied a whole bottle of gin into it, and the evening will definitely end badly if I don't get rid of it. Help yourselves to whatever you want, yeah?'

She hurries off, and Laura and I wander out onto the patio, where we find one of those outdoor furniture sets you see in lifestyle magazines but nobody has the money or space for in real life. There's a big L-shaped sofa, a table and a number of chairs. A large umbrella is carefully folded away in the middle. Jamie is sitting on the sofa, having what looks to be a fairly intense conversation with Sarah. I'm trying to work out which empty chair would be best to allow me to watch him unnoticed when Laura grabs my arm.

'Oh no. It's waaay too early for that,' she tells me firmly. 'If I let you settle out here then you'll be gone for the whole evening. You have to dance with me first.'

Reluctantly, I let her lead me back inside, where I carefully set my drink down on a sturdy-looking table before joining her in the centre of the room to dance. At one point, I'm vaguely aware of Sarah shouting something in the hallway before the front door bangs, but Laura isn't ready to let me go just yet, so we dance on.

It's probably around an hour and two pints of cider after we've started dancing that my bladder informs me that I need to find a loo. I remember seeing it as we arrived but, as soon as I walk out into the hallway, I realise I'm in trouble.

'Is this the queue for the toilet?' I ask the boy at the end.

'Yup. But I think someone's making out in there or something, because nobody has come out for ages.'

'Is this the only one?'

'There's one upstairs, but I think there's a queue for that one too.'

I run up the stairs to look, and he's right. The pressure in my bladder is getting intense, and I start jiggling my legs to try to alleviate the discomfort. It's no good though. If I don't get to a loo pronto then I'm going to have a very embarrassing accident. Looking around in desperation, I realise that this is the kind of house where the master bedroom is bound to have an en suite. All I need to do is find it. I know it's an invasion of privacy but I'm equally certain that Elodie's parents would rather I used their toilet than wet myself all over their carpet. All the doors apart from the bathroom have big 'No Entry' signs stuck on them, but I carefully open each one in turn until I spot an enormous double bed with, tantalisingly, a door next to it. I creep in and quietly close the door behind me, before pretty much sprinting across the room and bursting through the other door, my hand already unfastening the button of my jeans.

'Ow! Fuck!' a voice exclaims as the door collides with something.

For a moment, I'm frozen in horror. Standing in front of me, with blood pouring out of his nose, is Jamie Ferguson.

5

'What the fuck, Jessica?' Jamie exclaims.

'I'm so sorry. I didn't know anyone was in here,' I babble. 'Are you OK?'

'Of course I'm not OK! You just smacked me in the face with a door!' The blood is pouring out of his nose at a truly impressive rate and I realise that, whatever the rights and wrongs of this, I need to do something about that at least.

'We need to stop the bleeding,' I tell him. 'Sit down on the bath there, lean forward and pinch your nose on the soft part, just above your nostrils.'

He does as instructed, but the blood is still flowing. It's all over the front of his T-shirt and now dripping onto the floor.

'Give it a while,' I reassure him. 'It might take a few minutes but it should work.'

He doesn't reply exactly, but I assume the 'Mngh' noise he makes is assent. I grab some loo roll and hold it out to him.

'To stop any more going on your shirt,' I tell him. 'Hold it under your nose.'

Now that I've dealt with the immediate emergency, I realise that

I'm probably seconds away from another accident. What the hell am I going to do? I can't rejoin the queue for the main bathroom; that will end very badly. Equally, I can't move Jamie until he stops bleeding at least. Shit.

'Umm, Jamie?' I say.

'Yeah?' comes his muffled reply.

'I, err, really need to go.'

'Wha'?'

'I need to wee. Now.'

'Oh. Righ'.' He starts to get up. 'I'll wai' in de be'room.'

He's just about to open the door when a large droplet of blood splatters on the floor.

'Stop,' I tell him firmly, freezing him in his tracks.

'Wha'?'

'You can't go out there. You might bleed on the carpet.'

'Wha' you wan' me to do then?'

I sigh. 'Lock the door, sit back down on the bath and don't look.'

This is just fantastic, I think as he locks the door and I rush over to the toilet. My dream of getting Jamie on his own has finally come true, and so far all I've managed to do is injure him. To make things worse, I'm about to perform an intimate bodily function pretty much in front of him. It's about as far from my daydream of us snuggled up together as it's possible to get. At least I'm hidden from view by the shower cubicle as I hastily whip down my trousers and knickers and plonk myself unceremoniously on the toilet. The relief as I let go is immense, but I'm also scarlet with embarrassment. The noise seems amplified because I'm not alone, and of course a full bladder takes a while to empty, so it just seems to go on and on. By the time it finally finishes, my cheeks feel hotter than the surface of the sun. At least he appears to be as good as his word – he's in exactly the same position on the side of the bath, head down, when I emerge.

'How are you doing?' I ask him gently once I've washed my hands.

'I' seems to be gedding a bi' bedder,' he replies. 'Iss prob'ly broken dough.'

'Not necessarily,' I say as encouragingly as I can. 'But I think you'll probably have a black eye tomorrow, maybe two. People will think Sarah's been beating you up. Speaking of which, do you want me to fetch her?'

'She's gone 'ome,' he replies.

'Oh.'

I settle myself next to him on the bath. I do feel really bad about hurting him, but I'm not sure what to do that I haven't already done. Glancing down, I can see a reasonable amount of blood on the floor, but I'll be able to mop that up with loo roll once he stops bleeding. However, his white T-shirt hasn't fared so well, and I'm horrified to spot the Arcade Fire logo on it, which means it's bound to be one of his favourites.

'Let's have a look,' I say to him, after a few more minutes have passed. He carefully lifts his head and releases the grip on his nose. The initial gush has definitely stopped, but there's still a slow drip.

'Nearly there,' I encourage. 'Back into position for a few more minutes, and I reckon you'll be good as new.'

'Unlikely,' he replies as he grips his nose and dips his head again. I feel very awkward sitting so close to him and I'm aware that I'm fidgeting, so I take the opportunity to grab some loo roll, which I dampen under the tap and then use to wipe the blood off the floor between his legs. I'm filled with relief when he raises his head again after another few minutes and the bleeding appears to have stopped.

'Oh God, my T-shirt!' he exclaims. Now that he's no longer completely focused on stopping the bleeding, he's staring downwards in horror.

'Take it off,' I instruct him. 'We can wash it in the sink and try to get the worst of the blood out before it gets too ingrained.'

He's just started to pull it over his head, revealing a torso I'm struggling to keep my hands away from, when we're interrupted by someone banging on the door.

'Occupied, piss off!' Jamie shouts, and a male voice on the other side apologises. He gives me a tiny grin and I suppress a giggle.

'I think it might be beyond saving,' he says ruefully as he hands me the shirt.

'We'll never know if we don't try,' I tell him as I run warm water into the basin and plunge the T-shirt in. Immediately, the water turns dark pink.

'See? It's coming out,' I say as I wring the shirt out, empty and refill the sink and repeat the process.

After several goes, including rubbing soap into the shirt, it's a lot better, but there's still a very obvious pink streak.

'I think we may have gone as far as we can for now,' I observe. The water is now stubbornly clear, despite me rubbing over and over the stain with soap and rinsing it. 'Put it in the wash with some stain remover when you get home and that might get the rest of it.' I wring the T-shirt out thoroughly and hand it to him.

'You've done a good job,' he observes. 'There's just one small problem.'

'What?'

He holds the shirt at arm's length and, after a few moments, it starts dripping onto the floor.

'I'm not sure I can put it on like this.'

'OK. Hang on.' I start rootling through the cupboards.

'What are you looking for?' he asks.

'Hair dryer.'

'I don't think you're supposed to use them in bathrooms, are you? It's probably out there somewhere, if it's anywhere. Why don't

I hang it on the towel rail and let it drip for a bit. Once the worst is gone, I'll probably be OK to put it on.'

I consider my options. Now that he's stopped bleeding, he seems to have cheered up. I study his nose and, although there are a few stains around it from the blood, it doesn't appear to have any lumps on it, or be deviated to one side. In fact, it looks just as perfect as it ever has.

'Are you able to breathe OK?' I ask.

'It feels a bit snotty and sore, but apart from that, it's fine,' he replies as he hangs his shirt on the towel rail.

'I really am sorry,' I tell him.

'Don't sweat it. It was an accident.'

'What were you doing in here anyway? This is out of bounds, you know.'

'I could ask you the same question!'

'I was desperate, in case you didn't notice. The queues for the toilets are ridiculous.'

'Standard party rule,' he smiles.

'What do you mean?'

'It's not a party until someone has stormed out in a huff, someone else is crying in the kitchen and people are making out wherever they can grab a bit of privacy. Bathrooms are popular because you can lock the door.'

'Eww,' I say. The irony that I'm in a bathroom with a semi-naked man myself isn't lost on me, particularly as I can't take my eyes off him and my hormones are starting to make me feel quite giddy.

'Why did Sarah go home?' I ask. My plan is to calm myself down by talking about his girlfriend. By making her a real presence in the room, I hope I'll be able to resist the urge to run my hands over his bare chest.

'We had an argument. We've split up,' he tells me, matter-of-factly.

Oh damn. The hormones have just ramped up a notch.

'Lots of couples argue though, don't they? This is probably a temporary thing. She'll sleep on it and see sense in the morning.'

'I don't think so. She got all upset over nothing again and I told her I'm getting a bit tired of dealing with her emotions all the time. Her moods are like Jekyll and Hyde, and I don't think I can take any more of it. Given the names she called me as she left, I think we can be fairly sure she won't "see sense", as you put it. That's why I was up here. It was all super intense and I just needed a quiet space to chill for a minute. I started in the bedroom, but I felt like some kind of pervy stalker in there, so I retreated in here. I was just coming out when—'

'—when I arrived.'

'Exactly.'

I grab some more loo roll and gently wet it. 'I'm going to try to clean up your nose, OK?' I tell him. He nods and I gently start dabbing and wiping. He winces a couple of times, but I manage to get all of the dried blood off.

'There you go. Good as new.' Without thinking, I lean forward and place a gentle kiss on the tip of his nose.

'What did you do that for?' he asks.

'Shit. Sorry!' I can feel my cheeks heating up again. 'It's something my mum always did after I cut myself or scraped my knee. She'd wipe it clean and then give it a kiss "to make it better." I wasn't thinking.'

'It was nice.' He smiles. 'I'm not sure it totally did the trick though. You might need to try again.'

'Might I?' I laugh. 'Are you sure you're not playing to the gallery for sympathy now?'

'Me? Never!' He smiles again and part of me melts. I lean forward and place my lips against his nose again, letting them linger, closing my eyes and breathing in the scent of him as I do.

'Is that better?' I ask, a few moments later.

'It is,' he replies. 'The problem is that my mouth hurts as well. I wonder if that got caught with the door too.'

'Jamie Ferguson!' I exclaim. 'Are you *flirting* with me?'

'Do you know what, Jessica Thomas? I believe I am.'

'Which reminds me. How do you know my name?'

'What?'

'You've never spoken to me before. I didn't think you even knew I existed.'

'You're kidding, right?'

'No.'

'You are literally the coolest girl in our year.'

'Are you sure I didn't hit more than your nose with the door? You're sounding concussed.'

'Are you telling me you don't know?'

'Know what?'

'Look at Elodie, Sarah, and most of the other girls. They're all into the same things, and secretly competing against each other to have the best boyfriend, the latest fashion accessories, or whatever it happens to be. And then there's you, going completely against all of that and giving precisely zero fucks. You're just completely your own person, and that's why you're cool.'

'Oh.' He's read me completely wrong, but I'm not about to put him right. I quite like his interpretation of me, actually. I reach out and brush his lips with my thumb.

'Is it very sore?' I ask.

'You have no idea.'

Agonisingly slowly, he leans forward and brushes my lips with his. I've read lots of books where people talk about fireworks going off inside them when they kiss, but this is the first time it's happened to me. It feels *incredible*.

As the kisses deepen, I reach out and place my hands on his

chest. The feel of his skin against mine is electric, and I press myself further into him.

'Ow! Watch the nose,' he murmurs.

'Sorry,' I whisper back. I'm aware of his hands snaking under my top, which would normally make me freeze with insecurity, but I want him so much that I don't care. I crave the feel of his hands on me, and before I know what I'm doing, I'm pulling off my top as we stand up and press ourselves against each other. His hands move to my backside, pulling me against him, and I feel dizzy with desire.

* * *

'Fucking hell, that was intense,' he gasps a while later as he carefully withdraws from me. I watch, mesmerised, as he slides the condom off, ties a neat knot near the top, wraps it in loo roll and flushes it down the toilet.

To my astonishment, I'm completely naked. On the one hand, this isn't a surprise – we kind of took it in turns to remove each other's clothes – but now that I'm coming back to reality, I feel incredibly self-conscious all of a sudden, especially as I remember the bra padding. Thankfully, he didn't make any comment when he came across it, but I feel like a fraud for wearing it now.

'You are amazing, Jessica,' he tells me as I hurriedly start gathering my clothes together and covering myself up. 'Can I see you again?'

'I should bloody hope so! Just so you know, I'm not in the habit of ripping my clothes off for people I don't intend to see again.'

He reaches into his jeans pocket and pulls out his phone. 'Give me your phone number. I'll text you tomorrow and we can hang out.'

'I'd like that,' I tell him as I read out the number and he enters it.

'I'll be thinking about you all night,' he breathes huskily, leaning forward and kissing me again.

'I'll be thinking about you too,' I reply.

'You'd better go on ahead of me. I'll stay here for a bit longer until my shirt dries. I think we might need to fly under the radar for a bit, otherwise people will accuse me of having moved on too quickly.'

'You're right.' I kiss him hungrily one more time before getting to my feet and quietly unlocking the bathroom door. 'See you tomorrow.'

I feel like I'm floating as I descend the stairs in search of Laura. I've just lost my virginity to the boy of my dreams, and tomorrow is going to be the start of a whole new chapter for me. I don't think I could be any happier.

6

PRESENT DAY

Jamie doesn't choke on the champagne, more's the pity. As soon as the applause dies down, I slip out of the marquee and back to the kitchen. At least none of the guests appear to have recognised me; that's some kind of blessing, I suppose.

You'd think that, after twelve years, I would have managed to put it behind me and move on. And I did, by basically cutting all of them out of my life, even Laura in the end. Nothing but a completely fresh start was going to save me from the burning humiliation Jamie inflicted on me, and that's what catering college and my friendship with Alice has done. Now though, seeing Jamie up close, it feels like it all happened yesterday.

After I left him in the bathroom at Elodie's house, I spent the rest of the evening in a daze of happiness. Laura kept asking me what I was grinning about, but I couldn't tell her because of my promise to Jamie that we'd stay under the radar for a while, so I just made something up about being relieved that my exams were over, and the effects of the cider. I'm not sure she believed me, but I didn't care.

Jamie had reappeared after a while and I heard a few people

asking about his shirt, and him replying that he'd been clumsy and walked into a door. I felt a little flip in my stomach every time our eyes met, and when he surreptitiously winked at me, the elation was almost too much to bear. Not only was I going out with Jamie Ferguson, the love of my life, but we already had a secret.

When my phone pinged with a text from him the following morning, I rushed up to my room to read it. I'd already spent ages deciding what to wear for our first proper date, right down to my favourite underwear in case we 'did it' again. I opened the message and read:

Hi Jessica. Sorry but I won't be able to hang out with you today. Sarah came round this morning and we've had a long chat. We've decided to give things another try. I hope you understand. She doesn't know what happened, so I'd be grateful if you didn't say anything. J.

I can still remember every single feeling that passed through me. At first, I couldn't believe it. I reread the text several times in case there was a mistake, but the words were the same each time. He'd fed me a load of bullshit that I'd stupidly lapped up, before taking what he wanted and callously dumping me the moment his idiot ex-girlfriend fluttered her eyelashes at him. He hadn't even had the decency to tell me face-to-face, or even ring me up; he did it by text so he could avoid the fallout. That brought on the rage, and I flew out of the house and was halfway to his (yes, of course I knew where he lived; that's entry-level stalking) before I realised that there was no way confronting him could make things better for me. I could see it clearly: him standing there with his arm around Sarah, casually denying that anything had happened between him and me. He would have made me sound like a lunatic, and I was humiliated enough.

That was the point at which the tears had started, and they

didn't stop for weeks. I couldn't talk to anyone about what I was going through, and I hated myself for being so naïve and practically handing him my virginity on a plate. It was supposed to be one of the best summers of my life, but it ended up being the worst. By the time I started college, even Laura was starting to lose patience with me.

My unwelcome trip down memory lane is interrupted by a scuffle in the doorway.

'I'm sorry, you can't come in. This is a private area,' Ken, one of the chefs, is saying.

'I don't give a damn about that. Let me through,' an all-too familiar voice replies, and I slowly turn to face the speaker.

'The others may not have recognised you,' the woman says to me, 'but I'd know that face anywhere.'

I look her up and down. She's instantly familiar, but also different. The huge pregnancy bump is the first thing I notice, and I wonder if I should get her a chair. Her dark hair shines in the harsh overhead lighting; I suspect some expensive products have gone in there. She looks older, but her smile is exactly as I remember seeing it so many times. This reminder of my past is thankfully much more welcome.

'Hello, Laura,' I say.

'Twelve years without so much as a postcard, and that's all you've got?' she accuses.

'Well, I'd hug you, but you look like you're about to pop,' I tell her. 'We've just finished clearing up in here, so the last thing I need is you giving birth and making a mess. When's it due?'

'Not for another month, would you believe. It's like having an alien in there. Look at you, though. You look so... grown up.'

It's true that I do look quite different. While I'm by no means overweight, working around food all day every day does mean that I'm curvier than when I was at school. The longed-for breasts finally decided to make an appearance when I was eighteen. They're still not big, but I can wear a fitted top with confidence. My mousey hair now has blonde highlights, and I keep it fairly short in a pixie cut, which is much easier than forcing long hair into a hair net all the time.

'So,' she says expectantly, 'fill me in.'

'You first,' I reply with a smile, 'just in case you go into labour.'

'Fair enough. Highlights are a degree in Psychology from Nottingham University, job in PR where I met my husband, Kevin, and first baby due in a month.'

'Wow, that really is the abridged version!' I laugh. 'OK. Catering college and started this business with my partner, Alice.'

'Oho, your *partner* Alice. Are you a lesbian now?'

'Business partner Alice, and no, I'm not.'

'Oh right, sorry. It's just your summary didn't include relation-ship status, so when you said partner—'

'Relax, I get it. There's no relationship status to share though. I'm married to my work.'

'You're very good at it, if the wedding breakfast we've just had is anything to go by. I wish we'd had you at our wedding. We had one of those all-inclusive packages at a stately home and the food was dire.'

'How long have you been married? That's proper adulting, that is.'

'Two years. We spent the first few years saving up for the deposit on our house and then it was a few more years after that before we had the money to get married, so it's been a bit of a journey.'

'Do you still live locally?'

'No, Wolverhampton.'

'Bloody hell, that's the other side of the country! How did you end up there?'

'I probably should have mentioned that the PR firm is in Birmingham, so we need to be reasonably close to there. It's only a thirty-minute commute from Wolverhampton on the train. What about you?'

'I've got a flat in Canterbury. Nothing special, but it's enough for me. I assume, by the fact that you're here, that you stayed in touch with Elodie.'

'Yeah. I needed a new best friend after you vanished into your college and refused to come out to play any more, and Elodie was there for me,' she says, trying and failing to look suitably mournful.

'I'm really sorry,' I tell her. 'I had quite a lot of stuff to deal with and I think I just shut everyone out.'

'Shit happens. I'm just glad to see you doing so well. I can't believe Elodie didn't recognise you, though. It's obvious she doesn't have a clue who you are.'

'She was always much more your friend than mine.'

'I suppose so. Hey, Jamie Ferguson is here, did you see? I couldn't help noticing that he appears to be on his own.' She waggles her eyebrows suggestively.

'No, Laura. Just no, OK?'

'Are you sure? I was just thinking that if he's single, and you're single...'

'Leave it. I'm completely over him. Not interested.'

Thankfully, she takes the hint and lets it drop.

The guys are packing up the kitchen now so we grab a couple of chairs and settle in the corner of the marquee for a catch up. She introduces me to her husband, who seems nice but forgettable. I spot a number of my former classmates either on the dance floor or sitting at tables chatting, but none of them seem to be giving us more than a cursory glance, which is just fine by me. A few people do congratulate me on the food as they pass, which is nice. Elodie is completely wrapped up in Daniel, and I'm not sure she's even aware that there are other people here. It is lovely to see Laura again, and I'm really happy that we've been able to pick our friendship back up pretty much as if nothing has happened, but I'm not ready for this to turn into a full school reunion. Every so often, my eyes drift to the top table to see if Jamie has died from the concentrated force of my loathing for him, but he's engaged in conversation with Elodie's dad and looks like he won't be escaping any time soon. Maybe Elodie's dad is explaining to Jamie what a brilliant businessman he is at length and in considerable detail. That wouldn't be as good a punishment as Jamie dropping dead, but it would be a start at least.

* * *

The party is still going strong at eleven, but my part is thankfully done, and I start loading the last bits and pieces from the cold buffet into my ancient Volvo estate. Alice has been gently suggesting that I might like to think about replacing it because she thinks it gives off the wrong image, but it's never let me down, so I really don't see the point. The vans and kitchen trailers are long gone; they should be safely parked up at the unit by now. I dare to give Laura a squeeze, and we exchange numbers with all the usual promises to keep in touch. She's invited me up to Wolverhampton, but I suspect that won't happen because, quite apart from my fairly intense work schedule, she's going to have her hands full once the baby comes. I hope we'll manage fairly regular phone calls, though.

A few guests are starting to leave as well, so I wait for a gap before pulling out onto the lane. As the marquee and the field start to recede from view, I can feel myself relaxing. I turn on the stereo and begin singing along to the Abba CD that is currently in there. It's shiny, happy music, which is just what I need after the events of today. Even the fact that I'm on a single-track road with passing places, which I normally find very stressful, can't dampen my relief at having got away with it. I don't even know what I'd have said to Jamie if he'd recognised me. I try to play it out in my head.

Jamie: *'Hello Jessica. You're looking good.'*

Jessica: *'Fuck off, wanker.'*

Jamie: *'I guess I deserve that. If it means anything, I'm sorry, OK?'*

Jessica: *'So am I.'*

Jamie (looking hopeful): *'Really?'*

Jessica: *'Yeah. Sorry I met you, sorry I bought your bullshit, incredibly sorry I slept with you, but mostly sorry you haven't had the decency to die in a bizarre industrial accident...'*

My reverie is interrupted by a strange noise from under the bonnet. It's a kind of rhythmic banging, as if something is loose in there. Straight away, I start to lose power, and then there's a much bigger bang and the engine stops completely.

'Bloody hell,' I mutter grimly as I coast into one of the passing places and turn on my hazard lights. I turn the key to see if I can restart the engine, but the awful noises from under the bonnet make it perfectly clear that the only way this car is going any further is on the back of a breakdown truck. With a few more muttered curses, I reach for the AA card in the glovebox and my phone.

The universe has obviously turned against me. Not only do I not have any signal on my phone, but when I open the door slightly to turn on the overhead light so I can read the AA card, I notice that my cover actually expired just over a year ago. What the hell am I going to do now?

After a few minutes of paralysis, I realise that I'm probably just going to have to pay someone a fortune to rescue me. If I can get to somewhere with a signal, I can at least go online and do a bit of research. The question is, which way to walk? I passed through a village a mile or so back, and there might be a signal there, but I'm probably also only a mile from the main road, and there's bound to be signal there too. I'm still weighing up my options when I notice a pair of dazzlingly bright headlights coming up behind me. There's so little traffic on this road that I reckon it's got to be a wedding guest. Maybe they'll give me a lift to the main road.

I step out of the car to flag them down, but I needn't have bothered, as the car pulls in behind me, its engine burbling. As I walk up to the driver's door, the window glides down and I realise the universe still has one more joke up its sleeve.

'Are you OK? Do you need help?' Jamie asks.

7

Of course it's him; talk about an impossible situation. I briefly consider telling him that everything is fine, that I just stopped for a moment because something was moving about in the boot. I could do that – there is bound to be another guest along in a while – but then I see that his headlights are clearly illuminating the slick of oil oozing out from under my car.

'I'm no mechanic,' he observes as he gets out and spots the oil, 'but that doesn't look good. Have you called the breakdown service?'

'Yes,' I lie. I'll just tell him they're on their way and he'll leave me alone to wait for the next guest to rescue me.

'You must be on a good network,' he says. 'I haven't had any signal for the last few miles. Which one are you on?'

Why won't he just go away?

'Vodafone,' I tell him, hoping against hope that it's not the same network he's on.

'They're obviously better round here than EE then. How long did the breakdown people say they would be?'

'Oh, very quick. I explained that I was a woman on my own and they said they'd send someone straight over.' *Please, please just go away.*

'They always say that, but I'm not sure it means anything. Would you mind if I waited for them with you? I know you don't know me, so if you want to wait in your car with the doors locked, I'll just sit in my car behind until they come.'

Without waiting for an answer, he climbs back into his car and turns on his hazard lights as well. In the dark of the lane, the two sets of flashing lights make it look like the scene of a major accident. I climb back into the Volvo and try to work out what to do. After a while, another car comes along and slows as if it's going to stop, but I see Jamie's hand waving them on. It's a matter of moments before their tail-lights disappear round the next bend and Jamie and I are alone again.

This just keeps getting worse and worse. Jamie thinks he's being a white knight by waiting with me until the rescue service arrive, but nobody is coming. I've got no chance of hitching a lift with another wedding guest while he's sitting behind me, merrily waving them on. If I admit to him that I lied, he's going to want to know why. It's obvious from the way he's acted that he doesn't recognise me, so I'm going to look pretty stupid. I'm literally paralysed with indecision.

After twenty minutes have passed, each one of them agonising, I see him open his door and watch in the wing mirror as he approaches and taps on the glass. Maybe he's bored and he's going to leave me after all, I think. That would be a result. I wind down the window.

'I just wondered,' he says, 'whether it's worth giving the breakdown service another call to see how far away they are. Sometimes they need a little reminder, if you know what I mean.'

Now what? I try to think fast.

'Oh, umm, yes. That is a good idea. Why don't you go back and sit in your car while I do it? I don't want you to get cold and you know how long these people take to answer. I'll come and tell you as soon as I've got through.'

'Don't worry about me. I'll wait here.'

Of course he will. I feel like a fly caught in a spider's web; the more I wriggle to try to free myself, the worse the situation gets. I know – I'll pretend to make a call and maybe that will satisfy him. I pull out my AA card and carefully tap the number into my phone. It won't make any difference as I haven't got any reception, but it needs to look right. What if he's one of those weirdos who remembers telephone numbers for fun and knows the number for the AA off by heart? I saw this TV programme once where this guy came on and could basically recite the registration plates of every car every member of his family had owned in his lifetime. What a waste of brain space.

I press the dial button and hold the phone to my ear. Straight away, it gives me the no signal beep but I need to play act this like an Oscar winner. My dignity depends on it. I wait for a few moments, then look up and roll my eyes at him.

'We're exceptionally busy but your call is important,' I tell him, trying to get my level of sarcasm just right so as not to arouse suspicion. I've obviously struck the right note, given his amused look. I leave it for as long as I dare, including a few exaggerated eyerolls for Jamie's sake, before launching into my one-sided conversation.

'Oh yes, hello there. I rang earlier to report a breakdown? Yes, I'm just calling to see if you have any idea when you might get to me. Oh, I see. Yes, I imagine Saturday nights are a busy time for you. Another hour at least? OK, thanks for letting me know. Yes, if you can get someone sooner I would much appreciate it. Thank you.'

I mime hanging up the phone and turn to Jamie.

'They're exceptionally busy,' I tell him. 'The dispatcher said it would be another hour at least. Look, I'm very grateful to you for pulling up, but please don't feel you have to stay. I'll keep the doors locked. I'll be perfectly safe, I'm sure.'

He looks like he's struggling not to laugh.

'What?' I ask him, thrown off course by his strange reaction.

'It was a good performance, I'll give you that,' he grins. 'There were just a couple of, how can I put it, credibility issues.'

'What are you talking about?'

'How did the dispatcher know who you were? You didn't give a name, or even your membership number.'

Oh, bollocks.

'It's, erm, a new system,' I gabble. 'I asked the same question the first time I rang. Apparently, my mobile number is registered on their system so they knew it was me without having to ask for my details.' Despite prickling with the discomfort of piling lie on top of lie, I can't help but be impressed by my ingenuity under pressure. I almost believe myself.

'OK, I'll buy that,' Jamie concedes after pondering it for a moment. 'There's just one more tiny problem.'

'What?'

'There wasn't anyone on the other end of the phone, was there.'

'Of course there was!'

'There wasn't. I don't know if you've noticed, but we're in the middle of nowhere and it's very, very quiet. I would have heard the ringing, the automated voice you impersonated so beautifully, and even the voice of the person you were talking to. I didn't hear any of those things, but what I did hear very clearly was your phone dropping the call. Shall we stop play acting now so you can tell me what's really going on?'

Great. He's completely rumbled me and I've run out of lies to cover myself. I've got one roll of the dice left. Maybe, if I tell him the truth, he'll decide that I'm some sort of lunatic and decide to leave me to my fate. It's humiliating and part of me wants to laugh at the absurdity of it. Each time Jamie and I are alone, it ends up with me looking a complete fool.

'OK, fine,' I sigh. 'I don't have any signal either. Not only that, but I just discovered my breakdown cover expired just over a year ago. I lied in the hope that you'd leave me alone.'

'Why didn't you tell me when I pulled up?' He looks confused but not annoyed. 'You could have just said that you'd rather I left you alone if you didn't feel safe with me.'

'I didn't want to be rude.' *Well done, Jess. Lamest excuse ever.*

'And making me sit in my car for nearly half an hour for no apparent reason, that isn't rude at all?' He's still smiling as if this is all terribly amusing to him. Why can't he just get annoyed and storm off?

'You caught me unawares,' I tell him. 'I was improvising.'

'Have you got a side hustle as an actress?'

'No. Why?'

'I just wondered. You're a brilliant chef, we all know that. Based on the performance you've just given, I'd say you're also a fairly talented actor. Had we been on a busy road where I couldn't hear so easily, you'd have fooled me completely. Maybe you should consider taking it up.'

'Thank you for the careers advice.'

'OK, look. I think it's plain that you don't want me here, and I'm sorry for making you feel uncomfortable. It wasn't my intention. But I can't leave you without at least knowing that you're going to be all right. So, given that you have no mobile reception and your breakdown cover has expired, what's your plan?'

'Before you showed up, I was thinking that I either walk back to the village or I walk up to the main road. I'm bound to get a signal in one of those places.'

He looks horrified. 'Of all the nonsense you've spouted since I arrived, and there has been a lot of it, that is the most insane. Assuming you don't get flattened by a passing car on this tiny lane, have you never watched a single police drama on TV? Stories involving women wandering around the countryside on their own after dark tend not to have happy endings.'

'I was also thinking about flagging down a passing car and asking for a lift,' I reply defensively. 'Most of the traffic on this road at this time of night would be people from the wedding.'

'I'm someone from the wedding!' he exclaims.

I decide to play the card he's just given me.

'Yes, but you're also a man on your own. How do I know you're not going to pull into a farm track a little way ahead and chop me up into little pieces with the machete in your boot?'

'I'm starting to wonder if that might be best for everyone,' he murmurs before realising what he's said. 'I'm joking, I promise. I don't even have a machete in my boot. I'll show you.'

Of course he doesn't have a machete in his boot; whatever I think of him as a person, I know Jamie is perfectly harmless in that respect. However, if I can make him think that I genuinely perceive him as a threat, maybe he'll go.

'That's an ancient trick,' I tell him. 'I'm not falling for that.'

'For what?'

'The old "come and check that there's nothing in my boot" routine. Have you never watched a police drama on TV either? Here's how it goes: you open your boot, I bend down to look inside, and then you bundle me in and drive away. Turns out the machete was on the back seat all along.'

'Very good, Inspector Clouseau,' he laughs. 'You've got me bang to rights. Or at least you would have if there weren't a couple of fatal flaws in your logic.'

'Such as?'

'My car is a two-seater and, please don't take offence, but the boot is so tiny that you wouldn't fit in there even if I chopped you up first. So bundling you in there whole is definitely out of the question. You're good, but your police drama is going to have some serious continuity issues if you carry on down this line.'

Another car comes up behind us and Jamie waves it on.

'Why did you do that?' I ask him. 'They might have given me a lift.'

'They looked like murderers.' He's unable to contain his amusement now. 'Look,' he says when his laughter has died down. 'In all seriousness, let me help you. I'm here and, like I said before, there's no way I can leave until I'm sure you're going to be OK. Why don't I give you a lift up to the main road so you've got reception at least? Will you let me do that? If you're genuinely worried that I might attack you, I'll give you one of my business cards to leave in your car. That way, if you go missing, which I promise you won't, the police will be straight on to me.'

He fishes his wallet out of his pocket and pulls out a business card, handing it to me through the window. I turn the dome light back on and study the card. At the top there are the Jaguar and Land Rover logos, with the name of a dealership between them and *Jamie Ferguson, Sales Manager* in the middle of the card, with address and phone details below.

'It's all legit, before you ask. You can check online if you want,' he tells me.

'I would, if I had any signal.'

He sighs. 'OK, police drama hat back on. Let's say I'm a serial killer on the hunt for my next victim. I think I'd be planning it rather better than this, don't you? Randomly bumping into a stranger who's broken down doesn't seem a very clever victim selection method.'

'You could be a con artist,' I counter. 'This could all be an elaborate fake identity, with driving licence and passport to match.'

He laughs again. 'I could be, but I don't think you'd make rich pickings. I don't want to be rude, but your car hardly screams, "I'm a wealthy heiress", does it? Now, are you going to let me help you?'

I realise, unpalatable as it is, that he really is my only option of getting home before dawn.

'That would be very kind, thank you,' I say flatly, as I open the door and get out of the car.

8

Stepping into Jamie's car is like entering another world. Where the interior of my Volvo is most kindly described as 'lived in', the inside of Jamie's car is spotless. I'm almost scared to sully the buttery soft leather seat with my bum, in case I leave a mark or scratch it. As well as the overhead light, various parts of the cabin are illuminated with a soft blue glow. It quietly screams, 'expensive'.

Jamie closes my door and walks around the front of the car to his side, climbing in and settling himself behind the wheel. He closes the door and looks at me for a moment, a puzzled expression on his face.

'What?' I ask.

'Sorry,' he replies. 'I didn't mean to stare. It's just that you look really familiar, and I admit I've been trying to work out why. Do you ever get that? You see someone and you think you know them, and then you realise that they're not who you thought they were at all?'

I turn and look at him directly. Much as I hate him, he's still very good looking. His dark-brown eyes sit above his perfectly straight nose, making me think that I should have been a bit more forceful with the door the last time I saw him. It would have been nice to leave a permanent reminder of me.

'Umm, sometimes,' I reply. 'Are we going then?'

'Jessica Thomas. That's who you remind me of.'

Oh no.

'Who's she?' I ask stupidly.

'A girl I was at school with.'

My mind is whirling, and I can feel the bile rising inside me. This was a really, really bad idea. I should have forced him to go and leave me. If he works out who I am, there's no way this will end without me telling him a few home truths. Don't get me wrong, I have role played this scenario several times, especially in the early days, but in my head it always happened when I was the one in control, not when he was in the middle of rescuing me.

Sod it. What is the worst he can do? Chuck me out of his snazzy car and leave me to be rescued by literally anyone else? I might never see him again after tonight, and I know part of me will always regret it if I miss this opportunity. Feeling suddenly giddy with the recklessness of what I'm about to do, I open my mouth.

'Oh yes?' I say evenly. 'Tell me about her.'

'Why?'

'I'm curious. If I have a doppelgänger out there, I'd like to know a bit about her.'

'To be honest, I didn't know her that well. We had some classes together, but we didn't move in the same circles. She seemed nice though, if that helps.'

'Don't you think it's odd that you have such a clear recollection of someone you barely knew?'

'When I say that I barely knew her, I mean that I didn't really talk to her. I knew who she was, but we weren't friends, if you know what I mean. She dropped out of school before the sixth form, I do remember that.'

'Do you know where she went?'

'No. Like I said—'

'—you weren't close. I get it. You didn't move in the same circles, you didn't have any conversations with her, you didn't sell her a load of bullshit about how she was the coolest girl in your year, and you *definitely* didn't dump her by text message the morning after you fucked her in Elodie's bathroom.'

The sudden silence in the car after I've dropped my bombshell is deafening. The dome light has gone out now, but I can still see Jamie's face in the glow from the dashboard. He looks like I've slapped him, and there is a long pause before he speaks again.

'Elodie introduced you this evening,' he says numbly. 'She called you Jess…'

'Which is short for Jessica. Well done,' I tell him, sarcastically.

'It's coming back to me now. I think Laura told Elodie that you'd gone to catering college,' he continues.

'That would make sense, given my current profession.'

'The thing in the bathroom at Elodie's party though, that wasn't serious. I mean, you knew that, right?'

He's got to be kidding me.

'What was it then?' I ask bitterly. 'A little distraction shag to help you get over your temporary breakup with your girlfriend? Is that it? Because, let me tell you, it was pretty fucking serious from my perspective.'

'But people hooked up all the time back then.'

'Not me. You were the first person I slept with, did you know that? Stupidly, you see, I believed all that shit you told me about how amazing you thought I was, and how you wanted to hang out and get to know me better. I was into you in a big way. God only knows why, but I was. There's no way I was going to hand my virginity over to just anyone, but when the boy I had the biggest bloody crush on told me he felt the same way about me, I thought I was safe. I thought it was the start of something good. You fucking broke me, Jamie, and I've hated you ever since. Do you understand?'

'Oh, Jessica—'

'It's Jess,' I snap.

'I'm so, so sorry. Why didn't you tell me it was your first time? I would never—'

'Because it never occurred to me at the time that you were just a slimy bastard telling me what you thought I wanted to hear so you could get into my knickers.'

'You really hate me, don't you.' It's a statement, not a question.

'I do, yes.'

'I don't blame you. After hearing that, I kind of hate me too right now. If it's any consolation, Sarah and I broke up again for good a couple of weeks later.'

'Why on earth do you think that would make me feel better? It just makes the whole episode even more pointless because it means you broke my heart for nothing.'

'Is there anything I can say? I get the impression that "sorry" isn't going to cut it, somehow.'

'Anything you could have said, you should have said twelve years ago.'

He smiles ruefully. 'No wonder you were so desperate to get rid of me when I pulled up behind you.'

'Exactly. Are we going then, or shall I let you go on your way so I can be rescued by someone who didn't shit all over me?'

He sits there without moving for so long that I'm starting to wonder whether there's something wrong with him.

'There might not be anything I can say,' he tells me eventually, 'but there is something I can do. Have you got your driving licence with you?'

'Yes. What's that got to do with anything?'

'Can I see it?'

'Why?'

'Just show it to me, will you?'

With a growl of annoyance, I pull my purse out of my bag, extract my driving licence and hand it to him. He turns the dome light on and examines it, before taking a picture of it with his phone.

'What the hell did you do that for?' I ask, grabbing it back. 'Is this your equivalent of collecting scalps? "I always make sure to get a picture of the driving licence of every girl I've fucked. I have quite the collection, do you want to see?"'

He completely ignores me. 'Open the glovebox, will you? You'll find a form in there, as well as a pen. Can you hand them to me?'

'What is this about? You're acting really weird all of a sudden.'

'I'll explain in a minute. Form, please.'

I sigh and do as he asks. I watch as he copies the details from my driving licence onto the form, and then fills in some other boxes.

'Right, sign at the bottom,' he tells me, passing me the form and the pen.

'You're having a laugh. I'm not signing anything until you tell me what's going on and what this is. For all I know, you've decided that you haven't fucked me over enough and this is a deed of proxy to allow you to have me detained under the mental health act so I can spend the rest of my life in a padded cell dreaming of ways to kill you.'

'It's not that, although you were acting very strangely earlier. This car that we're sitting in isn't mine, OK? It belongs to the company I work for.'

'Lovely. What's that got to do with me?'

'It's a demonstrator and, if you sign this form, you're officially taking it for an extended test drive.'

I'm flabbergasted.

'Let me get this straight. You think this whole situation is some sort of *sales opportunity*? If anyone needs their head examined, it's you.'

'I'm not trying to sell you anything, I promise.'

'Just as well. Apart from the fact you're the last person I'd buy a car from, there's no way I could afford something like this. What does it cost, forty grand?'

'Eighty-eight. This one has a few extras, so it's actually ninety-five.'

'Bloody hell! Who spends that much money on a car?'

'We're getting off the point. You sign this form and you can go on your merry way.'

'I'm not driving this!'

'Why not?'

'Because... because it's worth nearly a hundred grand! What if I damaged it?'

'It's insured.'

'So I just take this car and leave you here. What happens to you?'

'Do you care?'

'Not hugely, but I've got a lot of stuff in the Volvo that I don't want stolen, and it sure as hell won't fit in here.' I glance around the car noting the total lack of storage space.

'Look. I have breakdown cover that covers any car I'm in. You take this one, I'll flag down the next wedding guest and call the rescue service once I get to the main road.'

'Listen, Jamie. I understand what this is,' I tell him a little less harshly. 'You feel bad and you want to make it up to me. But you can't, don't you see? You can lend me all the flashy cars in the world, but you can't undo what happened. This is very kind, honestly, but you'd do better deleting the picture of my licence from your phone,

ripping up the form and leaving me to it. I'm a big girl these days; I
can look after myself.'

'I can't do that.'

'Why not?'

'Because then I'm always the bastard in your narrative. I'm not
expecting you to forgive me, but I want to help, and this is a simple
solution to your problem. Even better, it doesn't cost you anything.
I'll get your car recovered to the dealership and ask one of the tech-
nicians to have a look at it on Monday.'

'And what will you do for transport?'

'I work at a car dealership,' he laughs. 'Transport is the least of
my worries.'

'Won't your boss be pissed off with you? It's obvious that I'm not
the kind of person who would be in the market for a car like this.'

'I am the boss, on the sales side at least. Give me your number;
I'll call you on Monday with an update on your car.'

'Will you actually call this time, or will you just text to say
you've changed your mind about helping?'

'You'll be swanning around in ninety-five grand's worth of my
employer's property. I'll call.'

'This doesn't change anything, you understand that? We aren't
suddenly going to be best buddies.'

'I know.'

'Fine.'

He hands me the form again and I sign it. He then takes me
through the controls of the car, which nearly has me running for
the hills again. It all seems ridiculously complex, from the way the
door handles pop out of the bodywork when you touch them, to the
space-age instrumentation on the dashboard. He even shows me
how to raise and lower the roof.

'It's the middle of the night. Why would I want the roof down?'
I ask.

'Because it won't be the middle of the night tomorrow, will it? You've got this car until Monday at least. Enjoy it, but be careful. It's pretty quick and I can't help you if you fall foul of the police, so keep an eye on your speed, OK?'

Eventually, once I'm settled in the driver's seat and have a vague idea of what everything does, I press the engine start button. The silence of the night is shattered by a loud snarl.

'I think the exhaust has a hole in it,' I call over the din.

'It's supposed to sound like that.'

'Why?'

'It's a sports car.'

'Fine. Are you sure you don't want me to give you a lift to the main road?' It seems the least I can do.

'You're all right. I'll flag down the next wedding guest.'

'Try not to get murdered. I need the stuff in my car.'

'I'll do my best, now go. I'll call you on Monday.'

'You'd better,' I tell him as I slip it into gear and pull away.

9

'What the bloody hell is that?' Alice exclaims as she opens the door to me the next day and spots the Jaguar. 'Where's the Volvo?'

'The Volvo died,' I tell her as I step over the threshold.

My initial anxiety about being behind the wheel of Jamie's idiotic sports car had pretty much evaporated by the time I reached the end of the lane and turned onto the main road. It may be worth nearly two thirds of my flat, but I have to admit it is very nice to drive. Last night, I was mainly enjoying having decent headlights, but I followed Jamie's advice this morning and drove over to Alice's house in Ashford with the roof down. Yes, it's totally impractical and ridiculously expensive, but I don't think I've ever had so much fun in a car. I do wish it were a little quieter though; the bellow from the exhaust every time you start the engine or put your foot down is a bit too attention-grabbing for me.

'What, and that's your courtesy car?' Alice continues as I follow her towards the kitchen. 'Remind me which breakdown company you're with. I need to take out a policy and then sabotage my car. Wait until Richard sees it. He may need to be alone for a while with a box of tissues.'

'Yuck, Alice! It's not so much a courtesy car as a guilt offering.'

'Someone must be feeling extremely guilty to hand that over. You didn't catch the groom shagging one of the bridesmaids, did you? That's about the only thing I can think of that would warrant it.'

'No, nothing like that.'

'Well, come on then. Spill the beans.'

Alice listens carefully as I tell her the story, from my massive crush on Jamie (leaving out the most embarrassing parts, obviously) through the events in the bathroom at Elodie's party and the text the next day, to him rescuing me last night. In a funny way, it's a relief to be finally telling someone else now that I've said my piece to Jamie. The fact that she wasn't there and doesn't know him helps, because I can distance myself from it a little, almost like I'm talking about someone else instead of me.

'Bloody hell, poor you,' she sympathises when I've finished. 'No wonder you didn't want to do the wedding.'

'I knew he would be there but, even if he hadn't been, there would have been enough people there that I remembered from that time. I've worked so hard to put it behind me, so I was worried about how I'd feel.'

'Why didn't you tell me before? I'd have done it for you.'

'You hate outside catering!'

'I don't hate it, exactly; I just prefer the shops, that's all.'

'You do hate it. The last time you came out with me, you whined from the moment we set up.'

'I still would have done it.'

I sigh. 'I know you would, but I don't think it would have helped. I would just have felt like a coward for not facing up to my past. What's done is done, and at least I got the opportunity to tell Jamie what I thought of him.'

'Very effectively, it would seem,' she smiles. 'So what happens next? I assume you don't get to keep it forever.'

'No. Jamie said he'd get one of his mechanics to have a look at my car tomorrow and then he'll give me a call, so I imagine I'll have to give it back then.'

'When's lunch?' Mia asks as she wanders into the kitchen in her pyjamas, eyes glued to the phone in her hand.

'Good afternoon, sweetheart,' Alice replies slightly sarcastically to her daughter. 'Lunch will be at two, when your father gets back from golf. In the meantime, you might like to say hello to Jess and then think about having a shower and putting some clothes on.'

'Hi, Jess,' Mia says without lifting her eyes from the screen.

'Hello, Mia. How are you?'

'Yeah, pretty decent actually. I'll see you in a bit.' She turns and wanders back towards the staircase.

'Richard and I think she might have a boyfriend,' Alice tells me conspiratorially once Mia is out of earshot.

'Why?'

'She's been suspiciously happy for a teenager all week, and she texted me twice to say that she would be getting a later bus because she was staying on at school to study in the library.'

'Maybe she's just really into her schoolwork at the moment.'

'Perhaps. The fact that I spotted her going into the milkshake bar in the shopping centre with a boy during one of these impromptu study periods tells a rather different story though, don't you think? Especially as they were holding hands.'

'Have you asked her about it?'

'God, no! Can you imagine the histrionics? She'd think I was stalking her.'

'Are you?'

'Of course not. I was picking one of Richard's suits up from the dry cleaners if you must know.'

'A likely tale,' I grin.

'Piss off. Anyway, don't say anything to her about it, OK? We're quite enjoying this calm between the teenage storms.'

I laugh. I love Sunday lunches at Alice's. When we first started up the business, I'd come over for lunch on a Sunday and then Richard would entertain Mia for an hour or so while we discussed the week's takings, what was working and what wasn't. Then, as the business grew, and particularly once the outside catering took off, Alice decided we needed Sunday lunchtimes to have a break from the business and just enjoy being friends. It doesn't often work out like that, of course; Richard and Mia regularly have to tell us off for talking 'shop' at the table.

Our dissection of Mia's blossoming romance is interrupted by the sound of the front door opening and closing, followed by Richard's booming voice announcing that he's home.

'Have you seen the penis substitute parked out on the road?' he asks as he strides into the kitchen and kisses Alice. 'Someone is definitely compensating for something. Hello, Jess. I didn't see your car?'

'That's because Jess is driving the penis substitute,' Alice tells him. 'It's quite an interesting story, actually. If you're a very good boy, go upstairs and change out of your hideous golf clothes before lunch, she might tell it to you when you come down.'

'She doesn't mean it,' Richard tells me with a grin. 'If you weren't here, she'd be ripping these clothes off me.'

'Yeah, and shoving them in the bin!' Alice laughs. 'I've never understood why you have to wear such ridiculous garb to knock a little ball about.'

'You have no romance in your soul, darling. Golf is the sport of kings.'

'No it isn't! Polo is the sport of kings. Golf is the sport of bank managers.'

'I don't think bank managers exist any more, do they? Anyway, we'll have to agree to differ. Is there time for Jess to take me for a quick run round the block in her swanky car before I change? Only if that's all right with you, Jess, of course.'

'Fine with me, or we can go out after lunch,' I reply.

'No, please take him now. He'll only have ants in his pants otherwise,' Alice laughs. 'You've probably got another twenty minutes or so before lunch is ready and I'll try to slow it down a bit. Go on, go and have fun.'

Despite his initial rudeness, Alice's predictions come true and Richard is mesmerised by the car; at one point, he made me pull over and wait until the road was clear so I could put my foot down to give him a feel of the acceleration.

'That car is something else,' he enthuses to Alice when we get back. 'I particularly like the way the air vents rise out of the dash when you start it, and the noise! That did things to me no car should do.'

'That's lovely, darling,' she smiles. 'Now please go and take that horrible clobber off. Lunch is practically ready.'

'I told you,' she remarks as soon as he's out of earshot. 'I'd be prepared to lay good money that he's already working out how to con me into letting him have one.'

'He'll need to find a spare ninety-five grand lying around if he wants that one,' I tell her.

'Ninety-five grand? That's obscene. He can forget about that then.'

* * *

In the end, neither Richard nor Mia reappear until Alice is ready to dish up and has yelled up the stairs a couple of times. Today's roast

is beef, and she's cooked it to perfection, with Yorkshire puddings, a selection of vegetables and crispy roast potatoes that I know will be beautifully fluffy inside. The gravy and horseradish sauce are passed round, and we savour the first couple of mouthfuls in silence.

'Mum, how would you feel about me becoming a vegetarian?' Mia asks after a while. She's made quite a dent in her helping of beef, so this seems a strange question to me.

'I'd want to know why you wanted to do it,' Alice replies, 'but I'd support you if you had a good case for it. Why?'

'Oh, no reason. It's just something I'm thinking about. The problem is that, although I don't like the idea of animals being slaughtered for food, I really can't imagine living without bacon.'

'That is a dilemma,' Richard agrees. 'Would it help you if I pointed out that all the animals we eat have eyes on the sides of their heads?'

'What on earth has that got to do with anything?' Alice asks.

'It means they're prey animals. They have eyes on the sides of their heads to give them a wide field of vision to see predators coming. Predators, on the other hand, have their eyes in front. A narrower field of vision, but better perception of distance and so on to help with hunting.'

'And your point is?'

'Where are our eyes?'

'In front.'

'Exactly, so we're natural predators. God has designed the prey animals to be eaten and us to hunt and eat them. You don't want to be making God cross now, do you, Mia?'

Mia rolls her eyes.

'Don't listen to your father, Mia,' Alice tells her. 'If you feel strongly that vegetarianism is for you, you go for it.'

'However, if you get all preachy about it and try to guilt-trip me when I'm enjoying a steak, you'll be moving out into the shed,' Richard adds, causing Alice to join in with her daughter's eye rolling.

'So, Jess. Tell me about how you came into possession of such a fabulous car,' Richard asks me when we've finished eating and Mia has retreated to her room. 'I looked up the price—'

'—and we definitely can't afford one,' Alice finishes for him.

'I know. It's a pity, though. I feel I belong in a car like that.'

'If it's as fast as you say it is, you'd probably crash it. I'm too young to be a widow and Mia needs her father.'

'Maybe I can pull the same stunt Jess did. Even if I only had it for the weekend, it would be enough.'

'You might struggle with that. Jess was given it by a boy she had sex with at school,' Alice tells him. 'If you start having sex with other people, whether there's a flash car in the deal or not, I'm going to take a very dim view.'

'Really? You had sex with someone and got that car in return? Isn't there a word for that?' He smiles to ensure I know he's not being serious. I'm used to Richard's humour, so I'm not at all offended.

'Ha! I'd make a lousy prostitute, if that's where you were going, Richard. I believe the whole "sex as a transaction" thing involves payment at the time, not twelve years later.'

'I think I'm going to need to hear the details,' he replies.

I tell the story exactly as I told it to Alice. The good news is that it's getting easier each time. The not so good news is that Richard doesn't immediately come down on my side like Alice did.

'OK. I completely get why you felt, feel, the way you do,' he tells me after a long pause, 'but can I ask a couple of questions that you may find controversial?'

'Umm, I suppose so. Go on.'

'Did this Jamie guy know you had a crush on him at the time?'

'Of course not! The whole point of having a crush on someone is that they don't know, surely?'

'That's what I thought. Did he make any promises about this being the start of a relationship before you, erm, did the deed?'

'He didn't say anything explicitly, but I was certain it was what he meant. And then, afterwards, when he said he wanted to hang out with me—'

'Why are you asking these questions, Richard?' Alice challenges him.

'It's the lawyer in me, sorry. I always try to see both sides of the story. He told you last night that he thought it was just a normal hook-up, right, Jess?'

'Yes. I was gobsmacked.'

'OK. Here's the bit I think you might not like. I know you expected it to be the start of an amazing romance because you were already in love with him, but the important point here is that he didn't know that. So, it wouldn't be totally unreasonable for him to think it was just a casual thing like he described.'

'He dumped her by text!' Alice exclaims, outraged. 'You don't have sex with someone and then send them a text basically saying thanks but no thanks.'

'That was shitty, I agree,' he admits.

'So you're saying that part of this is my fault?' I ask him. I've always got on very well with Richard, but I've never been cross-examined by him before, and I don't like it at all.

'*Fault* is much too strong a word. I guess what I'm trying to suggest is that there were some fundamental miscommunications here, which led to you having very different understandings of what the encounter meant.'

'So you're saying he didn't take advantage of me? That I'm holding an unreasonable grudge?'

'Absolutely not, Jess! I'm just saying that he might not be the complete villain you've painted him as in your head. After all,' he grins, 'anyone who's prepared to lend you their car and wait for the breakdown service instead of you can't be all bad, can they?'

10

My head is all over the place when I leave Alice and Richard's house for the drive back to Canterbury. I've put the roof down again but even the bright sunshine and the wind in my hair aren't enough to distract me from going over and over Richard's argument in my mind. Have I been unfair to Jamie for all these years? As the lead singer of The Misfits, he did attract quite a lot of female attention; maybe he thought I was some kind of groupie. I try to remember every word that was spoken but, despite it being a pivotal moment in my life, I honestly can't recall every sentence. It all got a bit fuzzy when the kissing started. I know he said things to me when we broke off to catch our breath, but I was in no state to focus on what he was saying when all of my mind and body was fixated on what he was doing.

They say your first time is often disappointing, that it's sometimes uncomfortable, but it wasn't like that at all. It was nice, actually. My English teacher at school absolutely hated the word 'nice' and forbade us from using it in our creative writing because it was so anodyne, but it fits my memory of the sex perfectly. It wasn't unpleasant in any way but it wasn't earth shattering either. It was just nice. Jamie obviously liked it, as I do remember him saying it was intense at the end. But, of course, the reason that it was nice was because I trusted him, because I loved him, because I felt safe. He betrayed all of those feelings without a second thought.

The flash of hurt I still feel at that memory brings my main dilemma back into sharp focus, which is whether I've misjudged him, at least a little. His reaction last night made it clear that he genuinely didn't have any idea how I felt about him at the time, or even that it was my first time. I wonder whether he would have behaved any differently had he known those things. My sister, Molly, told me once that men are completely controlled by their 'dumb sticks' so, given that I'd clearly lit his fire, I imagine he probably would have gone ahead anyway. I suppose the question is whether it would have made him behave differently the next day if he'd known what a big deal it was for me.

I'm no further forward when I reach my parents' house. I realise that I'll face a barrage of uncomfortable questions if they see the Jaguar, so I park it on the next street. Despite both having left home, Molly and I still make the effort to visit on Sundays when we can. She's only three years older than me, but I somehow feel much younger than her, probably because she's a teacher who has done the whole 'getting married and starting a family' thing, whereas my chances of meeting anyone have been pretty much scuppered by the fact that I've been totally focused on building the business with Alice.

'Hello!' I call out as I let myself in with my key.

'Hello, Jessica love. We're in here,' my mother's voice replies from the sitting room.

The scene that greets me looks like it's come straight from the cover of a 1950s housekeeping magazine, only with better decoration. My father is sitting in his wingback chair with the Sunday newspaper on his lap. His slightly sleepy expression indicates that he was probably dozing until a few moments ago. My mother and Molly are perched on the sofa together with Molly's baby, Henry, on Mum's lap. The table in front of the sofa is largely covered by the teapot with accompanying milk jug and sugar bowl, a Victoria sponge cake with a few slices missing, and delicate china cups and saucers. My mum and dad have had this tea set for as long as I can remember, and it only ever comes out on Sundays. I think there were originally six cups and saucers, but a couple of them met with accidents over the years, so there are only four left now.

'Hello, Jessica. This is a nice surprise!' My dad says this every time, as if me pitching up on a Sunday afternoon were an unheard-of event, rather than something that happens pretty regularly.

'Yeah, I was passing and thought I'd check in to see if you were still alive.' I'm ashamed to say my response is just as formulaic.

'Why don't you have a cuddle with your nephew while I make a fresh pot of tea?' Mum stands up and holds the baby out to me.

I don't know what it is, but Henry seems to think I'm the next best thing to his mother. I've always assumed it's because I look a bit like her so he associates me with her, but it could equally be because I'm quite content to sit and babble nonsense at him for what feels like hours.

'Hello, gorgeous man, how are you?' I ask him as I gather him into my arms and he beams at me.

'He's a bit snotty, so watch your top,' Molly warns.

'Are you going to snot on my top?' I repeat as I gently sway him from side to side while he gurgles with delight. 'That wouldn't be very good, would it? For all you know, this might be Versace and totally allergic to baby snot.'

'Business must be going well if you're buying designer clothes,' she laughs.

'It is going well,' I agree, 'but not that well, you're right.' I turn back to Henry. 'Your mummy has uncovered my deception,' I tell him. 'I can't even remember where this top came from, so snot away to your heart's content.'

'We're trying to keep him distracted,' Molly tells me as I take Mum's place on the sofa. 'He's just started crawling and loves his new-found freedom. Unfortunately, he seems determined to get his hands on Mum's tea set this afternoon, so it's been a battle between him wriggling and wanting to be put down, and the rest of us stopping him from smashing the place up. I know it's all good developmental progress but I do kind of miss the days when I could put him down and he'd still be wherever I'd left him when I got back.'

'Where's Paul?' I ask her. Molly's husband is not a regular feature of Sunday afternoons but she assures us regularly that he comes as often as he can. From the way he sits and fidgets when he does come, it's usually fairly obvious that he'd rather be somewhere else though so, despite the fact that I get on with him reasonably well, it's a bit of a relief when he's not here.

'He says he's got marking to do,' she says, matter-of-factly. This is evidently for my father's benefit, because she then lowers her voice to a whisper so he can't hear the next sentence. 'He's just as likely to be watching porn, though.'

'Why?'

Molly addresses the next sentence in the same whisper to a happily burbling Henry. 'Daddy's probably feeling a bit pent up, isn't he? Ever since you were born, Mummy hasn't really been in the mood, no she hasn't!'

'It's been nine months,' I murmur back to her. 'Don't you think it's time to get back on the horse, so to speak?'

'I know I should, and I am trying. I still love him, of course I do, it's just that sex feels like another thing I have to tick off my to-do list at the moment, rather than something to look forward to. Anyway, who the hell are you to be giving me sex advice, Miss Perennially Single?'

'It's a fair cop,' I smile.

'What are you two girls whispering about?' Mum asks as she brings the refilled teapot through and places it on the table.

'I reckon the less we know, the better, love,' Dad tells her. 'It's just like when they were growing up. They were always whispering to each other and giggling, do you remember?'

'Jess was attempting to give me relationship advice,' Molly explains gleefully. 'I was just reminding her that it's a bit rich receiving sex therapy from a woman who would make a nun's love life look interesting.'

'Not in front of the baby, Molly!' my mother admonishes her.

'He's not going to remember, is he?'

'Well, probably not, but it's still... *inappropriate*.'

Now it's my turn to smile. Mum dropping the 'i' bomb is about as close as she gets to telling us off now that we're adults.

'How long after I was born did you and Dad restart things in the bedroom?' Molly asks, causing both my parents to flush with embarrassment. Few topics are off-limits in our family, but Mum and Dad are fairly prudish where sex is concerned.

'I can't remember,' Mum stammers after a tense couple of seconds. 'The usual amount of time, I suppose. Jessica, would you like a slice of cake?'

'No thanks, Mum. I'm still full from lunch.'

'And how is Alice?' she continues, obviously desperate to change the subject.

'She's fine. She and Richard suspect that Mia has a boyfriend. Alice saw them going into the milkshake bar in Ashford together.'

'That's a bit precocious, isn't it? How old is she, twelve?'

'She's fourteen, Mum.'

'Even still. I didn't even look at a boy until I was sixteen.'

'Who was that?' Molly asks. 'You didn't meet Dad until you were twenty, did you?'

'Incredibly, darling, despite being a hundred and four, I managed to grow up in sufficiently enlightened times that we didn't get married off to the first member of the opposite sex we clapped eyes on,' Mum tells her archly. 'I had a boyfriend or two before I met your father, and I was by no means the first woman he went out with.'

'OK, enough!' Molly laughs, clapping her hands over her ears. 'How on earth did we end up here?'

'I think it started with you being unkind about Jessica being single,' Mum reminds her. Another point to me, and I smile slightly. I love Molly, but we've always competed. It's what sisters do.

'Having said that,' Mum continues, turning to me, 'it would be lovely if you were to meet someone and settle down. Surely the business is well enough established that you could find some time for a social life?'

Molly smirks but I barely notice. I'm much more perturbed by the image of Jamie that's suddenly popped into my head, accompanied by Laura's voice saying, *If he's single, and you're single...* I hastily push it out. If I am ever going to meet anyone, it sure as hell isn't going to be him; there's a gulf a mile wide between possibly accepting that he isn't quite the bastard I've always believed him to be and us ending up together.

'...never so much as brought a young man home, did she, Jim?' My mother is still speaking and I realise I've completely tuned her out for a moment.

'What did you say?' I ask.

'I was just saying that we're not aware of you ever having had a boyfriend. Perhaps you're one of those people who just prefers their own company.'

'Asexual,' Molly murmurs, quietly enough to ensure Mum doesn't hear.

'Says the woman who'd rather leave her husband to find his

kicks on the internet than help the poor guy out,' I murmur back. 'I've just been really busy, that's all,' I tell Mum as soon as I'm certain Molly doesn't have a comeback. 'When I meet someone, you'll be the first to know, OK?' Another image of Jamie's handsome face illuminated by the dashboard lighting last night flits into my mind and I mentally slap myself.

'Just don't leave it too long, will you?' she urges. 'I long for more grandchildren and you're only seven years off being considered a geriatric mother, you know.'

'I don't think that's a thing any more, Mum, and I'm sure Molly will oblige in the meantime, won't you, Mols?' I turn back to Henry, who is starting to fidget and complain. 'You'd like a little brother or sister, wouldn't you?'

Molly shoots me a filthy look and I grin widely. This round has definitely fallen to me.

As soon as I leave them and turn the Jaguar towards home, my head fills back up with all the questions that I was wrestling with on the drive over here, only now I have the two points at which Jamie popped into my consciousness to add to the muddle. I'm reluctantly starting to accept that Richard may have a point, but what does that mean and, more importantly, where does it leave me? Have I spent the last twelve years mentally heaping burning coals on a man who didn't (fully) deserve it? What does that say about my own self-awareness?

One thing is for certain: the sooner I give this bloody car back and get Jamie out of my life, the better.

11

The call finally comes as I'm trying to wrestle the week's grocery shopping into the tiny boot of the Jaguar. My mood isn't helped by my awareness of the man in the next row openly watching me struggle. He probably thinks I'm an idiot for buying such an impractical car, and part of me wants to go over, explain that it isn't mine and generally give him a piece of my mind. At least I'm reasonably confident manoeuvring it; it has sensors everywhere to tell you when you're getting close to things, so if he's hoping I'm going to entertain him some more by making a complete pig's ear of reversing it out of the space, he's going to be sorely disappointed.

'Hello?' I say more brusquely than I mean to after pressing the accept button.

'Jess, it's Jamie. You sound like you're in the middle of something. Would you prefer if I called back later?'

'It's fine,' I tell him through gritted teeth as I give up, dumping the final bag in the passenger footwell and closing the boot.

'How's the Jaguar?' he asks.

'Not very well suited to the supermarket run, it turns out,' I tell him.

'Ah, yes. I suppose most of our F-Type customers have other cars for that kind of thing. Anyway, I have an update on your Volvo. It's bad news, I'm afraid.'

'You're consistent, I'll give you that.'

'What do you mean?' He sounds genuinely confused.

'This is only the second time you've ever contacted me by phone, and it wasn't exactly great news last time either.'

The pause on the other end of the phone before Jamie clears his throat and carries on lets me know that my barbed remark has hit its target.

'Yes, well. I asked our chief technician, Simon, to take a look at your car. As I mentioned before, I'm no mechanic so a lot of the stuff he reported back to me about big ends and conrods went over my head. But the summary is that something important that shouldn't have come loose came loose, causing lots of other things inside the engine to break into several pieces and do untold damage to yet more things they should never have come into contact with. Did you hear any banging before the engine stopped?'

'Yes, there was a rhythmic banging for a few seconds and then the engine just cut out.'

'That ties in with what he said. The long and the short of it is that your car needs a new engine.'

Great.

'How much will that cost?' I ask.

'If we did it? The parts alone would cost way more than the car is worth, I'm afraid, and that's before you add on the workshop fees. The only way we could see to make it remotely viable would be to use a second-hand engine out of another car that had been scrapped, but that's not something we would be able to do here because our work all comes with warranties and so on that means we have to use new parts.'

'Wouldn't taking one from a scrap car just be replacing one knackered engine with another?'

'Not necessarily. There are places that specialise in salvaging undamaged parts from insurance write-offs. So, imagine a car like yours that has maybe been involved in a heavy rear-end collision. The car may be written off, but there's nothing wrong with the engine. It can be used again.'

'OK, that sounds like an interesting possibility. How do we do that?'

'Simon spoke to a mate of his who runs a repair shop not far from here. Unfortunately, even going that way is going to cost a lot more than your car is worth. I wanted you to know that we'd done the research, though.'

I sigh. 'So basically my only option is to buy another car.'

'I'm afraid so, yes.'

'And what about the Volvo? What do I do with that?'

'If you like, we can arrange to have it scrapped for you. There will be a small fee, I'm afraid, unless...' he pauses again and I can just hear him riffling through sheets of paper.

'Unless what?'

'Sorry, I was just looking for the paperwork so I had the details. Now, please don't think I'm treating your misfortune as a sales opportunity, like you said on Saturday, I'm really not, but I suddenly remembered we've just taken a car in part-exchange that could be perfect for you. It's a Land Rover Discovery Sport. The guy who owned it is a regular customer of ours, and he takes good care of his vehicles. It literally came in this morning, so we haven't had time to prepare it or anything, but I could arrange for you to test drive it with one of the sales guys if you were interested.'

'This sounds a bit too convenient to me,' I tell him suspiciously. 'My car is uneconomical to repair but you just happen to have the perfect replacement that came in today? Bit of a happy coincidence from your point of view, isn't it?'

'Honestly, there's no pressure from me. We won't have any trouble selling it; I just thought it might be a good fit for you. There's lots of room inside for your equipment and it's four-wheel drive, so well suited to events like Elodie's wedding where you have to take it off road. Having said that, there is something I do need from you today, I'm afraid.'

'The Jaguar?'

'Sorry.'

'Don't be. It was really kind of you to lend it to me and to get my car picked up and everything. What time did you get home in the end?'

'Just after three in the morning. Your fake phone conversation was spot on; the breakdown people were having a busy night, so it took them a while to arrive.'

I'm glad he's on the phone so he can't see my flush of embarrassment as I remember the events of Saturday night.

'I do appreciate it, really,' I tell him. 'If it's any consolation at all, I took my business partner's husband out for a ride in the Jaguar and I think he'll be a customer of yours as soon as he finds the money and a way to persuade his wife.'

There's a laugh from the other end of the phone. It's deep and rich, and the sound of it stirs something in the pit of my stomach.

'I'll look out for him,' Jamie tells me.

'I'll be expecting commission, naturally.'

He laughs again. 'I'll see you later then?'

'Yes, I'll get it back to you this afternoon. I assume I should bring it to the address on your card?'

'That would be perfect, thanks.'

* * *

When I get home, I unpack the shopping and put a load of washing on before logging on to my laptop to begin the search for a new car. After an hour, I'm no further forward. I don't know what any of these cars are, or whether they're any good or not, and I'm both bored and depressed. At least I don't have any evening events this week, so I can probably live without a car for a little bit, although it's going to cost me a small fortune in taxi fares. Unfortunately, using the Mad Hatter vans to get to work and back is out of the question as we load them up each evening with the next day's shop deliveries, and then they have to stay plugged into the mains to keep the fridges running overnight before the drivers pick them up at six in the morning.

I did look up what a Land Rover Discovery Sport was, and I hate to admit that it does look immensely practical. However, apart from the fact that all the ones I've found cost way more than my savings, I'm very resistant to Jamie benefiting from this. In despair, I call Alice.

'Hey, Jess, what's up? Bored on your day off?' she asks when she answers her phone.

'I wish. Jamie rang earlier and the Volvo has had it, so I've been looking at cars and I need someone sane to talk to.'

'And you chose me because…? I don't know anything about cars. Richard deals with that.'

'I know, but I don't have a Richard. The closest I have is Dad, and he's at work.'

'I'm at work!'

'That's different. I know you have time to talk to me, because I'd be there if anything important was happening. Plus, I'm not really after car knowledge. My problem is more emotional.'

'If you're going to tell me that knackered old Volvo has huge sentimental value and you'll do everything in your power to save it, I'm not your woman. You know how I feel about that thing.'

'It's not the Volvo, it's Jamie.'

I can almost hear her ears prick up. 'Go on.'

'He tried to sell me a car.'

'He's a car salesman. They do that.'

'I know, but it's all a bit convenient, isn't it? "Your car is dead, but here's a new one I just happened to have lying around"? Plus, I've done a bit of research on the car he's suggested and I'm certain it's going to cost much more than I've got saved. And, on top of all of that, I just don't want him to give him a pound of my money. It seems so *unfair* that he should get to swan back into my life twelve years after shitting all over me and profit from it, no matter how kind he's been.'

'OK, I get you. Let's go through these one at a time.'

'Thank you. I knew you'd understand.'

'I honestly don't think you should read anything untoward into him offering you a car. In fact, I think it would be odd if he didn't. How many cars do you think they sell a week?'

'No idea.'

'Me neither, but I expect it's quite a few. So I don't think he'd need to stoop to sabotaging your Volvo to make a sale if that's what you're worried about.'

'I wouldn't put it past him.'

'Yes, but you have such a low opinion of him that I could suggest he was a drug dealer and you wouldn't put it past him.'

I laugh. 'It's a fair cop, but even if he has the perfect car for me, and he hasn't sabotaged mine just to make a sale, the point remains that I still don't have nearly enough money to buy it.'

'Nobody does. That's why finance was invented. Next? Oh yes, about you giving him money. He doesn't own the dealership, does he?'

'No, he's the head of sales.'

'So the money isn't going into his pocket, is it? It'll be going into the company's bank account.'

'I guess so.'

'Also, if he's still feeling guilty, you might be able to screw him down on the price a bit, which would be to your advantage. Think of it that way.'

I sigh. 'OK, thank you. I suppose I'd better give him a call and arrange to look at this thing then.'

'Have fun!'

* * *

Unsurprisingly, Jamie sounds delighted about my change of heart and assures me he'll do everything he can to make the price of the Land Rover competitive. I'm still feeling distinctly uncomfortable as I nose the Jaguar into one of the few free parking spaces at the dealership and check it over to make sure I haven't left anything behind. Being rescued by Jamie was bad enough, but now I'm literally on his turf. It feels like putting my head in the lion's mouth, particularly as I have no idea what to expect. I bought the Volvo privately from a lovely old guy who had had to give up driving because of his eyesight. Dad came with me and paid him with cash, which I repaid from my savings later. This is nothing like that and I'm all alone. At least I don't have to see Jamie; he was tactful enough to book me in with one of his sales guys, someone called Ian. I announce myself to the receptionist and take a seat in the waiting area. A few minutes later, a man gets up from one of the desks and strides over to me.

'You must be Jess,' he tells me. 'I'm Ian. Is it OK if I call you Jess?'

'Yes, that's fine,' I reply.

'Great stuff. I gather you know my boss, Jamie, so you won't be surprised when I tell you he's asked me to take extra care of you. Would you like a tea or coffee to begin with?'

'I'm fine, thank you.'

'Great, well let's show you this car.'

Irritatingly, Jamie is proved right. The Land Rover is perfect for what I need and, a little under an hour later, after Ian has explained the finance plan and assured me that they cannot possibly sell me the car any cheaper than the price Jamie has given him, I pay the deposit and sign my name on the dotted line. I don't know whether Ian has some sort of secret button under his desk, but seconds after I slide the signed agreement back across the desk to him, Jamie appears. He's wearing a dark-blue suit and looks even better than he did in his wedding clobber, damn him.

'How did you get on?' he asks. 'I hope Ian took good care of you?'

'He did, thank you,' I reply, as coolly as I can.

Ian obviously picks up on the slightly frosty atmosphere, as he makes an excuse about needing to file the paperwork, thanks me for my business and disappears, leaving Jamie and me on our own.

'I know you said I would be the last person in the world you would buy a car from, but I genuinely believe the Land Rover will be a good fit for you,' he says. 'I'll ask the workshop to prioritise it so you get it as soon as possible. How are you getting home?'

'I'll call a cab.'

'Let me drop you. I don't have any appointments for the rest of the day. It's the least I can do for our latest valued customer.'

'I don't want to put you to any more trouble,' I tell him. I don't tell him that the real reason, apart from not wanting to spend more time with him doing his Mr Nice Guy act, is that I'm not wild about him finding out where I live. I know I'm being ridiculous; as well as the documents I've just signed, the paperwork for the loan of the

Jaguar also had my address on it, but there's a big difference between him knowing my address and actually seeing where I live.

'It's no trouble at all,' he replies, smiling widely. 'Let me grab some keys and I'll be right with you.'

After we've loaded the stuff from the Volvo into the shiny SUV he has plucked from somewhere and I give him my postcode for the satnav, a single thought is playing in my mind. He's either a phenomenally good actor or he's a genuinely nice person trying, in a clumsy way, to atone for his past behaviour. God, I hope it's the former. The latter doesn't bear thinking about.

12

I have escaped from Jamie, or at least I'm trying to. He did call a week or so after I picked up the Land Rover, ostensibly to see how I was getting on with it, and the conversation was incredibly awkward and stilted. A month has passed since then and I haven't seen or heard any more from him, so life has pretty much returned to blissful normality. Unfortunately, the Land Rover, which I have to admit I'm very pleased with, does still remind me slightly of him every time I clap my eyes on it. So, as part of my ongoing effort to get him completely out of my head, I registered on a dating app and I'm going on a date this evening.

Alice did try to encourage me to sign up on some dating apps a few years ago, but the whole idea of effectively becoming some kind of menu item for unknown men to peruse and rate filled me with horror. However, this one is supposed to be purely for single, professional people, and I've been matched with Luke, who lives in Herne Bay. The app doesn't give away too much information about your matches; the idea is that you find out about each other when you meet but, judging from his profile picture, I'd say he's mid-thirties. We've exchanged a few messages and he's been perfectly polite, so we're meeting at a pub near Whitstable. I was a little disappointed when he first suggested it, as I know there are some cracking restaurants in the town, but maybe it's better for our first date to be somewhere where the food takes a step back, allowing us to concentrate on getting to know each other. I hope that's his reasoning, anyway.

Alice and Laura are both much more excited about it than I am. Laura still hasn't had the baby, and is getting increasingly tetchy about it, but I'm really enjoying being back in contact with her and we talk fairly regularly. She's demanded a blow-by-blow account of the evening at the first opportunity, even if she's in labour. Alice was all for coming round and going through my wardrobe with me to help me select a suitable outfit until I reminded her that I am, in fact, a grown-up and perfectly capable of dressing myself. She is going to call me at 9 p.m. precisely, though, just in case things are going badly and I need an excuse to escape. We've agreed that the signal for 'everything is fine' will be if I answer and say, 'Hi, Alice, I'm with someone right now, can I call you back?', but if I say anything else, she'll invent an emergency.

I give myself one final check-over before leaving the flat. I've gone for a casual look with skinny jeans, a fitted top and a light-brown leather jacket. I've kept the make-up minimal as well: a little eyeliner and a flick of mascara, with neutral lipstick.

The pub is busy when I get there, but the car park is massive and it doesn't take me long to find a spot. I give Luke's name to the woman at the welcome desk and she leads me to a table tucked away in a remote corner of the dining room. My initial relief at seeing that he is already there is short-lived. His profile picture must be an old one, because he's forty if he's a day, and the dark hair in the photo is more salt and pepper now. He's also wearing a pair of deeply unflattering glasses with heavy, black, plastic frames, which make him look a little like a spy from the 1960s.

'Jess, lovely to meet you in person at last,' he says as I take my seat. I notice that he didn't bother to get up to greet me, another mark against him. He stares at me, openly appraising, which I decide to forgive as I kind of did that to him just now.

'I hope you don't mind me saying, but your photograph really doesn't do you justice. You're even more beautiful in the flesh,' he remarks after a moment.

'Thank you,' I smile. I'm desperately trying to think of something equally complimentary to say without openly lying when I realise that he's no longer focused on me but is instead gesticulating at one of the waitresses, trying to get her attention.

'How can I help?' the waitress asks when she comes over. Her words are friendly enough, but I can see the irritation in her eyes and I try to give her a sympathetic look. I know from my catering training that restaurants serve clients in a particular sequence to prevent the kitchen being overwhelmed by a flurry of orders all arriving at the same time. Luke blatantly trying to jump the queue is messing with the system.

'I'd like a glass of tap water and what would you like, Jess?'

'A small glass of white wine, please.'

'I never drink in these places,' Luke explains to me smugly when the waitress has gone. 'The markups they charge are astronomical. Your glass of wine, for instance. How much is that?'

'I didn't look,' I admit.

He searches through the menu. 'Here we are, house white is seven pounds ninety-five for a small glass. You could probably buy the whole bottle in the supermarket for less than that.'

I'm tempted to explain about overheads, staff costs and so on, but I can see he's not interested. These are statements of fact to him, rather than opportunities for debate.

'What do you fancy to eat?' he asks. 'I'm going to have the prawn cocktail and a rump steak I think.'

'You seem very familiar with the menu,' I observe. 'Do you come here a lot?'

'I've been a few times. These places are all the same though, aren't they? You could walk into any one of them and I'd guarantee you they'd have prawn cocktail and rump steak on the menu.'

'You're probably right,' I agree. 'I tell you what, I'll join you and have the same.'

'Not a vegetarian then? That's a relief.'

I can't decide if he's shy and overcompensating, or whether he's actually a prime arsehole. 'Benefit of the doubt,' I murmur under my breath. 'So, Luke, tell me a bit about yourself,' I try. 'I know from your profile that you like reading, the cinema, long walks and food.'

'Confession time,' he smiles. 'Everyone puts those things, don't they? I mean, I can read, obviously, and I've been to the cinema a couple of times, but my work is very mentally demanding, so I like to really switch off when I'm not working.'

'I see. And what is it that you do?'

'Electronic shelf-edge labels.'

'I'm sorry?'

'You know, when you go to the supermarket, and there's a label on the shelf under the baked beans to tell you how much they are? I work with those, only the ones we do are electronic rather than printed. They're all connected to the store wi-fi, which means that the store can react instantly to price changes without having to print new labels and deploy staff to attach them to the shelves.'

'I think I've seen them on the continent,' I tell him. 'Little boxes attached to the shelves with liquid crystal displays.'

'Those are old school,' he scoffs. 'These days it's all about e-ink.'

'E-ink?'

'Like on a kindle. See, the problem with the liquid crystal ones you described is that they need a constant source of power, and they're limited to displaying prices. E-ink displays only need power when you want to change them, so they're much more efficient, plus you can put anything you want on there. Prices, descriptions, barcodes, the list is endless.'

Thankfully, we're interrupted by the arrival of the waitress with our drinks, and Luke takes the opportunity to give her our food order. I try not to wince when he orders his steak well done, and he looks distinctly disapproving when I ask for mine to be medium rare.

'I like my food properly cooked,' he declares when the waitress has departed again, before launching back into his monologue about electronic shelf-edge labels. I semi-tune him out, and his detailed explanation of the difficulties of operating shelf-edge labels in freezer cabinets is thankfully interrupted by the arrival of our starters. I've made a fair number of prawn cocktails in my time; Luke is right that they never quite seem to come into or go out of fashion. The secret, in my book, is plenty of juicy prawns and just enough sauce to bind them together and flavour the lettuce. This, sadly, is not like that. A few limp prawns are engulfed in an ocean of over tangy sauce that obviously came out of a bottle, and the lettuce is starting to brown at the edges, so it's patently been sitting around for a while. Luke notices none of this and shovels his in with gusto. I take a few mouthfuls, but it has a weird artificial flavour that I really don't like, so I set it aside.

'Aren't you finishing that?' Luke asks.

'I'm watching my figure,' I lie. 'I love prawn cocktail, but it's so fattening. It was lovely just to have a little taste though.'

'Shame to let it go to waste,' he tells me, pulling my dish towards him and swiftly polishing off what I've left. By this time, it's more than obvious that Luke and I are not going to be meeting again. The only thing keeping me here is that I am actually starving. I suppose he might also make an amusing story to tell my grandchildren, if I ever get that far.

He's moved beyond the mechanics of how shelf-edge labels work now and is telling me all about the clients he's working with and the number of air miles he's earned jetting around Europe with his job. I'm nodding and smiling while taking a mental inventory of the contents of my fridge to work out what I can knock together when I get home. I've realised that my prawn cocktail lie about watching my weight means I'm barely going to be able to make a dent in my main course either. I check my watch and discover that it's not even eight o'clock. If I'm still here by the time Alice makes her rescue call, I may well have unexpectedly stabbed Luke to death with his steak knife.

'That was a cracking bit of grub,' he announces a while later when he's polished off a steak that looked so dry, it must have been like eating cardboard, along with all of his chips and most of mine. I managed to eat half of my steak, but it was ferociously chewy. Frankly, I just want to leave as soon as I can without seeming openly rude. My opportunity comes when he disappears to the loo.

'I'm really sorry, I've got to go,' I tell him when he returns, trying to look as sad about it as I can. 'My sister just rang. She's looking after my dog and he's just been sick everywhere.' It's a total lie, but I can't stand him any more.

'I wouldn't worry about it,' he replies, completely unperturbed. 'Dogs are sick all the time. Just tell her to leave it and he'll probably eat it all back up again.'

'I do worry about it, because he's got a condition and the vet told me he needs to come in if he's ill.'

Luke is obviously irritated because he's been eyeing up the dessert menu.

'Well, I suppose if you really have to go,' he says unhappily. 'Shall we get the bill then?'

'Please.'

He gesticulates at the waitress again, but this time I'm actually pleased. The sooner she comes over and we get out of here, the sooner I can put this behind me and do something about rescuing what's left of the evening. When the bill arrives, he rummages in his wallet and produces a load of vouchers, which he leafs through carefully before placing them on the table.

'That should cover what I had,' he explains. 'I don't leave tips on principle.'

I no longer care enough about him to find out what bizarre principle that is, so I settle my part of the bill, adding a generous tip for the poor waitress. As soon as we get outside, I take a huge breath of fresh air, delighted to be free.

'I had fun this evening. Let's do this again,' he tells me, leaning in for a kiss, but I pretend not to notice and turn towards my car.

On the way home, I call Alice.

'Oh dear,' she says as soon as she answers her phone.

'What makes you say that?'

'It's not even eight thirty and you're calling me from the car, I can tell. Was it that bad?'

'Worse. Still, if you ever need to know about electronic shelf-edge labels, I can point you to just the right man. How many questions do you think he asked about me?'

'None?'

'Yup.'

'I'm sorry.'

'Yeah, me too. Total waste of an evening. Tell me about you.'

'I've got some news actually, but I'm not sure you're going to like it.'

'I'm already in a bad mood; I don't imagine you can make it any worse.'

'I took a booking just as we were closing up. A new client for you and the external catering team.'

'Oh yes?'

'Yes. It's an evening do for a car dealership in Canterbury. They're launching a new model and want us to provide canapés and serve drinks to their invited guests.'

I know the answer to my next question before I even ask it.

'Which dealership?'

'The Jaguar Land Rover one, of course. Look, I know you don't like Jamie, but this could be a good opportunity for us. Would you rather I did it?'

I try to weigh up which is worse: seeing Jamie again or listening to Alice whine about how much she hates doing outside catering. It's a close contest.

'It's fine,' I tell her after a pause. 'I'll do it.'

13

'You're making it up!' is Laura's first reaction when I phone her and tell her about the disaster date with Luke.

'I wish I was,' I reply.

'Oh dear. So no second date for shelf-edge label man, as he will forever be known?'

'Definitely not. I'm starting to wonder if I'm just designed to be single.'

'You can't believe that based on one bad date.'

'This isn't my first time around the dating block, you know. Luke is just the latest in a collection of bad dates.'

'You should have taken my advice and snapped Jamie up at the wedding,' she admonishes.

'I don't think so,' I tell her firmly.

'Why not? You were, like, totally obsessed with him at school, and now you can't raise a flicker of interest? It's not as if he's sprouted an extra head or anything. In fact, I thought he'd grown into himself and looked better than ever. What am I missing here?'

'Nothing you need to worry about. You concentrate on getting that baby of yours out into the world.'

'Ha. There's no sign of that at the moment. In fact, I've sent Kevin out to get me a hot curry to see if we can move things along. Anyway, stop trying to change the subject. Come on, spill.'

I sigh. She's not going to let it go, and she was my best friend at the time. I ought to have told her back then, really.

'Do you remember the party at Elodie's after we finished our GCSEs?' I ask her.

'Not specifically, but there were a lot of parties at Elodie's over the years.'

'I'll take your word for it. That was the only one I was invited to.'

'That's not true. I distinctly remember her asking me to bring you along to more, but you were doing your "I'm off to college and ditching all my school friends" routine.'

'Fine, it was the only one I came to then. Anyway, the point is there was an incident at this party involving Jamie and me.'

'Really? How come you never said anything?'

'It didn't end well. I was embarrassed and wanted to forget all about it, forget all about him.'

'Oh, Jess.' She's put her sympathetic voice on. 'What happened? Did he give you the brush-off?'

'Not until after he'd had sex with me in Elodie's parents' bathroom.'

'*What?* Wait a minute. You had sex with him? You had sex with Jamie Ferguson *and you never told me?*'

'I'm sorry. Like I said, it didn't end well. He dumped me by text message the next day, and I felt so stupid for letting myself be taken in by him. I couldn't tell you because I felt so ashamed of myself for being such a mug.'

'Why would you be ashamed? If anyone should be ashamed, it's him. Wasn't he going out with whatshername at the time?'

'Sarah.'

'That's her.'

'They had a big row at the party and she went home. He told me they had split up.'

'She was pretty volatile. I think they split up a lot, to be fair. So how did all of this come about? It's very out of character for you to go from nought to sexy in the space of a single evening. Did you have any boyfriends before? I can't remember, I'm afraid. Baby brain.'

'No.' I fill her in on needing the loo, smacking Jamie's face with the door, helping to sort out the nosebleed and trying to clean his shirt. I gloss over the actual sex as much as I can but then go in heavy on the text message of the following morning.'

'What a bastard,' she murmurs when I've finished.

'Yeah, that's what I thought too.'

'I'm noticing past tense here.'

'It's complicated.'

'I bet it isn't. I reckon you clapped eyes on him at the wedding and your hormones went into overdrive just like they always used to. You're probably practising signing with his surname again, aren't you?' she laughs.

'Nothing like that.' I fill her in on the breakdown and Jamie's rescue.

'Let me get this straight. He rocked up, you gave it to him with both barrels and he still helped you out?'

'I think he felt guilty.'

'So he should! Taking advantage of you when you were completely lovestruck.'

'Yeah, but here's the complicated bit. He didn't know I was completely lovestruck, did he? He had no reason to believe it was anything more than a casual hook-up. How many other girls in our year did he sleep with, do you think? He was never short of interest.'

'A few, I would imagine. I know Elodie shagged him at least once.'

'Really?'

'Yes. I love Elodie, but she was as indecisive where boys were concerned as she is about everything else. As soon as she started going out with one guy, she'd start wondering whether someone else was actually better. I don't think she ever went out with Jamie officially; she just tried him on for size if you know what I mean. I have no idea how Daniel actually managed to get her to commit to marrying him. Anyway, none of that is relevant to you. How are you going to square Jamie the bastard with Jamie the knight in shining armour?'

'I don't know. My plan was to move on and put him back in my past, but now he's booked me to do an event at his work, so I have to talk to him and see him again.'

'Interesting. Given that you've made your opinion of him ruthlessly clear, why would he do that?'

'Maybe he likes my food.'

'Of course he does, it's delicious. But I'm sure there are other companies owned by people who haven't told him how much they hate his guts that also make nice food. Why not spare himself the hassle and use one of them?'

'Perhaps he still feels guilty.'

'Let me tell you something I've learned about men. They aren't very good at guilt. Guilt only happens for a few brief moments between being caught and coming up with some bullshit justification for their behaviour that shifts the blame onto their accuser.'

'That seems like a bit of a sweeping generalisation, Laura.'

'It may be but, like most generalisations, it has more than a grain of truth to it. Men are simple creatures and they like an easy life. Jamie played his "get out of jail free" card when he said he thought it was just a casual thing, even if he now knows you didn't.

In addition to that, he rescued you when you were a damsel in distress. Why invent reasons to spend more time in your company and make his life deliberately difficult, when he could just walk away and tell himself he's paid his debt? I'll tell you. It's because he likes you.'

'Your baby brain must be even worse than you thought. None of what you've just said makes sense,' I tell her firmly.

'It makes perfect sense. Remember, underneath the sharp suit is a very simple creature, like all of his sex.'

'What does Kevin think of you running men down like this?' I can't help asking.

'It was Kevin that explained it to me,' she says. 'He told me, "If a man is being mysterious and complex, it's because he's trying to hide something breathtakingly simple".'

'So you think Jamie is doing this because he wants – what? To be friends? To be *lovers*?'

'Maybe.'

'There's just one problem with that, which is that hell will freeze over before I get romantically involved with Jamie Ferguson again.'

'Don't you think you're being a little hard on the guy? You've admitted yourself that maybe you had expectations back then that he didn't know about and, yes, the text was bad, but he seems to be working his arse off to try to put that right, don't you think? Why not cut him a little slack?'

'Do you know how most murderers are caught?' I ask.

'No, and what's that got to do with anything?'

'They get caught returning to the scene of the crime.'

'I'm pretty sure that's an urban myth, and I still don't see what it has to do with Jamie.'

'If I let him back into my life, I'm effectively returning to the scene of the crime.'

'That metaphor totally doesn't work,' she laughs.

'OK, let me try a different one then. Let's say you went to a restaurant where the food was awful and you got food poisoning. How likely would you be to go back?'

'Nice try, but that one doesn't work either.'

'Why not?'

'Because it doesn't sound to me like the food was awful at all. The problem, if we're sticking with this latest clunky metaphor for you and Jamie, is that you had a lovely meal but the restaurant texted you out of the blue and cancelled all your future bookings. And that's the heart of your problem. You have unfinished business with him.'

'Any business between me and Jamie is definitely finished.'

'He doesn't seem to think so and, if you're properly honest with yourself, I don't think you do either. Otherwise it wouldn't be "complicated" like you described.' I can practically hear her making the air quotes.

'So what do you think I should do?'

'Cut yourself some slack. Cut him some slack. See where it goes. He's got to be a better prospect than Luke, hasn't he?'

'Joining a convent would be a better prospect than Luke,' I retort.

'Fair point. OK, final two questions. Ready?'

'Go on.'

'Do you think Jamie is good looking?'

'I guess so.'

'I need yes or no.'

'Fine, yes.'

'And do you think he's a good person based on your interactions with him since Elodie's wedding?'

'Yes,' I tell her reluctantly.

'Think about those things. I've got to go now as Kevin's just arrived with our takeaway. Love you.'

'Love you, too.'

* * *

The conversation with Laura has left me even more unsettled than I was after Richard challenged me, so I'm feeling decidedly anxious when I dial Jamie's mobile the next day.

'Jess, hi!' he answers after a couple of rings. He sounds excited to hear from me, which reminds me of my conversation with Laura and makes me distinctly uncomfortable.

'Hello, Jamie. I'm ringing to follow up on the booking you made with my colleague Alice. Is now a good time?' I'm using my most professional voice to try to convey to him that this is strictly a business arrangement and nothing more.

'I was doing admin so it's an excellent time. What's up? There isn't a problem, is there?' He's obviously picked up on my tone because the excitement has gone, but now there's a different edge to his voice. I'm not sure, but it almost sounds like disappointment. It's not reassuring.

'No, nothing like that. I just wanted to find out a bit more about the event and what you were looking for so I can put together the costs for you.'

'Ah, right. For a moment there, I thought you were going to tell me that you couldn't do it, which would have been a bit embarrassing given how much time I've spent bigging you up to my boss. Anyway, I'm very glad you can do it. Basically, Land Rover are launching a new model and all the dealers have to reveal it on the same day. We've decided to go for an evening event, where we've invited pretty much everyone who's ever bought a car from us. We'll have the new model in the showroom and the sales guys and I will all be on hand to answer questions and hopefully take a few orders. What we'd like from you is a selection of canapés and some people to hand out drinks. We'll get in some Prosecco, orange juice and sparkling water as well as glasses, so it's just a question of offering people a drink when they arrive, providing the canapés and circling around with them.'

'We can do that. How many people are you expecting?'

'Probably around eighty over the two hours. They won't all come at once; they'll drift in and out through the evening.'

'OK, so a selection of hot and cold canapés for eighty people to be served over two hours, plus staff to hand them round and pour drinks. Anything else?'

'That sounds about it.'

'And what did you have in mind in terms of budget?'

'I'm not entirely sure at this point. This is a premium car though, so we're looking at something rather more impressive than some Kettle chips and peanuts, if that makes sense.'

'I get it. So, if I were to say to you baby baked potatoes with sour cream and caviar, ham and Dijon mini-croissants, minted feta and pine nut filo rolls, would I be on the right lines?'

'They all sound delicious, so I'm going to say yes. Do I get a tasting in advance?'

Having relaxed a little, I'm now back on edge. Is this him trying to engineer another meeting, or am I being over suspicious? I wish Laura hadn't said anything now, because I'm second guessing everything he says and I don't like the way it's making me feel.

'Do you need one?' I ask eventually.

'Honestly? No, but it might put my boss's mind at rest if he could come along and see what he's going to get.'

That seems a reasonable explanation, I suppose.

'OK. Leave it with me,' I tell him. 'I'll email you a proposal with a suggested menu and costs. Once you're happy with that, we can arrange a tasting at one of our shops for you and your boss. How does that sound?'

'Perfect, thank you.'

It takes me over an hour to draw up my list of recommendations, taking dietary requirements and staffing into account, but in the end, I'm confident that what I've put together is just the right blend. I've included some lower priced items that look pretty, such as cheese puffs, but included enough of the crowd pleasers like mini Yorkshire puddings with roast beef and horseradish to make the overall effect feel 'premium'. I review the costs one more time and then realise what I'm missing.

'Hello again, Jess,' Jamie's voice comes down the line and I can practically hear his smile, damn him.

'Hi, Jamie. I've put together your proposal, but I realised I don't have your email address.'

'It should be on the business card I gave you.'

'I don't have that to hand, I'm afraid.' I binned it a few weeks ago, but something stops me from telling him that. For some reason, I find that I don't want to hurt his feelings by admitting that I never expected to have anything more to do with him after I bought the Land Rover.

He reels it off and I write it down in my diary against his booking, drawing a large box around it so it stands out. Now all I have to do is work out whether there genuinely is unfinished business between us, whether he's got a hidden agenda, and what on earth I do about it if he has.

14

'These are fabulous, Jess. Just the kind of thing we're looking for,' Jamie's boss, Gerald, enthuses as he pops another mini potato in his mouth. 'I was worried it was just going to be cheese and pineapple on sticks, and some manky mini sausages.'

'Which just goes to show how much you trust me,' Jamie retorts. 'I told you she was good.'

'Where cars are concerned, I trust you implicitly,' Gerald replies. 'You've got a track record there, but what evidence have I got to trust you where food is concerned? For all I know, you couldn't tell the difference between a hot dog and a fillet steak.'

'I'm glad you like them, Gerald,' I smile. I don't usually get nervous when customers come in for a tasting, but I'm definitely on edge this evening. Gerald isn't a problem, but I'm very conscious of Jamie sitting next to him. I've been trying to read him ever since they walked through the door, searching for any evidence that this is about more than the food, but he's completely inscrutable. I'm also painfully aware of Alice watching the proceedings from the doorway into the kitchen.

'There's just one small issue,' Gerald tells me, fishing my

proposal out of his jacket pocket and spreading it on the table between us. 'It's, umm, a little more than I budgeted.'

Oh, Gerald. You're so predictable.

'This kind of quality doesn't come cheap, Gerald,' I explain. 'Out of interest, how much does this car you're launching cost?' I already know the answer to this question because I've done my homework. A quick internet search of upcoming Land Rover launches revealed not only the model but the price range.

'The starting price is a hundred thousand pounds, give or take,' Jamie offers.

'That's a lot of money,' I reply. 'I imagine that the kind of people who can afford that would be somewhat disappointed with, what was it you said? "Cheese and pineapple on sticks".'

Gerald sighs. 'You're right. But I can't justify this to the business. Are you sure there isn't any wiggle room on the price?'

I look him in the eye. We both know what's happening here, and I can see the amusement on Jamie's face as his boss and I prepare to lock horns.

'What did you have in mind, Gerald?' I ask.

'If you could see your way to a ten per cent discount, I think I could sign this off here and now.'

I paste on my most regretful face. 'I can't do ten, Gerald; I'd be making a loss.' That isn't quite true. Canapés are incredibly profitable, so we'd still be making a healthy sum at ten per cent, but that's not how this game is played.

'What could you do for me then?' Gerald asks.

'Realistically? Three per cent, and that's cutting my margins to the bone.'

'That's a shame,' he replies. 'I think what you've produced here is amazing, and just right for the launch, but I'd need six per cent to make it even remotely viable from my perspective.'

'Let me talk to my business partner for a moment,' I tell him, before getting up and ushering Alice into the kitchen.

'What are you doing?' she whispers as soon as we're alone. 'You could have just given him the ten per cent he asked for. Now he's on the brink of walking out.'

'He's not going anywhere and that's not how this works, as you well know. If I'd given him the ten per cent straight away, he would have known that he probably could have got more and then he would have gone away with a sour taste in his mouth. By making him work harder for a smaller discount, I'm giving him the impression that he's a shit-hot negotiator and he'll be crowing at Jamie about it for days.'

'This is one of the many reasons I don't like your side of the business. In the shops, people come in and pay the price we ask. There isn't any of this haggling.'

'To be fair, a lot of the catering customers just pay the price as well, but Gerald obviously likes a good haggle. It's fine, I can handle it.'

'What's your plan then?'

'Well, you and I are having a tense conversation in here about what we can afford to knock off, obviously, and then I'm going to go out and offer him five per cent. He'll smell blood and dig in at six, at which point I'll look over to you, you'll shrug and I'll capitulate.'

'Have you pulled your un-mates rates trick again?'

'I was tempted, but no.'

'Your Jamie is hot, by the way.'

'He's not my Jamie, and I'm sure I don't know what you mean.'

'Of course you don't. Are you ready to wrap this up then?'

Gerald is looking expectant as I rejoin him and Jamie at the table.

'Look,' I tell him. 'Jamie's been a good friend to me recently, and

I really want to help you out. Because of that, we've agreed that we will offer you five per cent, as a one-off. How does that sound?'

'I'm really sorry,' he says, looking every inch as regretful as I did earlier. 'Six would have been doable at a stretch, but five makes it just too expensive. Thank you for your efforts, though. It really is a pity because your food is truly delicious. Another time, perhaps.' He folds the piece of paper and puts it back in his jacket pocket before starting to get to his feet.

'I guess I should have known you'd drive a hard bargain,' I tell him. 'You don't get to where you are in your field without knowing how to negotiate.'

'It's just business. Nothing personal.'

'Hey, no offence taken. I admire it. In fact – and my colleague is going to haul me over the coals for this as soon as we're alone – I'll give you your six per cent if you're happy to place the order with us now.' I turn to Alice, knowing that Gerald and Jamie's eyes have also shifted to her, and struggle to suppress a giggle as she throws up her hands in mock horror and flounces into the kitchen.

'Someone definitely isn't happy with you,' Gerald observes, grinning. 'Fine. You have a deal.'

We sit back down at the table while I write the order up in our order book, clearly marking in the discount. When I'm done, I pass the book across for his signature.

'A pleasure doing business with you,' Gerald says as I staple the credit card receipt to his copy of the order and hand it to him. 'Now, I've got to go, but I'll leave Jamie to sort out the practicalities with you, if that's OK?'

'No problem. I look forward to seeing you at the event,' I reply as I lead him to the door, holding it open for him.

'That was an impressive piece of negotiating,' Jamie observes as soon as Gerald has disappeared.

'Thank you.'

'He would have gone to five per cent though, if you'd really dug your heels in.'

'I'll let you into a little secret,' I tell him with a smile. 'I would have done it at ten. Alice's histrionics were just play acting.'

Jamie tilts his head back and his laughter fills the shop.

'You are a piece of work, Jessica Thomas.'

'As the man said, it's just business. Nothing personal. You won't tell him though, will you?'

'Don't worry, your secret is safe with me. To be honest, I think he'd probably offer you a job if he knew. I do have one question, though.'

'What?'

'When you told him I'd been a good friend to you lately, did you mean that or was that all part of the act?'

It takes me a while to come up with an answer. When I said it, it was very much a throwaway line to justify why I was giving in to Gerald, but I'm reluctantly coming to the conclusion that Jamie has been a good friend, despite my efforts to prevent him. I think about what Richard said, as well as my conversation with Laura as I look into Jamie's eyes, trying to figure him out. It's obvious what he wants me to say, but am I ready to say it?

'I'm not interrupting anything, am I?' Alice asks as she breezes through the shop, car keys already in her hand.

'No, we're just discussing the practicalities of the event,' I lie smoothly.

'OK, well don't forget to lock up on your way out.'

'Will do, thanks, Alice,' I call as the door closes behind her.

'Well?' Jamie asks, when the silence starts to become oppressive.

'You have been a good friend to me, it's true,' I tell him. 'I'm not sure that makes us friends though. That's your real question, isn't it? You want to know if we're friends now.'

'Yes.'

'Why?'

'What do you mean?'

'Why do you want us to be friends? You barely know me. Is this part of your guilt trip? Because that isn't a good basis for a friendship.'

'You say I barely know you, but that isn't true.'

'I'm not talking about knowing me in the Biblical sense!'

He blushes. 'That's not what I meant.'

'Tell me what you know about me then.'

'Professionally, I know that you're a superb chef and a formidable businesswoman. Personally, I know that you're fiercely independent—'

'What? How on earth could you know that?'

'Umm, possibly because you made it very clear that you didn't want my help when your car broke down? I've never met anyone so stubborn.'

'Thanks a bunch! Anyway, it's not that I wouldn't have accepted any help; I just didn't want help from you.'

'Which brings me on to my next point. You're a straight talker when you're not play-acting phone conversations with non-existent people or haggling with my boss. I reckon you're a proud person but also not afraid to re-evaluate a situation and see it from a different perspective. These are all qualities I admire, which means I like you. I'd like you to like me too.'

I smile. 'You were doing quite well until the last sentence. Bit needy, Jamie.'

He laughs again. I do like his laugh. When it dies away, he fixes his eyes on mine and suddenly looks very serious.

'I really am sorry about what happened at Elodie's. I behaved like a dick.'

'Since bumping into you again, I've been doing quite a lot of thinking and I'm not sure I'm completely blameless either,' I admit.

'I think the fairest thing to do is chalk it up to poor communication. Can I ask you a question?'

'Of course.'

'You need to be totally honest with me. I'll know if you're lying. Did you really think I was cool, or was that just a line you fed me to make me feel good?'

'I really thought you were cool. I still do, actually.'

I study him carefully, but I can't see any signs that he's not telling the truth.

'You made me sound like this strong, independent person with zero fucks to give, but all I was really doing was trying to fly under the radar and not be noticed.'

'Hm. You might have been trying very hard not to be noticed, but it didn't work. You were different from the other girls somehow, and that made you stand out.'

'Yeah, I know. They had tits and I didn't.'

'I wasn't talking physically. There always seemed to be this competition about who was going to go out with who. It wasn't just the girls; the boys were just as bad. And you just seemed to rise above it all, totally uninterested. In fact, Sarah was convinced you were a lesbian.'

'Charming!'

'That's getting off lightly from her. You should have heard what she had to say about some of the other girls.'

'I didn't really know her, but it doesn't sound like I was missing much.'

'She was all right. She just had lots of issues and that made her lash out sometimes.'

'Can I ask you another question?'

'Sure.'

'Did you ever think about me, you know, afterwards?'

'Are you serious? You were the reason that Sarah and I split up!'

'Why?'

'The morning after we... you know...'

'Had sex.'

'Yes. She came round, all tearful and apologetic, saying how much she loved me and wanted to make it work. I genuinely didn't know what to do, because I meant what I said to you about hanging out. You were so cool the way you dealt with the nosebleed, I seem to remember the sex was pretty awesome, and I was excited about getting to know you better, but on the other hand I had history with her, and I felt a responsibility for her.'

'Poor you,' I say sarcastically. 'Which of the adoring women to choose?'

'It wasn't like that. Anyway, I took the coward's way out. I couldn't face the hysteria if I told her it was over, and so I sent you that text because I assumed, wrongly as it turns out, that you and I were just a casual thing. It was a mistake. I knew that almost straight away, but by then it was already too late. When Sarah and I split up properly a couple of weeks later, I texted you and tried to call you to tell you, but—'

'I'd blocked your number.'

'Which is entirely reasonable.'

'What a mess,' I murmur.

'Yup. So when I saw you after the wedding, I thought maybe this was my chance to correct the mistakes of the past.'

'Hang on. Are you suggesting that maybe we pop back into the kitchen and get it on, see if you can avoid being a dick this time?'

'That wasn't what I was suggesting, no.'

'Just as well. Apart from the fact that the food hygiene people would close us down in a nanosecond, I'm not having sex with you again, however awesome it was for you. That ship has definitely sailed, do you understand?'

'I know, but would you let me buy you a drink, perhaps?'

I feel like I'm standing on the edge of a precipice. I could turn him down and walk away; that would definitely be the safe option. But I've realised that Laura, damn her, is right. Jamie and I do have unfinished business and, if I walk away now and cast aside his olive branch, what does that say about me? Also, despite the fact that I have no intention of ever going to bed with him again, hearing that I was awesome has stroked my ego more than a little.

'Sure,' I tell him. 'Why not?'

15

Despite Jamie's assertion that this is just a friendly drink, it does seem weirdly date-like walking into the pub with him. I feel like everyone is assuming we're a couple, even though nobody so much as glanced up when we came through the door.

'I'll get these if you want to find us a table,' Jamie offers when we reach the bar. 'What would you like?'

I hesitate for a moment. I quite fancy a glass of wine, but part of me wonders whether it would be safer to stick to soft drinks. I'd never forgive myself if I got drunk and snogged him again, or worse. This thought brings the scene in Elodie's bathroom crashing into my mind. *What the hell am I doing letting Jamie buy me a drink?*

'Is everything all right? You look like you've zoned out,' Jamie says, looking at me quizzically.

'Are you sure you're not a murderer?' I blurt, trying to deflect away from the reel that was playing in my head which I've somehow convinced myself he could also see.

'I'm sure. What's that got to do with anything?'

'I was just wondering whether this is your MO. You buy the drinks, your signet ring pops open and a little bit of powder goes in.

Next thing, I'm unconscious and you're preparing to chop me up in your cellar.'

He bursts out laughing. 'OK, you've got me. However, there are just a couple of your usual tiny flaws.'

'Which are?'

'I'm not wearing a signet ring and I don't have a cellar.'

'You haven't ruled out wanting to chop me up though.'

'That's because I might have to go through with that part if you don't actually choose a drink.'

He grins and I relax. *This is fine*, I tell myself firmly. *Just two friends enjoying some banter*. 'I'll have a glass of white wine, please.'

'Tell me something,' I continue once we're settled at a table with our drinks. 'How come you're selling cars rather than living the glamorous, rock-star life as lead singer of The Misfits?'

He's just about to answer when his phone pings. My eyes fall to the screen, but I'm too slow and don't get to see the sender.

'Do you mind if I deal with this?' he asks.

'Go ahead.' He reads the message and bashes out a quick reply before setting the phone down and looking back at me.

'Where were we?' he asks.

'You were going to tell me about what happened to The Misfits.'

His eyes twinkle with mischief. 'Oh yes. Which story to tell, though? Do you want the one where we're hugely successful but I develop a massive coke habit, spend months in rehab and then decide to just walk away from it all? Or would you prefer the one where we're also hugely successful but we start to have artistic differences and the band splits up, devastating our millions of fans? They're both much more interesting than the truth.'

'Tell me the true story first. If I decide it's too banal, I'll let you tell one of the others.'

'I guess you never heard us play, did you?'

'No. I wasn't one of the favoured ones. My crush on you had nothing to do with The Misfits. Or not much, anyway.'

'There's a reason so few people ever heard us.'

'Which is?'

'Quite simply, we were dreadful.'

'Really? But the favoured ones were always banging on about how deep and meaningful your lyrics were, and how your music challenged the status quo and other crap like that.'

'Obviously, we didn't know we were dreadful at the time. We actually believed the stuff you've just said, and we were convinced we just needed to find the right agent and we'd be off to the big time. We even applied to *X Factor*, thinking that might be our big break. It was *X Factor* that opened our eyes.'

'How so?'

'Hang on – if you really want to know this, we can't start there. It's like picking up a book and reading the last page first. So, when you were around, we were The Misfits, and we had, what did you call them?'

'The favoured ones.'

'Who would be like groupies, right?'

'Yes.'

'OK. So the band carried on once we reached the sixth form, but we changed our name. Martin, the bass guitarist, thought The Misfits was too adolescent and wouldn't stand out to potential agents. God, this sounds delusional now. Anyway, after a lot of humming and hawing, we changed it to Urban Dystopia.'

I burst out laughing. 'That is unbelievably pretentious!' I exclaim. 'I bet the favoured ones loved you even more.'

'It didn't do our image with them any harm, I admit. Anyway, do you remember Mr Price, the deputy head teacher?'

I nod and try to mimic his voice. 'Hemlines and necklines, ladies. Lower the first and raise the second.'

He smiles. 'That's him. He found out about us somehow, and suggested that the music teacher, Mrs Harris, came to hear us with a view to including us in the end of term concert.'

'And did she?'

'Yes. She was very polite, but no invitation followed. We told ourselves that she was too old and middle-class to understand our music, but that ought to have been the first alarm bell, really. Deep down, I think we all suspected we might be shit, but none of us wanted to be the first to admit it because that would seem like disloyalty.'

His phone beeps again, but this time he merely glances at the screen before turning it over so it's face down on the table.

'Were you really that bad?' I ask, trying to ignore the distraction.

'I'm afraid so. Let's start with Daniel, our drummer. Did you happen to notice him dancing at the wedding?'

'Not really. I was busy talking to Laura and trying not to be recognised.'

'If you'd have seen it, it would have been a clue. Let's just say I suspect Elodie would have had some impressive bruises on her feet the next day, because poor Daniel has absolutely no sense of rhythm.'

'That's a bit of a flaw if you're a drummer.'

'Yup. Add in a lead guitarist who is tone deaf and can only play three chords, as well as a keyboard player who failed his grade two piano, and you can start to imagine the scale of the problem.'

'Oh dear. What about you? Can you actually sing? I have this picture in my head of you screaming lyrics at random pitches, like some sort of musical Tourettes.'

'I can just about hold a tune, but I'm no Gary Barlow. Sean wasn't too bad, to be fair.'

'So you missed out on the school concert. Did you go straight from there to *X Factor*, or were there any other little diversions along the way?'

'It's all so embarrassing, looking back at it. We also made a demo CD and sent it to loads of top-flight agents.'

'Did any of them get in touch?'

'Of course not. Philistines, the lot of them. We were cutting edge, avant-garde. The world wasn't ready for us, obviously.'

'So then you applied for *X Factor*.'

'Yup.'

'And how did that go? Did you meet Simon Cowell?'

'Not likely. You have to get through two rounds of elimination before you even get close to the actual judges, let alone the TV show.'

'How far did you get, then?'

'We were pretty much laughed out of the first round. It was a total humiliation. The worst part was that they were talking seriously about putting us through for our "comedy value".'

'Ouch.'

'Yeah. It got worse when Mitchell, our tone-deaf lead guitarist, tried to challenge them.'

'Why?'

'Because they tore us apart. They dragged all the stuff we secretly knew but didn't want to admit into the open.'

'What did they say?'

'Funnily enough, I can remember it pretty much word for word. The main guy said "Listen, lads. Music needs three things: it needs rhythm, it needs a tune, and it needs lyrics that people are going to relate to. You have none of those things, literally none." Harsh, but ultimately fair.'

'He even hated the lyrics?'

Jamie stares into my eyes and drops his voice to a dramatic whisper. 'You're like a vampire, sucking me dry. Oh baby, I can't even cry. You make me want to lie down and die. Your love for me is just a lie. Your love... for me... is just... a lie.'

'Bloody hell,' I snigger.

'And that was one of the better ones.'

'And whose fault – sorry – responsibility were the lyrics?'

'We all worked on them together.'

'Mm. OK, I think I understand why your music career didn't work out. How did you get from there to your current job?'

'In some ways, that story is equally embarrassing. See, on the surface, I was this moody teenager who liked indie music and sang in a band. That was the cool part, or so I thought. But I was also a massive car nerd. Instead of watching hours and hours of porn, like a normal teenage boy, I used to spend my hours watching YouTube videos of car reviews.'

'Hold on. Are you seriously telling me that a teenage boy with what, in my albeit limited experience, appeared to be an entirely normal sex drive, never dabbled in any of the pornographic smorgasbord that the internet has to offer? I'm struggling to believe you.'

'Fine, there was some porn, but most of it was cars.'

'You weren't getting off to the cars though, were you?'

'Of course not. I'm not that much of a weirdo! But I knew all the models, how fast they were, everything. So, if I wasn't going to be a rock star, doing something with cars was the next obvious choice. As I told you before, I'm no mechanic, but selling cars? I reckoned I could do that. As soon as I passed my test and left school, I trawled my way around every car sales lot within commuting distance, asking if they had any jobs going. Of course, I was way too young to actually work on the sales side, but this one old guy, Steve Lord, offered to take me on probation as his assistant. It wasn't glamorous. Basically, my job was to keep the cars clean, prepare cars he'd bought to go on the forecourt, and do any paperwork he couldn't be arsed with. Some of the stuff I found in the cars that came in beggars belief.'

'Go on.'

'Knickers were a frequent find, usually tucked right under one of the front seats.'

'You mean—'

'Yup. It certainly taught me to treat any stains on the upholstery with deep suspicion.'

'That's disgusting!'

'It's the tip of the iceberg. I found all kinds of things, including used condoms, a small bag of weed and – this is the worst one – a turd.'

'Oh, God. Please tell me it wasn't human.'

'I didn't get it forensically analysed, but it would have to have been a terrifyingly large dog to produce something that size.'

'Didn't it smell?'

'I think it had been there a while. It was wrapped up in a tissue and stuffed in one of the door bins, with lots of other rubbish on top of it. There were quite a lot of fairly putrid things I found in that particular car, so the turd was probably just one of the components of the overall aroma.'

'How did you stand it?'

'For the most part, I enjoyed it. Not the turd, obviously, but Steve was a good boss and he knew I wanted to get into sales, so he took time out to train me. After a year or so, he began to let me take customers out on test drives, and that's how I met Gerald. Do you want another drink?' He indicates our empty glasses.

'I'll get these. What are you having?'

'Another pint of Harvey's, please. I'm not driving.'

The pub isn't particularly busy, so it only takes a few minutes for me to get the drinks. It's still long enough for Jamie to bash out a couple of messages on his phone, I notice. When I get back to the table, he glances at my glass of wine before looking back up at me.

'I'm not driving either,' I tell him. 'My flat's only a twenty-minute walk from here, so I leave the car at home if I'm coming into the Canterbury shop. Much less hassle than fighting with the traffic. Is there something you need to deal with?' I ask as his phone beeps again.

'No, sorry. It's fine.' Once again he turns it face down on the table.

'So, you met Gerald.'

'Yes, he was looking for a car for his son, who'd just passed his driving test. Steve and Gerald have known each other forever, and Steve thought it would be fun to get me to do the deal with Gerald, so he could get some customer feedback. The bastards had set it all up in advance. Anyway, it ended up backfiring spectacularly on Steve.'

'How?'

'Gerald was so impressed with me, he offered me a job with significantly higher pay.'

'I bet Steve didn't like that: being stabbed in the back by someone who was supposed to be his mate.'

'He was fine about it, actually. We're still good friends. In fact, if you'd have told me you didn't have the budget for the Land Rover, I would have recommended him to you.'

'And now you're the boss of the people that sell cars worth more than my flat. Pretty impressive at your age.'

'No more impressive than owning your own business. How did that come about?'

'It started when I met Alice at catering college.'

'What made you decide to go to catering college rather than staying on at school with the rest of us? It wasn't anything to do with what happened between you and me, was it?'

'No, you can relax on that one. I'd already decided to go to catering college before then. I just couldn't work out how trigonometry, literary criticism, or any of the rest of it was going to help me get a job. I wanted to learn practical stuff rather than writing any more essays about what Jane Austen had to say about the role of women in society. I would imagine myself in job interviews and the interviewer would ask, "What skills do you have that would make you a good fit for this position?", and all I would be able to reply is, "Nothing specific, but if you want to know how the subjunctive works in French, I'm your girl".'

'Do you know how the subjunctive works in French, then?'

'Not a clue!' I laugh. 'I was terrible at French.'

'Did you always know you wanted to cook?'

'God, no. It's scary really when I look back on it. We basically ruled out everything I knew I didn't want to do until we were left with catering or hairdressing, and I chose catering.'

'That sounds risky. What if you'd hated it?'

'I still had hairdressing lined up as a second choice, but thankfully I didn't need it. I found catering a real struggle to begin with because I didn't know half as much as I thought I did, but that's when I met Alice and we became friends. The rest is history.'

'And you started the business as soon as you left? What were you, eighteen?'

'Yes, it's only a two-year course. It was Alice's dream, really. To begin with, I was just going to work for her until I got enough experience to start out on my own, but we spent so much time together working on plans and proposals that she decided I ought to be her partner instead. She's also my best friend now.'

'And that works? What happens if you have a disagreement about something to do with the business? Doesn't that affect your friendship?'

'We don't disagree very often and, when we do, we rope in her

husband and daughter to referee. When I wanted to start the
external catering, Alice wasn't very keen. She thought it was a
distraction from our main business. So I had to put together a
proposal, as if I were going to the bank, and present it to the three
of them. Thankfully, they backed me on that one.'

'Hm. Watching you with Gerald tonight, I'm not sure I'd want to
go against you in a business decision.'

'It's lucky you sell cars and not cakes then, isn't it?'

As we sip our drinks, I'm very aware of his eyes on me, and I feel
suddenly hot. His phone has thankfully stopped pinging but I
realise I've let my guard down and I'm enjoying his company far
more than I ought to be. I'm definitely not going to have any more
wine tonight, that's for sure.

16

'You went for a *drink* with him?' Alice shrieks when I tell her on Sunday. 'So much for "he's not my Jamie".'

'He isn't. We're just friends.'

'If you say so. What did you talk about?'

'Nothing special. We were just filling each other in on what we've been up to over the last twelve years. It was good. Cathartic.'

'In what way?'

'I think we laid a lot of ghosts to rest. It turns out I made a bit more of an impression on him than I thought. He even tried to contact me a few weeks after the incident in Elodie's bathroom but of course I'd blocked his number so he couldn't get through.' I'm not telling Alice that he was also very complimentary about the sex; there are some things you don't tell even your best friend. I have to confess that, even though I have absolutely no intention of repeating the episode, being told I was 'pretty awesome' on my first attempt has buoyed me up no end.

'So what happens now?'

'Nothing. I do the event at the dealership and maybe we bump into each other every so often. Stop looking at me like that!'

'I'm sorry, but you're talking out of your backside.'

'Is this a business disagreement?' asks Mia as she wanders into the kitchen, tapping away on her phone. 'Do I need to go and get Dad?'

'No. Jess is trying to persuade me that the super-hot man she went for a drink with is just a friend,' Alice explains.

'Ugh. Old people sex. It's enough to put anyone off their lunch. When is lunch?'

'Soon. I'll call you.'

'She's got a bloody nerve,' I say to Alice. 'I'm twenty-eight; she makes it sound like I'm some sort of toothless geriatric!'

'To her, you are geriatric. Don't take it the wrong way. We were just the same when we were her age, weren't we?'

'I suppose so. What's happening with her boyfriend? Have you given her the safe sex talk yet? If the idea of me having sex appals her so much, you explaining it should be enough to tip her over the edge.'

'We think they've split up.'

'Oh, why?'

'She hasn't said anything to us, obviously. I mean, we're only her closest living relatives after all, but Richard overheard her running him down on the phone to one of her friends. Also, she's suddenly started eating meat again.'

'That does seem like a bit of a giveaway. Is she upset?'

'It's impossible to tell. There are so many reasons for her to be moody, you could pick one out of the air and have a decent chance of being at least partly right.'

'The joys of being a teenager, eh?'

'Mm.'

I'm pleased to have deflected Alice, as her line of questioning was making me uncomfortable. I really did enjoy catching up with Jamie, even though I felt slightly awkward when he insisted on walking me home at the end of the evening. Nothing happened; we kissed each other chastely on the cheek before he said good night and walked away. He was a perfect gentleman, which is why the incredibly filthy dream I had about him that night was such a surprise. I meant what I said about not reopening that particular door though; he may be 'super-hot', as Alice puts it, but I'm reminded of one of the few French proverbs I learned at school: *un chat échaudé craint l'eau froide*, which translates rather clumsily as, 'a scalded cat fears cold water'. Jamie may be perfectly safe now, but he scalded me pretty badly and I'm not going to be dipping my toes in the water with him any time soon, if ever.

'I'm going on another date, did I tell you?' I say to Alice as she brings the meat out of the oven to rest. It's lamb today, and the scents of garlic and rosemary coming off it are making my mouth water.

'With Jamie?'

'No. Stop pushing on that door; it's locked, OK?'

'You can't blame a girl for trying. Who is it then?'

'A guy called Nigel from the dating app.'

'What do you know about him?'

'Not a lot, but he seems nice from the messages we've exchanged. Also, unlike Luke, he's taking me to a proper restaurant.'

'Ooh. Which one?'

'The new French bistro that's opened up in Tankerton.'

'I've read about it. The reviews are excellent. When are you going?'

'Tuesday.'

'I look forward to hearing all about it.'

* * *

What I haven't told either Alice or Nigel is that this date is primarily a distraction. Jamie has occupied far too much of my head space since we officially buried the hatchet, so I'm hoping that going out on a proper date with someone else will help to push the reset button. Nigel has sounded genuinely nice on our conversations through the app, so I'm confident I'm not in for a repeat of the Luke experience at least. I park the car a little way up the road from the restaurant and I'm delighted to find him waiting outside for me, although I'm slightly puzzled to see that he's holding a carrier bag.

'Lovely to finally meet you, Jess,' he says, giving me a delicate kiss on the cheek. His aftershave is floral and slightly cloying, but the rest of him is exactly as he looked in his profile picture. He's tall, definitely over six foot, with light-brown hair, a prominent nose and light-hazel eyes that sparkle as he smiles.

'You too,' I reply. 'Shall we go in? I'm starving!'

He holds the door open for me and follows me through. The inside of the restaurant has definitely embraced the bistro vibe; the tables are covered with red, gingham oilcloths and the wooden chairs look like the owners raided several car boot sales; I can't see a single chair that matches another. The lack of carpet means it's also loud in here, but I'm smitten with the place already. While Nigel gives our names to the member of staff that greeted us, I cast my eyes over the other diners and what they're eating. They all look like they're having a whale of a time. This bodes very well indeed, and the food will hopefully be a world away from the stuff I had at the pub with Luke.

The waiter leads us to our table, near the back of the restaurant, and points out the blackboard with the menu on it. A jug of water, some bread and a slab of butter appear almost immediately.

'Oh, this is fabulous,' I declare after taking my first bite of the warm, crusty bread that I've slathered with soft, salty butter.

'It's not bad, is it?' Nigel agrees. 'I wasn't sure what to expect.

The reviews were good, but I haven't been here before, so it was a bit of a gamble.' He reaches into the carrier bag and pulls out a couple of bottles of wine.

'I didn't know whether you preferred red or white,' he explains, 'so I brought one of each. Of course, if you prefer something soft, I think they have all the usual things.'

'What the hell are you doing?' I ask, horrified, as he opens the bottles. 'Are you trying to get us thrown out before we even order any food?'

He stops what he's doing and looks up, evidently surprised by my outburst. He studies me for a minute and bursts out laughing.

'What?' I ask him.

'Sorry, I should have explained. It's a BYO restaurant. They don't have an alcohol licence so they expect you to bring your own bottle. Red or white?'

As I look round again, I can see that there are a variety of bottle holders next to the other diners, from simple carrier bags like Nigel's to full-on chilly bins, and my anxiety subsides.

'Really? In that case, I'll have a little bit of red, please,' I tell him. 'I've never come across a BYO restaurant before.'

'I think the concept originated in Australia and New Zealand,' he replies. 'It is gaining ground here, though. I guess it saves a good deal of faffing about with licences and so on.'

'Yes, but it must hit their profit margins because everyone knows the best markups are in the drinks.'

'I imagine they offset that with the savings of not having to run a bar. Some places charge you a flat fee for each bottle you bring, like a corkage charge. I don't know if they do that here.'

'It would be a bit rich. They haven't done anything. If they actually had to take the bottle and open it for you, that would be a different thing, wouldn't it?'

'I suppose so. What do you fancy to eat?'

The next ten minutes or so are taken up with perusing the menu on the board. It all looks delicious, and it takes me a while to make up my mind. In the end, I plump for the moules marinière followed by poulet à la Provençale, while Nigel orders Paté de Campagne and Steak Frites.

'So, have you been single long?' Nigel asks once we've given our orders to the waiter.

'Pretty much all my life,' I tell him. 'I'm a co-owner of a business, so there hasn't been a lot of time for socialising.'

I'm delighted to discover that Nigel is the polar opposite of Luke. He seems genuinely interested and asks lots of questions as I tell him about my work, friends (excluding Jamie, of course) and family life. Unlike Luke, he doesn't throw his opinions at me like they're statements of fact. I find him very easy to talk to.

'What about you? What's your story?' I ask him, as the waiter clears away the first course. Nigel has managed to score another plus point by offering me a bit of his paté for my professional opinion, and I reciprocated, only slightly unwillingly, with one of my mussels. The kitchen had obviously taken care with them, as they weren't even remotely gritty, and the sauce was so delicious, I had to hold myself back from finishing it, which wouldn't have left any room for my main course.

'Nothing very exciting, I'm afraid. I'm an optician. I married young, to the woman I thought was the love of my life, and we divorced a couple of years later. It was fairly amicable.'

'Do you mind me asking why you divorced?'

'Not at all. We just realised fairly quickly that we wanted different things out of life. I was ready to settle down and start a family, but she wanted to travel and have adventures. I believe she's currently in Thailand somewhere.'

'Shouldn't she have been upfront about the whole adventure thing before getting married?'

'She was, and I liked the idea of it when we talked about it, but when the reality of staying in shitty hostels in foreign countries dawned on me, I kind of went off it. I like my creature comforts, I'm afraid. A roof over my head, central heating, all the boring things. Do you like to travel?'

'I used to go on holiday with my parents when I was growing up, but that tended to be package holidays to sunny spots in Europe. There aren't that many appealing options for singles, so I tend to enrol myself on cookery courses in Italy and places like that.'

'That doesn't sound like much of a break from the day job.'

'It is though, because I don't have to think about it and there's always something new I can learn and bring back. I love wandering round the markets too. Somehow everything seems more vibrant and exciting in the sunshine.'

'I did enrol on something similar once,' he tells me. 'I thought I'd like to learn to paint, so I signed up to a two-week painting course in Tuscany. The food was lovely, but it became obvious very quickly that I have no artistic ability at all. You could have brought my paintings home, stuck them on a fridge and told people they were done by a four-year-old, and they would have believed you.' He smiles self-deprecatingly.

Our main courses arrive, and we continue to chat freely through both those and the puddings we decide we have to try, just to make sure that they're not a massive disappointment. By the end of the evening, I have no doubt that Nigel is quite the catch. He's attentive, I can see he's good looking, and he's excellent company.

All of which makes it a crying shame that, for some reason I can't quite fathom, I don't fancy him. At all.

17

Any fears I might have had about having to gently let Nigel down proved unfounded, as he called me the next day to say that he'd had a wonderful evening and really enjoyed my company, but felt he was looking for someone with more of a nine-to-five job who would be around in the evenings and at weekends more often than he suspected I would be. I tried to sound disappointed, but it was a relief. A month has passed and I haven't been on any more dates. After that night, I realised that I needed to get my head into a better place where Jamie is concerned before inviting anyone else into my life.

The problem is that, every time I think I've got him firmly back in the friend zone where he belongs, he finds a reason to call me about some detail to do with the car launch, and we generally end up having a long chat. It's not that I mind chatting with him – I really enjoy it – but I always end up feeling confused about him again. However, it's finally the night of the car launch and, from a catering perspective at least, everything appears to be going to plan. The canapés are going out at a steady pace, and Gerald made a point of coming out to the kitchen trailer earlier to tell me how delicious they are and how impressed he is with the professionalism of the servers. I haven't seen Jamie yet, but I have no doubt that he will appear at some point. This will be the first time we've met face to face since our drink in the pub and, annoyingly, I'm a little excited about seeing him again.

As much as I've tried to keep my barriers up, the lack of any other men in my life, plus Jamie's calls, makes it too easy for him to slip into my thoughts when I least expect it. I can't talk to Alice about it, as I know she'd tell me to stop messing about and jump on Jamie before he gets away, which is frankly totally unhelpful advice. Even if I wanted to talk to Laura about it, which I don't for the same reason, she finally had her baby last week, so I don't think she has mental space to listen to my relationship dilemmas. It's a little boy, and she and Kevin have named him Isaac. The obligatory newborn photos appeared on Facebook within hours of the birth, showing a delighted Kevin holding an angry-looking baby, with an exhausted and sweaty Laura in the background.

'Celeb alert,' Cara, one of the servers, tells me as she brings an empty tray back to the pass.

'Oh yes? Who?' I ask her.

'Only Ritchie Hart. He arrived in an enormous, fuck-off, chauffeur-driven SUV with blacked-out windows and a personalised numberplate. His new girlfriend, Miranda Leider, is with him too. She's even more glamorous in the flesh than in the magazines. I thought Emma was going to drop her tray of drinks, she was so starstruck.'

'Who is Ritchie Hart?'

'Oh come on, you must know him! He's the host of *Match Maker* on TV. Surely you watch it?'

'Sorry.'

'It's only, like, one of the biggest shows on a Saturday night. Every week, he gets ten members of the public who are looking for love into the studio and they have to answer a load of questions live on air. At the end, he matches two of them into a couple and they get to go on holiday together.'

'Sounds awful. Let me guess: all the couples hate each other and it's total car crash TV.'

'No! That's why it's so big. I mean, yeah, you do get some who hate each other and that's usually pretty funny, but he's had over twenty couples go all the way and get married so far. I can't believe you've never seen it.'

'Perhaps I should come inside and introduce myself,' I laugh. 'He'd have his work cut out with me.'

'Ha. Good luck with that. I read online that there's a two-year waiting list for the show, and it's pretty hard to get anywhere near him tonight as the sales guys have gone into some kind of feeding frenzy.

'Probably just as well. Knowing my luck, I'd be matched with someone I absolutely hated or who hated me, and then I'd be forced to go on holiday with them and end up serving out my days in some foreign prison after I'd murdered them.'

Our conversation is interrupted by the arrival of one of the other servers, Gisele. She's carrying a half-empty tray of mini salmon and dill cakes and looking flustered.

'Sorry, Jess. Ritchie Hart's girlfriend, Miranda, just asked if the salmon in the fishcakes was wild or farmed, and that wasn't in the breakdown you gave earlier. Apparently, Ritchie only eats wild salmon because of the additives in farmed fish.'

'Oh, for goodness' sake. Where on earth does she think she is? We're serving canapés in a car dealership, not tea at the Ritz.'

'What shall I say then?' Gisele is wide-eyed, obviously keen to do the right thing for the famous guests.

'Tell her the truth, which is that it's farmed but organic, so it's not pumped full of antibiotics or anything like that. Then tell her to take her head out of her arse and join the rest of us on planet Earth.'

'I might leave off the second bit, if it's all the same to you,' Gisele tells me before scampering off to impart the information to the golden couple.

'Not a fan of *Match Maker* then?' Jamie asks, appearing out of nowhere.

'Bloody hell, you made me jump. Where did you come from?' I ask. I'm very aware of my heart thudding in my chest and, frustratingly, it's only partly from the shock.

'Sorry, I was keeping out of the way to the side. I didn't want to be flattened by your server in her rush. I came out to see how you were doing. I reckon we've had around three quarters of the people we're expecting now, so hopefully you're in the same place.'

'Yes, that sounds right to me. Has it gone well?'

'Very. Gerald is absolutely over the moon, particularly as Ritchie Hart is in the middle of ordering the top of the range with pretty much all the extras. We're talking a quarter of a million quid's worth of car, give or take.'

'That's mad.'

'That's celebrity. So, what have you got against the lovely Miranda then?'

'Nothing. I have no idea who she is. I just think it's a nonsense demanding to know whether the salmon is wild or not.'

'People like that have totally different expectations to the rest of us. It comes with the territory.'

'I have nothing against people with exacting standards, and I'm all about organic, free-range food with traceable provenance, but if she knew anything about salmon, she'd know that was an almost impossible question to answer.'

'Why?'

'OK. You'd think it would be easy, wouldn't you? Farmed salmon come out of farms and wild salmon come out of rivers, right? But sometimes the farmed fish escape, and then they breed with the wild ones, so you catch one in a river and what have you got? Is it farmed, wild, or somewhere in between? Truly wild salmon are becoming increasingly rare.'

'I thought you could tell the difference from the colour of the flesh.'

'Amateur mistake,' I tell him with a grin. 'You could get any colour of flesh you want in farmed salmon just by adding the right dyes to the food. You could probably even have blue if you wanted it.'

'So how are you supposed to tell the difference?'

'The only way that I know of, and it's still a gamble because of the interbreeding, is to look at the tail of the fish.'

'What does that tell you?'

'Farmed salmon only have to swim around their enclosures, so they have pretty small tails. Wild salmon, on the other hand, have to do all that acrobatic stuff to get upstream and spawn, so they have much bigger tails to power them up the waterfalls.'

'Every day is a school day,' he smiles. 'What are you doing after this?'

'Why?'

'There's quite a lot of Prosecco left. Gerald's in such a good mood, he's suggested that the sales guys and me take a bottle each as a thank you. The problem with Prosecco is that you really have to drink the whole bottle when you open it, otherwise it goes flat. That's way too much for me, but I'd be happy to share it with you if you like.'

'I'm driving, sorry.'

'I thought of that. I could follow you home, you could leave your car there and come on to mine if you want. I've been working my socks off all evening, so if there were any leftover canapés, you could bring them too.'

'I don't know, Jamie. Having a drink in the pub is one thing, but—'

'I'm not trying it on, I promise. I'll call you a cab the moment you want to leave.'

I'm not sure what to say. On the one hand, the idea of spending some time with him after we pack up sounds very appealing, but I'm not wild about the idea of going to his flat. It almost feels like he's in control of the agenda if we do that, and that makes me uncomfortable. Plus, I think it's pretty unlikely that there will be any canapés left over, and I'm pretty hungry myself.

'It's a nice idea,' I tell him after I've thought about it and done a quick mental inventory of the contents of my fridge. 'I just want to suggest one small tweak if I may. I think it would be better if you came over to mine.'

'How so?'

'Because these canapés will definitely be all gone by the time we're done here, and I happen to know I have fish fingers, tartare sauce and fresh white bread at home.'

'Are you telling me that the great chef is offering me a fish finger sandwich?'

'Do you have a problem with that?'

'Absolutely not! It was just a surprise, that's all. I didn't think people like you ate lowly food like fish finger sandwiches.'

'A good fish finger sandwich is hard to beat, I reckon. So, shall I come and find you when we're all packed up and I'm ready to go?'

'I'll be waiting.'

* * *

In the end, the guests pretty much dry up by seven thirty, so we take the opportunity to tidy up and wipe down the trailer early and I'm ready to go by half past eight. Jamie gives me the address of his flat for my satnav in case we get separated, which turns out to be a good thing because we're only about two turnings away from the dealership before I completely forget which car I'm supposed to be following. My mind is preoccupied with trying to work out how I feel about having Jamie in my home. I'm also trying to remember whether I have any laundry drying on the radiators; the last thing I want is for Jamie's first impression to be a sea of knickers and bras. We might just be friends, but I'm still anxious to make a good impression. When I pull up outside his block, he's already parked up and is waiting for me, cradling the bottle in the crook of his arm and talking into his phone. He holds up two fingers to indicate that he's nearly done. Whatever the call is about, it seems serious, as he's frowning slightly.

'Sorry about that. Family issue,' he tells me as he climbs in and fastens his seatbelt. 'How's the car?'

'Very nice, thank you.'

'Have you tried out the four-wheel drive yet?'

'No, but Ian showed me how to work it, and I'm sure it's only a matter of time before I need to get out of a muddy field.'

'That reminds me, we're doing a track and field day at Brands Hatch in October, and Gerald asked me to ask you if you could do a lunch for the punters. It's a Saturday.'

'What's a track and field day?'

'Basically, we invite all the people who have bought cars from us in the last year, or who have ordered and are waiting for delivery, to come to Brands Hatch to get an idea of what the vehicles can really do. So we have some sports cars on the track, and there's an off-road course to demonstrate the Land Rovers. It's all sponsored by the manufacturer; they send the cars and instructors along with various goodies for us to give away. Gerald would like you to do the lunch.'

'But isn't there a restaurant there already?'

'We normally book one of the hospitality suites, but we aren't going to be the only people there. We share the day with other manufacturers, taking turns on the track and so on, so a couple of groups have to organise their own lunch. Gerald isn't generally a fan of that – he thinks having one of the hospitality suites gives a better impression – but he's got this bee in his bonnet about you doing something with a British theme to champion the British cars, see?'

'Give me the date and I'll check my diary. What do you need in terms of drinks?'

'We won't be serving alcohol, obviously, because they'll be driving. So, sparkling water, maybe some flavoured stuff, and tea and coffee at regular intervals. Can you do that?'

'I don't have a coffee machine in the trailer, but I can contact Mike from Better Latte Than Never and see if he's free. He's a bit of a miserable so-and-so, but he's got one of those little three wheeled vans with all the equipment built in and he makes a mean coffee.'

'Brilliant. Now, enough business. I've got Prosecco and fish finger sandwiches to think about. I'm starving.'

'Just as well we're here then,' I tell him as I turn off the road and swipe my entry card to open the gate into the car park. Thankfully, he doesn't seem to notice that I nearly drop the card in the process because my hands are so sweaty with nerves.

18
___

Jamie's presence seems to totally fill my flat; I repeated the mantra, *We're just friends* in my head all the way up the stairs, but I'm still acutely aware of him as I reach into the cupboard to bring out two glasses and hand them to him. It's not that my flat is particularly small; I'm just not used to other people, especially ones I have such complex feelings about, being in it. Thankfully, there weren't any stray pairs of knickers drying on any of the radiators, but I can sense him looking around and it makes me wonder what my home says about me. Having Jamie here makes me look at it in a different way. I'm sure it breaks all the Feng Shui rules (whatever they are), but my flat is comfortable in a kind of 'shabby chic' way. The living room has a squishy sofa that I picked up in a charity shop, along with a small TV and a large bookcase that is mainly filled with recipe books I've bought from various places over the years. The windowsills are festooned with pots containing different herbs. There are two places where I've spent serious money: my bed (which I won't be showing him) and the kitchen, where we are now. I hear the pop of the cork behind me and the scrape of the chair as

Jamie settles himself at my tiny kitchen table after handing me a glass.

'You might as well make yourself useful if you're going to sit there,' I tell him, handing him a board with the bread and a knife. 'Cut four slices from this. There's tartare sauce and lettuce in the fridge.'

'*Oui, Chef!*' he barks.

'Cut that out, idiot,' I laugh as I take a sip of the Prosecco, add some oil to a pan and place the fish fingers in it.

'Interesting,' he remarks, watching me.

'What?'

'Why fry them rather than grill them or bake them?'

'Because I'm hungry, and I haven't got time to wait for the grill or oven to heat up.'

'Oh.' He sounds disappointed. 'I thought maybe it was some cheffy secret.'

'Jamie?'

'Yes?'

'It's a fish finger sandwich. Stop overthinking it.'

'Can I ask you a different question then?'

'If you like.'

'Where do you see yourself ten years from now?'

'That's a bit deep. What brought that on?'

'I was thinking about it when I was talking to you earlier. You're twenty-eight and you already co-own your own business. Where do you go from here? What's the next challenge?'

'Does there have to be one? It's been pretty challenging just getting to here.'

'We've got, what, another forty years before we reach retirement age? If I told you that you were going to spend the next forty years doing this, how would you feel about that?'

'I don't think I look at it that way,' I reply after a pause. 'Alice and I make a yearly plan every January so we've got something to aim for, but I don't have any grand strategies beyond that, and certainly no forty-year plan. What about you? Where next for you?'

'Good question. On the one hand, Gerald isn't going to be around for ever. He's in his late fifties and he's never made any bones about the fact that he'd like to retire as soon as he can afford to. I reckon I'd have a decent shot at getting his job if I wanted it, but I'm not sure that I do.'

'Wouldn't you have to buy him out?'

'No. We're part of a chain of dealerships. He's the boss of our branch, but he doesn't own it.'

'So why don't you want his job?'

'Because that really is a dead end unless I win the lottery and can buy the whole chain. Assuming I don't, where would I go from there? Also, I kind of miss dealing with the customers since I became a manager. I've been toying with the idea of starting out on my own.'

'Can you afford to?'

'What do you mean?'

'At the moment, I imagine you get a regular salary, the swanky cars you drive about in, maybe some other perks like bonuses and a pension plan. If you start on your own, all of that goes out of the window, at least for the first few years. Trust me, I've been there and it's hard going. I was lucky, because I was living at home and my parents were supportive, but you've got a mortgage and other bills to pay, haven't you?'

'I do, but it sounds almost like the successful businesswoman is telling me not to start a business. Seems a bit counterintuitive, doesn't it?'

'I'm not telling you not to start a business; I'm just saying make sure you go into it with your eyes open. If I'd have known what a struggle the first few years were going to be, I think I might have turned Alice down and got myself a regular job working for someone else.'

'Do you regret it then?'

'Absolutely not. I love what I do and now that things are more stable, financially, I've got enough money to live pretty comfortably. I just wouldn't go through those first few years again.'

'A bit like a puppy, perhaps.'

'What?'

'My brother and his wife got a puppy some years ago. A labradoodle, cutest-looking thing ever. For the first six months, it drove them mad, chewing everything in sight, crying at night and peeing on the carpet – all the normal puppy things. I think there were several occasions when they came close to getting it rehomed because of all the carnage. It's three years old now and they absolutely adore it, but they still swear adamantly that they're never having another puppy.'

'I didn't know you had a brother.'

'He's a lot older so we were never in the same school.'

The conversation pauses as we turn our attention to assembling the sandwiches. Jamie cuts thick slices of bread, topping them with tartare sauce and lettuce from the fridge. I add the fish fingers when they're ready and we settle down to eat.

'God, this is good,' he murmurs after his first mouthful. 'I can't remember the last time I had a fish finger sandwich.'

'You can't go wrong with a bit of comfort food,' I agree as Jamie tops up my glass.

For a while, neither of us say anything as we concentrate on our food. I have an additional challenge, which is that it turns out a fish finger sandwich is a surprisingly difficult thing to eat without making a mess. Normally, this doesn't worry me, but I don't want to accidentally smear tartare sauce on my chin in front of Jamie. He doesn't seem to have the same reservations, and attacks his sand-wich with gusto.

'I've been thinking about it, and I reckon I'd get a kitten,' I tell him, when we've cleared up and settled ourselves on the sofa in the sitting room. My head is at that lovely stage where I've had enough Prosecco to feel the effect, but I'm still in complete control. Although I've started to get used to Jamie's presence in my flat and my nerves have settled, sitting so close to him on the sofa is doing things to me that I'm trying very hard to ignore.

'What?'

'Your brother and the puppy,' I explain. 'If it were me, I'd get a kitten rather than a puppy.'

'Because?'

'Don't get me wrong, I like dogs, but I don't really have the life-style for a dog. A cat, on the other hand, is more independent. You can leave a cat all day and it doesn't mind as long as it's got some-where warm and comfortable to sleep. Apparently, cats sleep for sixteen hours a day, did you know that?'

'I didn't. You're a veritable mine of information, Jess. First salmon and now cats.' He smiles and my insides flip. His dark-brown eyes are twinkling with amusement and I let my gaze travel down over his nose (still perfect despite my best efforts), his mouth and his neck. He's loosened his tie and undone his top button, and a wisp of dark chest hair is just visible in the gap of his collar. Now that I'm studying him properly, I have to admit that Laura was right; he's even more attractive than he was at school. The awkward, gangly teenaged-ness has gone; he's grown into himself and it's all I can do to stop myself from reaching out to run my hands over his chest. I have a tremendous desire to kiss him; I wonder what he'd do if I kissed him?

'I'd kiss you back,' he says.

'Sorry?'

'You just asked what I'd do if you kissed me.'

I can feel myself flushing crimson. I can't believe I said it out loud. Now what?

'If it's any help,' he tells me gently, 'I was kind of wondering the same thing myself.'

I'm suddenly paralysed with indecision. Part of me really, really wants to kiss him but there's another part that equally desperately doesn't want to. It's like my body and brain are pulling in separate directions. My body is threatening to act of its own free will, while my brain is fervently telling it that it would be a mistake, that Jamie isn't good for me. Something is going to have to give.

Fuck it. I lean forward and press my lips to his.

If this were a movie, we'd cut to scenes of fireworks going off and waves crashing on a beach, but the reality of kissing Jamie is not like that. Even though I can't really remember the details of what it felt like to kiss him twelve years ago, there is something almost familiar about it. It feels oddly like coming home. There's no awkwardness as our mouths open and our tongues meet, it's as if this is a well-rehearsed dance where we each know exactly what to do and when. It's lovely, and I can't get enough of it.

'Wow,' he says simply, when we come up for air.

'Yeah, that pretty much covers it,' I grin.

'There's something I need to tell you before this goes any further.' His face is suddenly serious and the joyful fizz inside me is replaced by a knot of worry.

'What?'

'My life isn't completely simple. I have other people who depend on me.'

'What are you saying? If you're married or in a relationship, this stops right here,' I tell him firmly. 'I'm not that kind of woman.'

'Relax, I'm not married and I'm not that kind of man either. But I do have a daughter.'

Whatever I was expecting him to say, it wasn't this. I sit back and let the information sink in.

'Why didn't you say anything before?' I ask eventually.

'I nearly did when we went to the pub, but I couldn't find a way to bring her up without it sounding forced. Plus, we'd only just buried the hatchet and I wasn't sure how you'd feel about me having a child.'

'I think you'd better tell me everything, don't you?'

'Her name is Elizabeth, Lizzie, and she's five years old. I met her mother, Simone, when I was working for Steve. I sold her a car, and, to cut a long story short, we ended up moving in together. Everything was going really well, so when Simone suggested trying for a baby, it seemed an entirely natural next step. Simone was never interested in marriage, so starting a family together felt like the commitment that would cement our relationship instead.'

'But you're not together now. What happened?'

'I don't think there was one thing in particular, rather a series of events that just broke us in the end. Lizzie was premature and had a very traumatic birth, having a newborn baby in the house was stressful, and we started to argue more and more.'

'I can understand that. I remember my sister saying how difficult it is when you're exhausted, you've tried absolutely everything and the baby still won't stop screaming. I think her husband definitely got it in the neck a couple of times when he said the wrong thing.'

'That sounds familiar, although we were rather more extreme. Simone was completely devoted to Lizzie and I felt increasingly shut out. I tried to help to begin with but, every time I did something that I thought would make her life easier, Simone made it abundantly clear that she felt I was meddling and somehow insinuating that she was a bad mother who couldn't look after her child. In the end, it became clear to both of us that we'd reached a point we couldn't come back from, so I moved out when Lizzie was eighteen months old. If I'm brutally honest, I think we were starting to drift apart before Simone got pregnant, but stupidly thought having a baby would bring us closer together. Anyway, they still live in the same house in Faversham, I see Lizzie regularly, and I think Simone and I are better parents for not living together. I wanted you to know now, because if you and I are going to take this further, you need to understand that she's an important part of my life.'

'Of course she is!' I exclaim, relieved that I haven't just unwittingly been adulterously kissing someone else's husband. 'Tell me though,' I continue more cautiously, 'things with Simone, are they definitely, one hundred per cent over? If there's even the vaguest possibility that you two might get back together, you need to be honest with me now. I'm not playing the Sarah game again.'

'I can promise you that Simone and I are not going to get back together,' he says solemnly, looking directly into my eyes. 'I'm all yours, if you want me. Well, apart from the bit that belongs to Lizzie, obviously.' He smiles.

Although I don't doubt his sincerity one bit, a door softly closes somewhere deep inside me. There is definitely more to this story than he's given me so far, and I need to protect myself until I'm certain I can trust him.

'I believe you,' I tell him, 'and I'm really grateful that you've been so honest with me. I really like you, Jamie, and I do want this, but—'

'It's OK, I understand,' he interrupts, pulling back. 'I'll call a taxi.'

'Shut up and let me finish. I was going to say that I want this, but you're going to have to be patient, and we're going to take it slow, OK? I can't afford a repeat of last time, so you're going to have to wait until I'm ready before we take the next step.'

He smiles. 'I reckon I can do that.'

'Is there anything else I need to know? Now would be a very good time to dust off any skeletons you have in your cupboards.'

'Nope. That's it. No other skeletons anywhere.'

'Good.'

I don't know why, but I suddenly feel awkward around him again. When we were kissing, I was swept up in the moment, but his revelations have kind of punctured the mood. I don't have a problem with him having a daughter at all, but it's like an invisible barrier has gone up between us.

'When you say you want to take it slow...' he begins after a few moments.

'Yes?'

'Does that mean that there is something?'

'What do you mean?'

'Well, if this was just a one-off thing, you'd be kicking me out around now, I reckon. But taking it slow indicates that this could be the start of something.'

I look at the hope in his face and I'm torn. I do want this, but I'm scared as well.

'I don't know yet,' I tell him, 'but don't be a dick this time, OK?'

'I won't.'

I can tell by his expression that there's more. 'What?' I ask.

'This taking it slow. We can still kiss though?'

My initial reaction is to tell him no, that I need more time. However, I can't deny the way he makes me feel when I look at him and, given what we've just been doing, imposing a ban on kissing now would be shutting the stable door long after that particular horse has bolted, wouldn't it?

I smile gently at him. 'I'd like that,' I say, as I lean forward and our lips meet again.

19

I'm not even through the door the next evening before the phone rings. The caller display tells me it's Laura and I briefly wonder if she's somehow sensed that something is going on with Jamie and me. I'm still not completely convinced that this isn't a massive mistake, particularly as I jumped out of my skin when his first text message arrived mid-morning., Thankfully, it wasn't a repeat of last time.

I'm thinking of you xx

I'm thinking of you too xx

What are you doing on Saturday night?

Working. Another wedding reception.

Nice. Try not to break down. I don't want you being rescued by anyone else. Sunday?

You'll be in trouble if I break down! Sunday evening's free.

Would you like to come round? I'm seeing Lizzie during the day, but I could probably rustle up something to eat. I'd love to see you.

I'd love to see you too. Don't worry too much about food as I will have had lunch with Alice and tea with my parents.

What on earth will we do if I don't feed you? We might have to talk to each other, or…

I like talking to you. Or… sounds even better xx

After that, it was a struggle to concentrate on the quiches and pies for the shops. Thankfully, even though I'm so familiar with our most popular products that I can pretty much cook them in my sleep, I still make sure I set timers just in case. Today would definitely have been a 'just in case' day as I've been very distracted. I know it was just kissing, but I feel like we're laying proper foundations for something much bigger this time. I meant what I said about taking it slow, but it was a struggle when every fibre of my being was begging me to take him to bed last night. I'm glad I didn't, but I'm not entirely sure how long I'm going to be able to hold out for.

'How are you?' I ask Laura as I close the door behind me and fumble for the light switch.

'Very, very sore,' she replies. 'I followed all the instructions, doing perineal massages and rubbing coconut oil into it when I was pregnant, and I still tore like a paper bag. I don't know how many stitches I've got down there, but it feels like it'll never be the same again. Going to the loo stings like buggery, and I'm bleeding buckets. According to the midwife, this is all completely normal, but I'm sure they never told me it was going to be like this. And that's before we get to my poor tits. Still, Isaac is an absolute sweetie. I never knew it was possible to love another human being so completely. I mean, I love Kevin, obviously, but this is totally different.'

'And how is Kevin?' I ask, keen to move the conversation on before Laura gives me any more gory details.

'He's being an absolute star. He bought me this doughnut thing to sit on, which really helps, and he's doing everything he can to make life easy for me. I'm up every couple of hours feeding Isaac, sometimes more, so he's attempting to keep on top of all the other stuff I normally do, such as cooking and laundry. He's not a brilliant cook and we had a bit of an incident where our white sheets suddenly turned pink, but he's trying hard and I really appreciate it. Anyway, enough about me and my mangled body. How are you?'

'Yeah, pretty good actually.'

'Oh yes? What do I need to know?'

'Jamie came over last night and, well, it's early days but I'm hopeful.'

'*What?* Wait a minute, back up here. I turn my back for, what, a week and you're dating Jamie now? The same Jamie that you firmly told me you wouldn't have anything to do with romantically?'

I grin. 'I changed my mind.'

'When?'

'Oh, somewhere around the first time that I kissed him.'

'And when was that?'

'Last night.'

'OK, so this is very new then. I was beginning to feel like someone who's been in prison for years, only to come out and find everything they thought was familiar has changed. Have you sealed the deal?'

'I'm sorry?'

'You know. Done the deed.'

'No. We're taking it slowly this time. I need to know that I can trust him before we go there. He has a daughter, did you know that?'

'Really? I take it he's not still with the mother.'

'No. They split up when Lizzie was eighteen months old.'

'Do you know why?'

'He said they argued a lot when the daughter was born, and it just got to the point where they couldn't carry on. He didn't give too many details and I didn't want to pry.'

'Hm. I think I would want to pry if I were you. Kevin and I have had a couple of humdingers recently, but it hasn't split us up. Do you think there could be more to it?'

'Such as?'

'What if he was unfaithful to her?'

'That's a bit of a leap, Laura.'

'Not necessarily. Home isn't all that happy, he starts looking elsewhere, she finds out...'

'That's not what he said happened. I don't think he's a cheater, Laura.'

'He cheated on Sarah with you, didn't he?'

'No. They split up, remember?'

'Only to get back together the very next day. Be careful, Jess, that's all I'm saying.'

I feel a bit deflated. This conversation isn't going the way I expected at all, and I'm starting to second-guess myself again. 'I thought you'd be pleased for me,' I say a little peevishly.

'I am! I really am. Sorry, I'm probably just a bit all over the place at the moment. Ignore me. Oh shit, I can hear Isaac crying. I'd better go and deal with him. Lovely to talk to you. Keep me posted, yeah?'

'I will,' I promise and hang up.

I know she meant well and thought she was looking out for me, but Laura has successfully punched a massive hole in my bubble of happiness. How would I feel if Jamie had been unfaithful to Simone? She's right; I could never trust a man who did that. I'm sure he's not the type, though. But then he did seem to get over splitting up with Sarah suspiciously quickly, didn't he? Am I making a massive mistake?

I try to put it out of my mind and focus on preparing my evening meal but the seed has been sown. I know I'm probably being paranoid, but I can't leave it. I reach for my phone and send him a message.

I need to ask you a question.

Sure. What's up?

Why did you and Simone really split up? Was it just the arguing or was there more?

There's a bit of a pause before his answer comes through.

I told you. We just weren't compatible in the end. Not sure what you mean by more?

Did you cheat on her?

He doesn't reply but my phone rings a moment later.

'What made you ask that?' He sounds slightly offended.

'I was telling Laura about you and she suggested there might have been more that you hadn't told me. It just sowed a seed of doubt in my mind so I thought I'd ask you directly rather than let it fester.'

'Will you believe me if I say no?'

'If it's the truth, yes.'

'I didn't cheat on her, I promise. I've never cheated on anyone and I wouldn't.'

'Some might say that you cheated on Sarah with me,' I challenge him.

'And they would be wrong,' he counters. 'She told me quite explicitly, just before she stormed out of Elodie's house, that we were finished. When you and I...' he peters out.

'Had sex. Why do you find that so difficult to say?'

'Because it sounds so clinical and cold.'

'I don't think we can call it making love, can we. Not in light of what happened afterwards.'

'Fair enough. But when you and I got together back then, I was a free agent. I didn't cheat on Simone and I won't cheat on you. I don't know what else to say, Jess.'

'I'm sorry. I do want to trust you, but I guess it's going to take time.'

'I get it, don't worry. Are we OK?'

'Yeah.'

'You don't sound sure.'

'I am. I'll see you on Sunday.'

'OK.'

I feel terrible as I hang up. I'm not even twenty-four hours into this supposed relationship with Jamie, and it already feels as if the wheels are coming off. A tear slips down my cheek and I brush it away. I know Laura meant well, but she has unwittingly done a lot of damage and the conversation with Jamie hasn't reassured me as much as I'd hoped. I believe him when he says he wasn't unfaithful, and I know that we're never going to get anywhere while the past still has a hold over me. The rational part of me knows that it was all a long time ago, and he's not the total villain I thought he was, but I've carried this hurt for so many years that it's difficult to just set it aside. Am I ready to let myself go and give him the trust he's asking for? Maybe it would be better to put a stop to this now before either of us gets too involved.

I'm still wrestling with my feelings a little while later when the intercom buzzer sounds to let me know that someone is at the gate to the car park. I'm not expecting anyone, or any deliveries, so my heart jumps into my mouth when Jamie's face appears on the video screen.

'What are you doing here?' I ask stupidly.

'I was in the neighbourhood. Can I come in?'

'I guess so. Park in one of the visitor spaces. I'll come down.'

I turn down the oven and grab my keys before running down the stairs to the ground floor and out into the car park. Jamie is standing by his car.

'Hi,' I say.

'Hi,' he replies. Neither of us seems to know what to say next, so there's a long pause. So far, so awkward.

'I have a hunch. Can I share it with you?' he tells me eventually.

'Please do.'

'On the phone, you said we were OK, but the tone of your voice told me a very different story. My hunch is that you've been pacing your flat, trying to work out if I am genuinely who I say I am, or whether I'm just the same bastard that hurt you twelve years ago getting ready to do it all over again. Your self-protective streak has kicked in and you've been telling yourself that maybe it would be easier to walk away before you find out. How am I doing?'

I smile guiltily.

'I thought as much. Here's the problem, though. I'm not the same guy that hurt you before. Well, I am, but you know what I mean. We may just be starting out, but I think we've got the makings of something really exciting here and I'm not going to give you up without a fight. I'll do anything.'

'Anything?'

'Just say the word. What do I need to do?'

A tear drips off my chin; I didn't even realise I was crying. He holds out his arms and I fold myself into his embrace, wetting his shirt in the process. He holds me close and we stand there for what feels like ages, neither of us saying a word. I can feel his cheek resting on the top of my head and my doubts and fears start to melt away. His arms feel strong around me, and I realise I'm practically clinging to him in return.

'I'm so sorry I doubted you,' I whisper into his chest.

'It's OK. It's going to take time, I get that.' He pulls back slightly and then plants a tender kiss on my forehead. 'All I need you to know is that I'm here and I'll do whatever it takes for however long it takes. Just tell me what you need and I'll do it.'

I tilt my head back and look up at him. 'If your hunch is anything to go by, you seem to be doing pretty well on telepathy alone so far,' I say.

He laughs gently. 'Don't push your luck. I'm a man, and I've probably just used up all my telepathic powers. It's probably safer if you just tell me in future.'

'I'll try.'

'Are we all right now, you and me?' His eyes are still full of concern, I notice. 'If there's anything more I need to say or do...'

'You've said and done everything you needed to. I'm sorry for being neurotic and dragging you over here.'

'Are you kidding? I have no idea how I was going to wait until Sunday to see you again so you gave me the perfect excuse.'

'Would you like to come up? I've got some shepherd's pie in the oven. I was going to freeze half of it, but you're welcome to it if you like.'

'I don't want to intrude.'

I laugh. 'You should have thought of that before you came rushing over to stop me dumping you!'

'Fair point. Yes please. I'd love some, if you really don't mind.'

'On one condition.'

'Which is?'

'You kiss me now.'

'With pleasure.' He dips his head and our lips meet. I'm aware that we're probably putting on quite the show for the neighbours, but I don't care. All I can think about are Jamie's strong arms around me, the delicate aroma of his aftershave in my nostrils, and his mouth on mine. I'm rapidly getting addicted to him.

20

'You look different,' Molly observes, staring at me as I settle on the sofa next to her at Mum's. 'Are you wearing make-up?'

'I might be,' I reply nonchalantly as I relieve her of Henry, who is beaming with delight. 'Paul at home on the porn again?' I ask, lowering my voice so Mum can't hear.

'I doubt he's got the energy,' she whispers back. 'Let's just say things in that department have restarted with something of a bang.'

'Really? Did you take pity on him?'

'No. I think it's got a lot to do with Henry going to nursery and me going back to work, even if it is only part-time.'

'How so? I would have thought that would just make you even more tired.'

'Several things, I reckon. I'm confident that Henry will sleep through the night now, so I'm sleeping much better, plus I stopped breastfeeding because he needs to be bottle-fed at nursery, which has probably had an effect on my hormone balance, and going back to work has made me feel like a semi-functioning adult rather than just a milk machine and care provider. So the mojo is back and Paul is a very happy man.'

'Lucky him.'

'It's not all about him. I'm quite enjoying being back in the saddle as well.' She grins.

'You're whispering again,' my mother scolds.

'Sorry, Mum. I was just saying that Jess looks different.' Damn, I thought we'd moved on from that.

'I'm wearing a little bit of make-up, that's all. Nothing to get excited about.'

'That's new. When did you start wearing make-up?' Mum asks as she reaches for a plate and the cake knife.

'I thought I'd make a bit of an effort for a change. I won't have any cake, thanks, Mum.'

'It's your favourite!'

'I know, and it looks delicious, but I had a big lunch at Alice's and I'm eating again tonight so I need to leave a little bit of room.'

'Going anywhere nice?' Molly asks.

'I'm meeting up with a friend, that's all.' I try to say this as casually as possible and focus on keeping a poker face so as not to arouse suspicion.

'Oh yes?'

'Just someone from school. We bumped into each other at Elodie's wedding and he's invited me round for something to eat.'

I realise my mistake as soon as the words are out. Molly's eyes have widened to the size of saucers.

'"He", you say? That would mean this someone from school is a boy.' She emphasises the word *boy* so I'm left in no doubt what she's driving at.

'Well done, detective,' I reply sarcastically.

'Anyone I'd know?' Molly asks carefully.

'I doubt it. You didn't really know anyone in my year, did you?'

'The only boy that comes to mind is that rock star one you were totally obsessed with. What was his name?'

'I wasn't obsessed!' I exclaim. This is all getting way too close for comfort.

'You so were. He was all you talked about when Laura came round. What the hell was his name?' She slaps her forehead in frustration.

'Jamie!' Mum exclaims triumphantly after a moment, waking Dad from his snooze. 'Jamie Ferguson.'

'Why are you shouting?' he asks. 'Who is Jamie Ferguson?'

'He's the boy that Jessica was obsessed with at school,' Mum explains. 'Molly and I were trying to remember his name.'

'What for?'

'I was not obsessed!' I repeat, even more strenuously.

'You were, love,' Mum chides. 'I remember emptying your bin once, and this piece of paper fell out. I could see writing on it, and I was worried it might be important and have got in there by accident, so I smoothed it out to look at it. It was just doodles mainly, but you'd written "Jessica Ferguson" in various styles, and some love hearts with "Jamie Ferguson" underneath them. I thought it was rather sweet, actually. It reminded me of when I was young and in love.'

'Were you spying on me?' I ask furiously.

'Of course not!'

'What would you call it then? Going through someone's bin sounds a lot like spying to me.'

'She's got a point,' Dad chips in. Now he's awake, he's obviously decided to referee.

'I told you. It fell onto the floor and—'

'Nonsense. You admitted yourself that you had to smooth it out, which means it must have been scrunched up when you found it. Most normal people wouldn't think anything of finding a scrunched-up piece of paper in a bin, but you mysteriously "thought it might be important" and had to smooth it out to read it?'

'I wasn't spying,' she repeats forcefully. 'It's just that you girls were so secretive when you were teenagers and I had to make sure you weren't getting into any trouble.'

'What?' It's Molly's turn to sound outraged now. 'Did you go through my bin as well?'

'Stop making me sound like a cross between a spy and some sort of vagrant. I just... checked things occasionally. It's what mothers do.'

'It's what nosy parkers do, more like.'

'You'll see. I bet you'll be just the same when Henry is a teenager.'

'I seriously hope not. It's a massive invasion of privacy, apart from anything else.'

'No, it isn't. If it's private, you shouldn't put it in the bin you know full well your loving mother is going to empty for you. If I hadn't come into your rooms and tidied up once in a while, you'd have drowned in your own mess, both of you.'

'One nil to your mother, girls,' Dad observes.

'Unfair!' I argue. 'You said I had a point earlier.'

'Yours was a penalty and you missed the goal. Your mother just scored.'

'Hm. And you're not biased at all, I suppose.'

'I know which side my bread is buttered,' he concedes.

'So, is it Jamie?' Molly asks, shattering any hope I might have had that the argument about bins and Mum spying on us might have deflected the original course of the conversation.

'It might be. Yes, fine, it's Jamie.'

'Ooh.' A delighted smile spreads across her face. 'Are you two a thing?'

My poker face completely collapses and I can feel the heat in my cheeks.

'It's early days,' I reply, blushing furiously.

'But that's brilliant, darling!' Mum gushes. 'I'm so happy that you've found someone after all this time. Your father and I were beginning to worry a bit, weren't we, Jim? When are we going to meet him?'

'Like I said, it's early days. I wouldn't rush off to get your wedding hat just yet.'

* * *

It takes me quite a while to make it over the threshold of Jamie's flat because we spend an inordinate amount of time kissing hungrily in the doorway. I'm still determined to take it slow but when he kisses like this, it's hard not to just think 'fuck it' and rip his clothes off.

'You'd better come in,' he grins when we finally break apart.

His flat is a surprise. I was expecting a cool, chic bachelor pad with lots of chrome and a muted colour palette, but that's not what I find. His living room is considerably larger than mine and, although the walls are painted in what looks like bog standard magnolia, there are bright rugs on the floor and a sofa big enough to sleep on. More colour is provided by the cushions scattered on the sofa, as well as some framed prints on the wall. There is a bookshelf crammed with a variety of books, including a number of children's books I notice, and there are framed pictures everywhere, all featuring a serious-looking, dark-haired young girl. There are some that include Jamie, as well as a few that include a striking looking woman that I'm guessing is Simone.

'Lizzie?' I ask, indicating one of the pictures.

'That's her.'

'I can see the resemblance. Does she come over here often?' I gesture at the children's books.

A look of sadness crosses his face. 'She's been a few times, but she's never stayed and Simone always comes too.'

'Really? You're Lizzie's father; surely you're capable of looking after your own child.'

'It's complicated. Simone has some attachment issues.' His tone of voice tells me I probably ought to let the subject drop, but the silence that replaces it is slightly uncomfortable and he clearly picks up on it because he continues after a few moments.

'Simone is still very protective of Lizzie and gets anxious about being separated from her. It's something she's recently started working on with the help of a therapist but we're still a long way from Lizzie being able to come here on her own. I've got a bedroom and everything ready for her when she does, but I don't think that will be for a while.'

I can see that he doesn't want to talk any more about this right now, so I decide to change the subject. 'What's for dinner?' I ask.

'You said you wanted something light, so I've got some salmon, new potatoes and I thought I'd make a salad.'

'That sounds perfect. Do you need a hand?'

'I don't know. I might get all nervous and shy having a chef in my kitchen watching me cook.'

'Oh, get over yourself!' I laugh.

'Fine. You can come and talk to me, but you're not to touch anything, OK?'

'*Oui, Chef!*' I reply.

'Very funny.'

It turns out that Jamie is actually a pretty accomplished cook, so I find myself quite happily admiring the view of him while he works. I'm particularly impressed to see that he mixes his vinaigrette dressing for the salad from scratch; I'll admit I was expecting him to fish a bottle of pre-prepared gloop out of the fridge.

'This is delicious,' I tell him sincerely as we start to eat. 'Where did you learn to cook?'

'Simone is French,' he explains. 'The first time I cooked for her, she was absolutely horrified. She was wrestling pans out of my hand and barking *"Non! Pas comme ça, Jamie!"* After that, she wouldn't let me cook anything until she'd taught me how to do it properly.'

'I know she's the mother of your child and everything, but she sounds like a total control freak,' I observe.

'She is a bit,' he laughs. 'I'm not speaking out of turn, by the way. She would fully agree.'

I know I should let it go, but I'm still not completely relaxed about her, which makes me want to know everything.

'You speak fondly of her,' I observe carefully. 'Do you get along better now?'

'Purely as co-parents,' he tells me firmly.

'How does Lizzie feel about you not being together?'

'She can't really remember when we were together so I don't think it worries her. Lots of her friends' parents are divorced or separated so it's not as if her situation is unusual.'

'I guess I was lucky in that. My parents are still disgustingly happily married,' I tell him. 'Thinking of which, I kind of let the rabbit out of the hat this afternoon, and they're demanding to know when they're going to meet you. I've told them firmly that it's early days and we're taking it slowly, but you know what parents are like.'

'That's OK. I told Simone about you as well.'

'Really? What brought that on?' Although I'd be lying if I didn't admit that talking about his ex makes me uncomfortable, the fact that he's told her about me is positive, isn't it?

'If things get more serious between you and me, I'd like you to meet Lizzie at some point. I thought it best to start laying the trail of breadcrumbs with Simone early, so she has time to get used to the idea, otherwise she'll only get anxious. Now, why don't you go and relax next door while I clear up in here and put some coffee on?'

I offer to help but he practically shoos me out of the kitchen, so I decide to continue my exploration of his sitting room. The bookshelf doesn't offer much more; the books on the lower shelves that I haven't already checked out are pretty standard coffee-table fare but I'm intrigued to notice a large rack of CDs.

'I didn't know anyone had CDs any more,' I call.

'Sentimental value. I dread to think how much I spent on them back in the day, so I can't bring myself to get rid of them, even though I never listen to them.'

I'm not at all surprised to spot a number of Arcade Fire albums as my eyes travel down the rack. I'm aware of Jamie coming into the room and I sigh with pleasure as he wraps his arms around me from behind and rests his chin on my shoulder.

'Are you still into Arcade Fire?' I ask.

'No. It's all a bit intense for me now. I'm more of a mainstream pop fan these days.'

'Do you want to know something incredibly sad?'

'Go on.'

'I bought all their albums back then too. I don't have them now, but I used to listen to them and try to memorise some of the lyrics, so I could appear knowledgeable if we ever had a conversation.'

His lips nuzzle the side of my neck and I savour the sensation. The temptation to grab his hands and move them upwards onto my chest is intense, so I concentrate on the CD rack once more to try to distract myself. A CD case with a handwritten label catches my eye, but I can't quite make out the writing on the spine so I pull it out to examine it. On the front, written in marker pen, are the words *Urban Dystopia*.

'What's this?' I ask, turning and handing Jamie the CD. 'Is this your demo?'

I can't help laughing as he blushes with embarrassment.

'I'd bin it, but I can't take the responsibility for ruining someone's life if they accidentally came across it and played it,' he tells me. 'It's like nuclear waste; it needs to stay firmly locked up for around ten thousand years until nobody knows what to do with a CD any more.'

'Put it on then.'

'I can't. The CD player is broken.'

'I think you're lying.'

'Fine,' he sighs. 'Just don't blame me if you suffer permanent mental scarring.'

'I'm sure it's not that bad.'

He turns on the stereo system and places the CD on the tray, before turning back to me.

'I don't think I can do this. You might not ever want to see me again.'

'Just play it,' I urge.

Jamie's face is a picture of misery as he watches the CD tray slide back into the player and presses the button to start it. I notice him reach hastily for the volume control and turn it down.

'Oh no you don't. Put that back.'

He sighs deeply and, after a few moments, the stereo starts to make the most bizarre noise. It sounds very much like a group of toddlers have been let loose in a room full of musical instruments. It's kind of thrashy, but in a totally uncoordinated way. When the vocals start and it becomes obvious that they also have no relation to any of the other things going on, it's too much for me and I begin to giggle uncontrollably.

'I'm sorry, Jamie,' I gasp, 'but this is awful!'

'I warned you.' Thankfully, he's laughing along with me.

'Does it get better later on?'

'Nope.'

'OK. I'll put you out of your misery. You can turn it off.'

'Did you really send that to people?' I ask once the noise has stopped.

'We did. Utterly delusional, I know.'

'It's a shame, because I think you'd have quite a nice voice if you had something intelligible to sing along to. Do you still sing?'

'Only when I know there's nobody listening.'

That's what he thinks. Unfortunately for him, I've decided that I would like to hear him sing something I might have chance of recognising, and a plan begins to form.

21

'You're taking him where?' Alice asks cautiously when I outline my plan to her during the week.

'A karaoke night. I've found a pub in Maidstone that does them.'

'Oh, Jess. Is that a good idea? If he only sings when he's sure nobody is listening, putting him in front of a load of people who definitely will be is not going to make you very popular.'

'I'm not going to hold a gun to his head and force him to sing. I'm just going to present him with the opportunity and encourage him a bit. I've thought this through. I'll drive, which means he can have a bit of Dutch courage, and they do food so we can have dinner. I'll pretend to be surprised by the karaoke.'

'That won't work.'

'Why not?'

'Why would you flog all the way to Maidstone for pub grub when you could just go out somewhere in Canterbury where neither of you have to drive? He's going to be suspicious as hell.'

'Hm. You're right. I'll have to think of something.'

'I'm still not convinced this is a good idea, you know. People can be unpredictable when you force them out of their comfort zone. How would you feel if he sprung something like skydiving on you?'

'I've always vaguely fancied having a go at that.'

'OK, bad example. I know, what if he took you to a football match?'

'Yeah, I'd be royally pissed off.'

'Isn't that what you're doing to him?'

'No, because this is doing something he used to enjoy, in a nice setting, with beer and food thrown in. Plus I'll turn the adoring looks up to eleven if he actually does it, so he'll be having his ego stroked as well. Perfect night out for a man, I reckon.'

'Sounds like Russian Roulette to me but I'll bow to your considerable experience and knowledge where the opposite sex are concerned. Oh no, wait a minute...'

'Ha ha. Like I said, I'm not going to force him. If he genuinely doesn't want to do it, then we can just listen to the other people and have a nice evening out. I reckon he will though.'

'I hope you're right. Are you going to invite him to lunch on Sunday if he's still speaking to you after this?'

'I think he's working this weekend. I will find a Sunday though, I promise. It's not as if you've never seen him before.'

'I know, but I haven't met him *properly*. This is the first time you've got further than a casual date with any man since I've known you. It's a big deal.'

'Now you're sounding like my mother. She told me that she and Dad had been worrying about me. What's that about? Worry about me if I'm an alcoholic, a gambler, or putting the GDP of Columbia up my nose, but since when has being single been cause for concern? Lots of people do it.'

'Hey, I'm not dissing you for being single. All I'm saying is that you going out with Jamie is a seismic shift from the woman I've got used to. It's a good thing, Jess. Let's just hope your karaoke antics don't scare him off.'

'He's a man, not a rabbit.'

She laughs. 'I'll remind you of that when you take him to bed. Let's think of some phrases, shall we? "At it like rabbits", the Ann Summers Rampant Rabbit. I hope for your sake he has at least some rabbit in him.'

'Don't hold your breath for that one. Slow and steady, that's how this is going to play out.'

I don't dare tell her that a surprising amount of my time, both when I'm awake and asleep, is spent imagining exactly what she's just alluded to.

* * *

'Where are we going?' Jamie asks, as we join the M2 heading for London on Friday evening. His head has been buried in his phone up to this point, but the change in engine note has obviously roused him.

'Out for dinner,' I reply. 'Have you finished your messages now?'

'Yes, sorry. Simone was just updating me on Lizzie's day. I know we're going out to dinner, but where? I assumed it would be somewhere local.'

'It's a surprise. Wait and see.'

It's just as well I have the driving to concentrate on, because Jamie is looking seriously gorgeous tonight. He's wearing a long-sleeved, light-blue shirt with the sleeves rolled up over dark jeans, and I can't help glancing down and admiring his forearms. His hands are resting lightly on his thighs, and my imagination is conjuring up all sorts of other places I could think of for him to put them. Thankfully, he seems completely unaware of how flustered he's making me.

'You're a good passenger,' I remark after a while. 'Alice is terrible. I won't drive her any more, because she keeps flinching and shouting, "Look out!" at things I've already seen.'

'I can do that if you like,' he offers with a grin.

'You can try. It's a long walk back to Canterbury from here though.'

'Good point. Plus, some of the people in the other cars look like murderers,' he laughs. 'You're actually a very reassuring person to be driven by, unlike some of the people I've been out on test drives with over the years. I feel quite safe.'

'What's the worst test drive you've ever done? Has anyone ever crashed?'

'Not with me, thankfully, but it does happen. Most people are pretty careful when they take cars out on test drives, but you do get the occasional idiot. Funnily enough, it was the elderly that frightened me the most.'

'Why? I can't imagine they'd be wanting to drive like hooligans.'

'No, they don't. But they don't always have very good reactions either. There was one guy I went out with who didn't go above thirty-five miles per hour for the whole test drive. People were overtaking him and hooting, and he just kept muttering, "maniac" each time. I think I aged about five years during that one.'

'Did he buy the car?'

'He did, and he was involved in an accident within the first month. From what I heard, he was in the wrong lane on a roundabout and, rather than following the road markings, he just cut across all the lanes without looking and was rammed in the side by an HGV.'

'Goodness. Was he all right?'

'Yeah. It was the end of his driving career though, and not before time.'

'It must be difficult to give up your licence, don't you think?

That's your independence. I remember when I first passed my test and got a car. It was so liberating; I could just go anywhere whenever I wanted. No more figuring out bus routes and worrying if some pervert on the bus was going to come on to me. That's a lot to give up, isn't it?'

'It is, but if you're getting to the stage where you're in danger of driving the wrong way down a motorway, it's definitely time to stop. My mum always says she will move into a flat in Canterbury as soon as she starts to feel unsafe behind the wheel so she can walk or take buses.'

'Tell me about your parents.'

'There's only Mum. Dad died of cancer a few years back.'

'I'm sorry.'

'Yeah, it was pretty grim. He wasn't that old so it was a shock. Mum's coped really well though.'

'Do you see her often?'

'It's not easy, because of work and Lizzie, but I speak to her several times a week and try to call in at least once a month. My brother lives quite close to her, so he and his wife drop by fairly regularly, and she's got lots of friends. She'd like you.'

'Did she like Simone?'

'Umm, no. I think it's fair to say that they didn't see eye to eye at all. Mum thinks Simone is incredibly uptight, but she puts up with her for Lizzie's sake, and Simone thinks my mother is always judging her.'

'Can I ask you a serious question?'

'Of course.'

'How do you see me fitting into all of this? You seem to have enough trouble fitting everyone important into your life already and I'm just going to add an extra layer.'

'Sometimes the extra layer is the bit that makes the rest palatable,' he replies after considering for a moment. 'Like the icing on a slightly burned cake.'

'Oh, that's good. Well saved,' I laugh. After that, my conversational ability dries up somewhat, because Jamie has moved his right hand and is resting it lightly on my thigh. All of my brain that isn't concentrating on driving is completely focused on the sensation of it: the gentle pressure and the warmth.

'Here we go,' I tell him as I swing into the car park.

'Why have you brought me all this way to go to a pub?' he asks. 'You know we have several very nice pubs in and around Canterbury, don't you?'

'Yes, but this one has a secret. Come on.'

* * *

I'm slightly taken aback by how busy it is when we walk in. I was expecting a few drinkers and a couple of people taking turns on the karaoke, but the place is buzzing and I'm glad I rang to make a reservation because there are very few tables that aren't occupied.

'It's karaoke night tonight,' the server explains as she leads us to our table, 'so there will be some singing in a bit. Are you here to sing?'

'Absolutely not,' Jamie tells her at the same time as I'm saying that we haven't decided. Jamie looks horrified.

'Oh no,' he says, as soon as we've settled. 'Please don't tell me you've brought me here to do karaoke.'

'You don't have to do anything you don't want to. I thought it might be fun, that's all. If you'd rather not, then we can just listen to the others and enjoy some dinner.'

'Are you going to sing?'

'I'm not the one with the rock star past.'

'OK,' he says after a bit. 'Here's the deal. I'll sing if you do.'

'That's not fair!' I exclaim. 'At least you can have a drink or two first to calm your nerves.'

'You should have thought of that before bringing me here under false pretences, shouldn't you?'

Our conversation is interrupted by the MC introducing the first singer, who gives us a very convincing version of 'Kings and Queens' by Ava Max. At the end, there's lots of cheering and whooping from the group she's evidently come with, and enthusiastic applause from everyone else. If everyone is like her, we're up against some serious competition and I definitely won't be taking to the stage, whatever Jamie's deal is. However, the chap who follows her has clearly had a few already, as he slurs his way tunelessly through a Robbie Williams number.

'You ought to sign him up for Urban Dystopia,' I giggle to Jamie, who is making surprisingly rapid progress through his first pint.

'He'd certainly add another dimension,' Jamie agrees as he flags down a passing server and asks for a refill. 'Back in a mo.'

He disappears off into the crowd, presumably to the gents given that his pint glass is empty already. I sip my Coke and listen to a couple of women murdering Beyoncé's 'Single Ladies'. He appears oddly pleased with himself when he gets back, but just shrugs nonchalantly when I ask him what's up, so we turn our attention to the menu. It seems the house speciality is pies, so Jamie orders a steak and mushroom and I ask for chicken, bacon and leek.

'I'm going to stick my neck out and say that one of those two women has just split up with her boyfriend,' Jamie observes, looking over at the singers.

'What makes you say that?'

'It's a classic breakup track, isn't it? Plus, I don't see a particular group supporting them, which means they're out on their own. A girl and her BFF having a few drinks and a drunken sing? Post breakup recalibration for sure.'

'Interesting theory. Are you some kind of secret psychologist?'

'No. I just like trying to work out what's going on in people's minds. It's probably a sales thing.'

'Do you get many breakups in your dealership? Couples unable to agree on what colour they want and deciding their marriage is over because of it?'

'I can give you a much better example than that. We had a couple come in wanting to trade their Range Rover for two Jaguars. Why do you think that was?'

'Because they were divorcing.'

'Exactly.'

'I think I've underestimated your work.'

'Really? How?'

'Because I've always thought of people who sell cars as pretty two-dimensional. The customer comes in, you try to upsell everything you can and it's a simple competition between how much you can screw out of them and whether they see through you.'

'That's a bit harsh. We do actually want our customers to go away happy. That way, they will hopefully come back.'

'It's more than that though, isn't it? It's about finding out what their motivation is for spending a shit ton of money on something they could pick up for a fraction of the price if they went somewhere else. I don't mean to be rude, Jamie, but most of us don't have the kind of money you charge for what is basically a way to get about.'

'You're right. People have all sorts of different motives. Some just buy the new model of the car they've always had. Others want something with a prestige badge on the drive. Sometimes—'

We're interrupted by the karaoke organiser's voice coming over the microphone.

'Our next song is a bit of a classic,' he announces. 'We're going
to go back to the seventies, with "Summer Lovin'" from *Grease* sung
by Jamie Ferguson and Jessica Thomas. Come up to the mic, guys.'
My mouth drops open and Jamie grins wickedly.

22

'What the bloody hell?' is all I manage as he grabs my hand and starts dragging me towards the stage.

'You brought me here to sing, didn't you?' he replies simply. 'So that's what I'm going to do. But, like I said, if I'm singing then you are too.'

'You are a bastard, Jamie Ferguson, and I may well leave you here after this.'

'You're just pissed off that your little stunt backfired. You'll enjoy it, trust me.'

I don't really have a choice, I realise. All eyes are on us as the MC gives us two microphones and cues up the track. My heart is in my mouth as the familiar introduction begins to play. I don't know if I can do this; this was never part of the plan.

Jamie sings the first line confidently at me and I'm momentarily distracted by his voice, which sounds nothing like the Urban Dystopia demo. He's gone full-on Michael Bublé smooth.

Oh shit. I'm supposed to be singing now.

I stammer my line out nervously, and he comes straight back in with his next phrase, giving me a salacious wink that almost makes me laugh.

What happens next takes me completely by surprise, as the whole pub erupts into the chorus with us, and I begin to get carried away with their enthusiasm. My nervousness fades as Jamie and I make our way through the verses, with the other pub customers joining in with the chorus parts. We don't get the harmony of the final bar completely right, but it doesn't seem to matter if the cheers and whoops from the audience are anything to go by. When it's over, we bow (awkwardly in my case), I grab Jamie's hand and we flee back to our table where our pies are waiting for us.

'Well, ladies and gentlemen, I'm sure we can all agree that was a star turn from Jamie and Jess there,' the MC is announcing. 'Who's next? Ah yes, we're going back even further to 1964 and "You've Lost That Lovin' Feelin'" sung by Tamara and Kelsey. Come on up, ladies.'

'It's another classic from the breakup duo,' Jamie enthuses, his eyes sparkling as he indicates the same two women who were singing Beyoncé just now. I'm not sure how much is down to his enjoyment of the evening and how much is down to the beer he's consumed, but he's evidently having a whale of a time.

'You were awesome,' he tells me as we begin to eat.

'Thanks. I was really nervous to begin with but I kind of got into it. Where have you been hiding that voice, though? That was amazing. If Simon Cowell had heard that, he would have signed you up straight away, I reckon.'

'I don't know about that, but I was surprised how much I enjoyed it. This wasn't the worst idea you've ever had, do you know that?'

'Praise indeed!' I laugh.

'What's interesting,' I tell him a little bit later as he starts his third pint, 'is that there aren't actually that many people singing, given how busy it is. Besides you and me – and I've sung enough for one night before you get any ideas – it's basically the breakup ladies, Ava Max-a-like and a couple of others. You'd think more people would get up and have a go.'

'I suspect karaoke is more fun as a spectator sport. You ought to have another go, though. You have a lovely voice. How about this: if I get up and do one more, will you?'

'I don't know, Jamie. Sometimes it's better to quit while you're ahead.'

'No pressure but, as another song has it, "you've got one night only".'

'This isn't going to be a thing then? For all you know, this pub is packed with A&R people, and we're going to be accosted in the car park by them all trying to sign you.'

'I doubt the A&R people are scouring karaoke pubs for the next Adele when they're already inundated with demos from serious talent like Urban Dystopia.'

'Good point.'

'Right. I'm going to put my name down for one more. If the server comes, can you order me the apple pie with vanilla ice cream please?'

I watch him with amusement as he makes his way over to the MC. Talk about an about-face. I'm not complaining, though; I got what I wanted, which was to hear him sing.

'I've ordered,' I tell him when he comes back.

'Great. Now, don't be annoyed with me, but I put you in the slot after mine, just in case you change your mind. I've told the MC you probably won't want to sing, but I didn't want you to miss the opportunity.'

'I don't think I'll be changing my mind.'

He doesn't reply, but starts crooning 'One Night Only' softly.

'You can cut that out,' I say, as sternly as I can, but he only laughs and carries on.

It turns out that a few more people have evidently filled themselves with enough Dutch courage to take a turn on the stage, so we've finished our puddings by the time the MC calls Jamie up again.

'We're going for a ballad now, ladies and gentlemen,' the MC announces. 'Fun fact for you all: this song is mainly associated with either Josh Groban or Westlife, but it was actually written by Rolf Løvland of Secret Garden. Please put your hands together for Jamie Ferguson and "You Raise Me Up".'

Jamie is grinning as he takes the microphone. 'I'd like to dedicate this song to a truly amazing woman. This is for you, Jess.'

He fixes his eyes on me as the introduction plays and he quietly starts to sing the first verse. The atmosphere between us suddenly feels charged, and I think the other people in the pub must have picked up on it too, because they fall completely silent.

I'm unprepared for the crescendo when he hits the chorus. His voice soars and he appears to be completely inhabiting the song now, but he never takes his eyes off me. The other people in the room seem to melt away, and it's as if we're the only two people in here. I'm mesmerised by him and I can feel tears pricking my eyes. When he gets to the key change, he really lets rip and I'm vaguely aware of a ripple of applause from the audience before he brings it back down very gently to the ending. I've heard the song countless times and I've always considered it to be a little over the top, but I've never heard it sung like that, and directly to me. The applause is deafening and I automatically get to my feet to give him a standing ovation. This is about so much more than the song, though. Any final reservations I have about him have disappeared, and I have no doubts about how I want this evening to end.

'So, Jess,' the MC says when the applause finally dies down.

'Jamie asked me to leave the next slot free in case you wanted to reply to that. Would we like to hear what Jess has to say, ladies and gents?'

The chant goes up straight away. 'Sing! Sing! Sing!' the audience is practically baying and it's like I'm being pulled to the stage by an invisible magnet. I'll have to reply, there's no doubt about that, but what song will tell him how I feel? The lyrics from 'Lady Marmalade' by Patti Labelle spring to mind but I think they might be a bit obvious.

I'm momentarily paralysed with indecision before inspiration strikes and I give my song choice to the MC. It's pure schmaltz, but that makes it the perfect reply. I just hope I can do it justice and convey the meaning to Jamie.

'Right then everyone,' the MC is saying, 'we're in for another ballad as we're going back to the eighties and the song "Wind Beneath My Wings" from the film *Beaches*. I'm sure you don't need any more information than that.'

The introduction plays and the audience whoops as I deliver the opening line. As I continue through the first verse, I'm suddenly struck by terrible doubt. The words are completely inappropriate for what I want to say and I think I may have made a huge mistake. I can't look at Jamie until we get to the chorus.

I practically sigh with relief when we finally get to the chorus and I lift my eyes to meet Jamie's; the audience erupts as I sing the lyrics that made me choose this song.

The rest of the song passes in something of a blur, but the audience obviously love it if the noise at the end is anything to go by. They're cheering, whooping and banging the tables, chanting, 'Jess and Jamie! Jess and Jamie!' It takes the MC a few goes to calm them down.

'That was something else, you two,' he says eventually. 'That's true love right there, ladies and gentlemen, isn't it?'

The audience erupts once again.

'I think we'd better pay the bill and get out of here,' I tell Jamie when I've fought my way back to the table. 'Always better to leave them wanting more rather than outstaying our welcome, don't you think?'

'Good idea.'

There's a brief kerfuffle where Jamie tries to pay and I have to explain to him very firmly that this was my treat and I'm quite capable of paying, and then we're out in the relative calm of the car park.

'Can I ask you a question?' Jamie says, as I turn the car towards home. 'Did you mean it, what you just sang?'

'Did you?' I reply.

'You know I did.'

'Good. So did I.'

Silence falls as we contemplate what just happened. I know we're still a long way from saying, 'I love you' to each other, but something meaningful has definitely shifted. The time for taking it slowly is done; I want all of him.

I'm nervous but excited as we pull up outside his flat. The atmosphere in the car is heavy – we haven't spoken a word to each other since our initial exchange – but that just makes it even more clear to me that the time for talking is over; I need to *show* him how I feel. I turn to him, eagerly anticipating the first kiss that will lead to more, hopefully so much more.

I don't know whether to cry with disappointment, laugh hysterically or scream in frustration. Jamie is fast asleep.

23

'That is the funniest thing I've heard in ages!' Laura hoots down the phone when I tell her about it the following Monday. 'Honestly, Jess, you've made my day. What did you do?'

'I woke him up, kissed him good night and sent him into his flat.'

'Did he drool in his sleep? Please tell me he drooled. There's you, thinking he's in this magical moment with you, while he's snoring and dribbling. I think I'm in danger of wetting myself.'

'I'm glad you think it's funny. I was so frustrated I had to—' I stop as I realise what I'm about to divulge.

'You had to what?' Laura giggles.

'Never mind. Too much information, and no, he didn't drool.'

'Oh God, it just gets better and better. There are literally tears running down my face from laughing so much. Poor you, having to substitute a quick bit of self-love for your night of unbridled passion. Why didn't you go in with him and chivvy him along? I'm sure he'd have woken up pretty quickly if he'd known what was on offer.'

'Because our first time should be special, and, "Hey, Jamie, wake up because I want to have sex with you" doesn't give me that vibe.'

'It's technically not your first time.'

'You know what I mean. But you're right: I want it to be more than some hastily arranged towels on the floor in someone else's bathroom.'

'So what are you going to do?'

'I'm not sure. The moment has kind of passed now, and I don't know how to create another one without it seeming forced and artificial. I've made such a big point of telling him that we're not going to rush into anything that I don't think he'll do anything unless I pretty much throw myself at him, and I don't want to come across as desperate.'

'You're overthinking it. Put some nice lingerie on, go over there with a bottle of fizz and seduce him. Job done.'

'That won't work.'

'Why not? I'm pretty sure that's how most people do it.'

'OK, let's say I do that. What if he's unprepared and doesn't have any condoms? What happens afterwards? "That was lovely, Jess; now piss off back to your own flat please" isn't exactly how I want this to end.'

'You could buy the condoms, you know. This is the twenty-first century, after all. You could also invite him to yours.'

'Yeah, but it doesn't solve the problem that I've either got to tell him upfront that he's staying the night, which gives the game away, or we're back at someone having to leave afterwards.'

'I'm sure sex never used to be this complicated.'

'Yeah, well it's a big deal. Let's just say it's been a while.'

'I've got it,' she cries enthusiastically. 'What about a hotel?'

'What, the whole "Mr and Mrs Smith would like to check in for an hour" routine? Sounds icky.'

'That's not quite what I had in mind. What about a weekend

away then? You could rent a cottage or something. Nothing icky about that.'

'Hang on. We haven't even spent the night together and you're planning a romantic getaway? It's a bit soon for that.'

'You don't tell him it's a *romantic* getaway. In fact, it's probably better if you plan for it not to be. Just a weekend away together where you have the opportunity to jump on him if the mood takes you. You just need the right pretext.'

I consider it for a few moments. It's actually quite a good idea. My mind fills with images of long walks to country pubs, delicious sex in front of an open fire followed by ice cold champagne in a hot bath and more sex in an enormous four-poster bed with fluffy pillows.

'That sounds more promising,' I tell her. 'Where to go, though? Norfolk is nice, and not that far away, or we could go north, I suppose.'

'Or...'

'Or what?'

'You could come this way. If you do that, you'll even have the pretext for the trip, which is that you want to see me and Isaac.'

'Don't take this the wrong way, Laura, but when I think "top holiday destination", Wolverhampton doesn't really make the list.'

'Don't diss my home city. Anyway, you don't have to stay in Wolverhampton itself. There are lots of nice places not that far away. Ludlow is really pretty, and that's only about an hour from here. Shrewsbury is also nice, and you've got the villages in and around the Long Mynd to explore round there.'

'What's the Long Mynd?'

'Part of the Shropshire hills. It's beautiful, you'll love it. Please come this way. It would be lovely to see you and have a catch up, if you can fit me in between all the sex you're going to be having, obviously.'

'OK,' I laugh. 'I'll think about it and talk to Jamie.'

'Honestly, Jess, I think this is the perfect solution. You've got me as the excuse for the trip so he won't suspect a thing. Book somewhere with two bedrooms to keep up the illusion, and make sure you've got contraception sorted in case he hasn't. Although I'd be wary of any man who didn't come prepared, so to speak.'

'I don't know. If he's prepared, that kind of says he was expecting it.'

'If he isn't prepared, he's a fool.'

* * *

Alice, unfortunately, is less than impressed with Laura's and my plan.

'In my experience, when someone spends as much time as you are planning the perfect romantic encounter, it always goes horribly wrong,' she tells me.

'It's not a romantic encounter, just a weekend away.'

'This is me you're talking to, remember. Did I ever tell you about when Richard proposed to me?'

'No, what happened?'

'He planned this massively romantic surprise weekend away, and he really pulled out all the stops, bless him. He booked us into this swanky, Michelin-starred hotel near East Grinstead with champagne, flowers and chocolates in the room, four course dinner in the restaurant, the lot.'

'That sounds lovely. I'd be up for that.'

'It was a lovely idea, I agree, which is why I still cringe thinking about it now. The problem was that I used to suffer with crippling migraines every month around the time of my period. I'm talking vomiting, the works. Sometimes they were so bad that I'd literally spend the whole night in the bathroom, and they used to wipe me out for three full days.'

'I don't remember you ever having a migraine.'

'No. They stopped completely when I got pregnant with Mia. I guess something changed in the hormone mix but I've never had one since. Anyway, poor Richard hadn't factored in my monthly cycle. So there I was, enjoying a hot bath with a glass of champagne and looking forward to an incredible dinner when whammo, it hit. I didn't leave the bedroom until we were due to check out the next day and even then it was iffy. Poor Richard was absolutely devastated.'

'Did he still propose?'

'Of course not! He was going to do it at the end of dinner; the poor man had talked to the kitchen and they had made a special chocolate box for the ring and everything. Proposing to a woman who's lying in bed and moaning that she wants to die is hardly the same thing, is it? He invited me round for fish and chips the next weekend and did it then. Much simpler and just as effective.'

'I'm not expecting Jamie to propose. I just want something a bit more special than a quick bonk in either his flat or mine. I don't think that's too much to ask.'

'As long as you don't have the period from hell all weekend, and he doesn't have a migraine or food poisoning. You'd better tell him to starve himself for twenty-four hours beforehand, just to be sure.'

'That's a terrible idea,' I laugh. 'Can you imagine? There's me, trying to look all seductive in a negligée or whatever, and he's so hungry that all he can focus on is Deliveroo.'

'Just keep it low-key, that's all I'm saying. If you build it up into a big thing, you'll only feel even more let down if it doesn't happen the way you want.'

'That's why I like Laura's idea. Even if we don't get it on, there's still lots to do. Plus I get to spend some time with her and the baby. It'll be fine, trust me.'

Now that the idea is in my head, I like it more and more. Pushing Alice's concerns to one side, I call Jamie in the evening.

'How much notice do you need to get a long weekend off?' I ask him.

'A couple of weeks. Why?'

'I was chatting to Laura earlier. She's invited me up to visit her and the baby and I wondered if you'd like to come. I thought we could make a mini break of it. Travel up on the Friday, see her at some point over the weekend, and spend the rest of the time exploring before coming back on the Monday. What do you think?'

'Sounds fun. Where does she live? It's somewhere near Birmingham, isn't it?'

'Wolverhampton, and before you say there isn't much to explore round there, she suggested we stay somewhere in Shropshire. It's beautiful, apparently. Have you been?'

'Mum and Dad took us to Aberystwyth on holiday a couple of times when we were growing up. I think we stopped somewhere in Shropshire to break the journey and have something to eat.'

'Is it nice?'

'I can't remember. Sorry. All the scenery tended to blur into one, and we just wanted to get there. It's a bloody long way, I can tell you that.'

'How can it be? It's just down the road from Birmingham!'

'I was talking about Aberystwyth. You're right, it's probably only three or four hours to Shropshire.'

'Are you up for it then?'

'Absolutely. Did you want me to book something?'

'No, I'll do that. You can research things to do and places to eat.'

'I'll need to know where we're going to be staying.'

'I haven't got that far yet. I'll send you the nearest town when I've found somewhere. Right, what about dates?'

After a bit of diary juggling, the first weekend that we can both get away turns out to be nearly three weeks from today, as I have a wedding next weekend and Jamie is committed to work the weekend after. I'm a little disappointed, but it also gives me an opportunity to follow Laura's advice and organise contraception before I ring her back to check she's going to be around. She's delighted, and I have to say I'm looking forward to seeing her too. I probably wouldn't have bothered to slog all the way to Wolverhampton on my own, but doing it as part of a long weekend with Jamie makes it something to look forward to.

However, finding somewhere to stay proves much harder. There is just so much choice, from cosy-looking converted stables, through granny annexes (which I swiftly rule out as not private enough for what I have in mind), to beautiful cottages. Every time I find something I like, I pore over the reviews to glean as much information as I can; a rat-infested shithole is not going to be conducive. After an hour or so, I've narrowed the list down to three, all of which are available for the weekend we've chosen.

The Retreat is part of a barn conversion and looks absolutely stunning, with one of those Victorian-style, free-standing baths, a traditional farmhouse kitchen with Aga and an open fireplace. In the end, I reluctantly rule it out because some of the reviews warn that the lane you have to go down to get to it is absolutely tiny, you regularly encounter tractors coming the other way and then have to reverse for miles. That sounds like much too much stress.

The next one on the shortlist is Summer Cottage, just outside Ludlow. Again, there's an open fireplace, but the kitchen is modern with fan oven and induction hob, which is less romantic but probably more practical than the Aga. I don't plan for us to be eating in much, but it's handy to know we can if we want to. After checking the listing and photos carefully, I realise there's no bath though, and I kind of feel a bath is a must for this type of weekend, so I strike it out as well.

That leaves me with Cherry Blossom, another barn conversion near Ludlow. Although it's single storey, they've left the roof beams exposed, which gives a lovely impression of space. The kitchen, sitting area and dining area are all in one open plan room, with a wood burner in the fireplace at the end. There are two double bedrooms, one with en-suite shower room, but there's also another bathroom with the all-important bathtub. The reviews are universally positive, saying how cosy it is, and a fair few of them mention an excellent pub within walking distance.

After another trawl of the rejected properties to make sure I haven't missed anything, I take the plunge and click the 'Book now' button. Now all I have to do is stop myself jumping on Jamie before we go away.

24

Considering that the main purpose of this weekend is to get naked with Jamie, I seem to have spent a small fortune on clothes. Tracking down matching knicker and bra sets proved surprisingly difficult, as most of them seemed to feature either large quantities of satin and lace or see-through panels or both, none of which are really me. I did toy with asking Alice, but I knew I'd be in for another lecture about setting myself up to fail if I told her how much work I was putting into this, and I suspect Laura only has eyes for full-support maternity knickers and those magical bras that unclasp easily for breastfeeding at the moment. Unless Jamie has a whole maternity fetish going on, I don't think those will do it for him. After a lot of trawling, I eventually found some cotton sets that I hope will look good, but are also practical enough to wear all day. As well as the lingerie, I've bought a couple of new tops that I like to think flatter my figure, and a pair of three-quarter length white jeans. I've never owned white jeans before, as they always seemed totally impractical, but these look especially good under the dark Breton-striped top I'm wearing. I have packed for all occasions and all weathers, with shorts, jeans, T-shirts, jumpers and a raincoat. I think the only thing that could catch me out would be snow but, as the forecast is for sunshine and temperatures in the high teens, I think I'm fairly safe there.

'I don't know why I let you drive when you keep picking me up in these clapped-out old bangers,' I tease him as he places my bag into the boot of the immaculate Range Rover he seemed to think was essential for our weekend in the country.

He's looking typically handsome in jeans and a rugby top, with a pair of sunglasses perched on his head. My insides do their customary flip as I put my arms around him and kiss him. The last three weeks have been a real exercise in self-control and there has been more than one occasion when I've nearly given in to the temptation to go with the flow, but I've just about managed to hold my nerve.

'I've already put the postcode into the satnav, so we're good to go,' he tells me as I climb up into the car and settle on the soft leather seat. 'Ready?'

'As I'll ever be. How long does it say it'll take to get there?' I ask as he pulls out of the car park.

'There's a bit of traffic on the M25, but it's predicting just over four hours. We can stop for lunch on the way if we want to.'

'Let's see. I'd rather get there and get sorted, wouldn't you?' Realising what I've just said, I glance nervously across at him, but my unintended double-entendre goes completely unnoticed because he's concentrating on the road.

'I've created a Spotify playlist we can sing along to,' he tells me once we're out on the motorway. 'I put in a few more *Grease* numbers, as well as a selection of chart hits and well-known songs from other musicals.'

'Let's see.'

He hands me the phone and I scroll through. He's evidently put nearly as much work into this as I have my wardrobe, as there's practically enough in here to get us all the way. I select 'We Don't Talk About Bruno' from *Encanto* to start us off, and we duet quite happily through a wide selection of songs until we reach the M40, when we decide to give our voices a rest.

'OK, here's a question,' I say after we've travelled a few miles in silence. 'Let's just say that there had been someone at the karaoke night, either A&R or maybe some members of a band whose singer had just died unexpectedly, and they'd come up to you and made you an offer. What would you have done?'

'I don't think that's very likely, do you?'

'Humour me.'

He considers for a while.

'I'm guessing, from your silence, that it wouldn't be a flat "no",' I prod him eventually.

'I think it probably would be, actually. I was just indulging the fantasy, and there were too many things that didn't work.'

'Such as?'

'Lizzie, for one. That life involves lots of irregular hours, time away on tour, promo stuff. I'd never see her.'

I feel a slight pang of guilt. 'Do you feel bad about leaving her this weekend?'

'No! That's not what I meant at all. I'm really looking forward to it, but going away for the occasional weekend is different from being on the road with a band. Does that make sense?'

'Absolutely. But there are singers out there who manage to have a family life as well. Let's say you were super rich and could afford tutors for her.'

'Take her with me, you mean?'

'Yes. I'm sure lots of celebs drag their children around with them. You just need an army of nannies and so on.'

'That doesn't sound much like family life to me. And you're forgetting that Simone would never let me take Lizzie on the road.'

'Fair point, but let's say Simone had some sort of epiphany and didn't mind. Then what?'

'Are you coming? I wouldn't do it unless you were there.'

Now it's my turn to be silent for a while and contemplate the fantasy.

'That's a hard one,' I reply eventually. 'I'd want to support you, obviously, but I think I'd be bored. Plus, you might turn into a massive knobhead and start shagging all your groupies.'

'I would only have eyes for you.' He turns to me and grins.

'You are such a bullshitter!' I laugh.

'It doesn't matter anyway,' he continues. 'Even if you said you were coming too, I'd still say no.'

'Really? Why?'

'I don't think I want it any more. When we were doing Urban Dystopia and The Misfits, the idea of the celeb lifestyle sounded really attractive. Fame, money...'

'Girls,' I prompt.

'Yeah, probably. But look at someone like Ritchie Hart. Do you think he's happy?'

'I don't know him.'

'Neither do I, but look at his life. On the one hand, he has fame, success and money, so he can have pretty much whatever he wants. The best table in a restaurant? No problem, Mr Hart. Fly away to a secluded villa by private jet? When would you like to leave, Mr Hart? Glamorous girlfriend is also a tick.'

'It's sounding pretty good to me so far.'

'Yes, but the other side of the coin is that his life is much more restricted than most people's. He's probably got a dietician whose sole job is to slap him if he so much as looks at a tub of butter—'

'—or a farmed salmon,' I interrupt.

'Exactly. He can't just go down the shop for a pint of milk and the daily paper, because he'd be papped all the way there and back, and I suspect the glamorous girlfriend is actually high maintenance and not a lot of fun.'

'Hm. When you put it like that, it doesn't sound quite so appealing.'

'No. So, going back to your original question. Do I want that life? Not really. I'm quite happy singing in the shower, thank you.'

'Oh, hang on a sec, my phone is vibrating,' I tell him with a smile. I lift it to my ear and say, 'Hi! Simon, great to hear from you. How's LA? Yeah, sorry, I know you could make him a star, but he's just said he's not interested.' I turn to Jamie and mouth, 'Simon Cowell, wanting to make you an offer.'

'Do give that up,' he laughs. 'I don't know if you've noticed, but this car is exceptionally quiet so I can hear that there's nobody on the other end. Is having imaginary phone conversations with non-existent people part of your whole vibe?'

'Sod off,' I laugh back. 'But you're right. I hadn't noticed but it is very quiet in here. I suppose that's what you get when you lay out house money for a car.'

'The secret is that this car has noise-cancelling technology built in. There are speakers all over the place whose sole job is to cancel out any unwanted noise.'

'You're winding me up.'

'I'm not.'

'But how do they know which noises to cancel? What if they started cancelling me by mistake?'

He laughs again. 'In a Range Rover, nobody can hear you scream.'

'Exactly. Might be a useful trick for parents of young children, though. You should definitely put that in your ad campaigns.'

'I suspect muting your children is probably against the law. If you can afford one of these and don't like your kids, the easiest thing is just to send them in another car.'

'How the other half live, eh?'

* * *

As the miles tick by and we get closer to our destination, the reality of what I hope we're about to do starts to sink in and the excitement and nervousness combine like a heavy weight in my stomach. I'm glad Jamie doesn't suggest stopping for lunch again, as I really don't think I could eat a thing at the moment. When we finally pull up outside Cherry Blossom, I'm barely able to take in how pretty it all is because every nerve in my body feels like it's fizzing. I'm so wound up, I can barely breathe. I'm amazed Jamie hasn't noticed the tremor that's crept into my voice over the last few miles, but he seems as relaxed as ever.

'Let's go and have a poke around before we unload the car,' he suggests as we climb out. My legs feel a bit like jelly, and I'm certain that's only partly due to sitting down for so long. He bounds into the house ahead of me and I follow behind, trying desperately to calm my nerves.

'This is lovely,' he observes as he casts his eye around the open-plan living space. 'It's a beautiful conversion, isn't it? They've kept the character of the barn while also including all the mod cons. I bet it's a nightmare to keep those beams free of spider's webs though.'

'They probably have stepladders, or really long dusters,' I reply feebly.

'Right, let's check out the sleeping quarters.' He sticks his head in each of the bedrooms, calling out his approval before locating the bathroom.

'I think you should have the bigger room, as you booked it,' he tells me when his inspection is complete. 'They're both nice so I won't feel hard done by at all.'

My heart is in my mouth as I take his hand in mine.

'Umm, Jamie?' I murmur.

'Yes? Are you OK? You look a bit pale all of a sudden. Do you need to lie down for a bit?'

'The thing is, I wondered whether you might like to share the same room as me.' I look for the spark of comprehension in his eyes, but there's nothing.

'You know I'd love nothing more,' he tells me seriously, 'but I'm not sure I'd be able to keep my hands away from you, and I know you want to take it slowly, so it's probably better that I sleep in the other room.'

'What if we didn't take it slowly any more?' I ask him, and finally the spark appears.

'What are you saying?' he replies, and his voice is suddenly hoarse and shaky like my own. He wraps his arms around me and, although we've pressed against each other like this many times before, there's a sense of anticipation this time that makes me bold. I slip my hands under his rugby shirt onto the warm skin of his back.

'I'm suggesting we take the brakes off. Have you got any condoms with you?'

'In my wallet, in the car,' he breathes.

'Well done, boy scout,' I murmur as my lips brush tantalisingly against his. 'Luckily for you, I'm prepared as well, so you can leave them out there. Now, which room did you say was the bigger one?'

25

We made it to the bed, just. Some of our clothes are still in the living area, but I was determined that there would be a bed involved this time. As soon as we both knew what was going to happen, we couldn't seem to undress fast enough and what followed was frenzied and intense. Slow and languorous will have to wait for another time, but we have the whole weekend, I remind myself as I slowly start to recover from the gasping, crying out and shuddering ecstasy.

'Bloody hell,' Jamie breathes, flopping on the bed next to me and pulling me gently into his arms.

'Worth waiting for?' I tease as my heart rate begins to slow.

'You have no idea how much I've dreamed of doing that,' he replies. 'It's been like this delicious torment, wanting you so badly but having to restrain myself.'

'Does it make it worse or better if I tell you that we would have done this three weeks ago had you not fallen asleep on the way back from the karaoke?'

'Oh, God. Really?'

'Yeah. I thought there was this amazing sexual tension in the air on the way back from the pub, and I was like "tonight's the night", and then it turned out you'd just nodded off. Bit of a mood killer,' I laugh. 'This is better though, don't you think? Let me ask my previous question again: would you like to share the same room as me this weekend?'

'What do you think?'

Even though I'm completely satisfied, the feel of his skin against mine is incredible, and I'm loving the sensations that are flooding through me. I could happily stay right here for the whole weekend.

* * *

'I guess we should probably get dressed and unload the car,' Jamie murmurs a while later. I'm not sure, but I think we may have fallen asleep briefly, as the light outside appears to have shifted.

'Mm. Just five more minutes,' I reply, pulling him closer to me.

'How's this for a suggestion? I know we were planning to eat out tonight, but I don't think either of us probably wants to do that any more. Why don't we find a supermarket and I'll cook something. You can relax, have a bath if you want, and I'll call you when it's ready.'

'I need champagne,' I tell him.

'What?'

'It's a fantasy I had when I was looking for somewhere for us to stay. I'm in a lovely hot bath with lots of bubbles, and you bring me ice-cold champagne.'

'I reckon I could manage that. Did you notice the shower, by the way?'

'No, what about it?'

'Let's just say I think it's large enough that we might be able to squeeze in a fantasy of mine as well.'

'Down boy!' I laugh, as I become aware of his mounting

arousal and pat it playfully. 'None of these fantasies are going to come true if we starve to death.' His talk of food has made me realise that I haven't actually eaten anything since breakfast and I'm ravenous.

'It's not going to go down if you keep patting it like that,' Jamie remarks. He gently disentangles himself from me and starts gathering his clothes together while I watch him from the bed, admiring his physique. I'm quite tempted to grab him and pull him back in, but a rumble from my stomach brings me back to earth and I reluctantly get up and start getting dressed as well.

I don't think my hand leaves Jamie's thigh as we make our way towards the superstore suggested by the satnav, and I'm eager for this trip to be as short as possible. I might be hungry, but I want to get him back and undressed again even more.

'What are we thinking?' I ask as we push our trolley into the store. 'Steak, chips, maybe some mushrooms and tomatoes? Something easy to cook, I reckon. I don't want you slaving over a hot stove when you could be slaving over more important things.'

'Point taken,' he grins. 'Steak and chips it is. We also need the all-important champagne and a bottle of wine to go with our dinner. What about dessert?'

'Ice cream. Pure indulgence and no faff.'

'Gotcha.'

When we get back, we do at least manage to unload the car and put the shopping away before retiring back to the bedroom. The frenzied urgency of earlier is gone now, and we take our time enjoying the intimacy of exploring each other's bodies, using our hands and mouths to find each other's pleasure points. The conclusion, when we get there, is even more satisfying, and I'm so relaxed afterwards that my limbs feel heavy and languid. It's the most blissful sensation.

'Can I ask you something?' I say to Jamie, propping myself up on my elbow. His eyes fall to my breasts as the duvet falls away and he begins caressing one lazily.

'Sure. Fire away.'

'When you rescued me after Elodie's wedding, you must have realised how I felt about you.'

'You made it pretty clear that I was not your favourite person, yes.'

'Why didn't you just leave me there?'

He sits up, and his expression is suddenly serious.

'You honestly don't know, do you?'

'No. Tell me.'

'I knew, even as I was sending that text the morning after we got together at Elodie's party, that it was unforgivable. I think I also knew, deep down, that I was getting back together with Sarah for the wrong reasons. I've thought about you so many times since then, wondering what might have been.'

'I can tell. You thought about me so much that you didn't recognise me until I told you who I was,' I remind him.

'That's not fair! You have to admit, you do look different. Plus, I wasn't expecting to see you, was I? It's a well-known thing that people are harder to recognise when you see them out of context, and it had been twelve years, Jess. Anyway, back to your original question. There were three reasons why I didn't leave you. One, because it's not in my nature to drive off and leave people stranded on their own in the middle of nowhere when I can help. Two, because I could tell how much you loathed me and I wanted to do something, anything, to show you that I wasn't the person you thought I was.'

'And three?'

'Three, because I felt like fate had brought you back into my life to give me a second chance.'

'Optimistic, given how I felt.'

'Justified though, given our current circumstances.'

I lean across and place my lips gently on his for a moment.

'For what it's worth,' I tell him, 'I'm glad you didn't drive off.'

'Me too,' he replies, 'more than you can imagine. Now, how about you run that bath and I'll see if the champagne is cold.'

I'm aware of his eyes on my naked body as I slip out of bed and head for the bathroom, but I don't feel awkward or self-conscious. I'm trying to think of the word as I turn on the taps and pour a generous measure of bubble bath into the tub.

Appreciated, that's the word. Along with everything else this afternoon, it's a feeling I could definitely get used to. I watch as the bath fills, and then slip into the delicious warmth of it, letting the bubbles cover me so that only my head is above the water. I hear the pop of the cork in the other room, and Jamie appears with two glasses a few moments later.

'How does this compare to the fantasy?' he asks as I take a sip of the champagne, savouring the chill and the popping of the bubbles in my mouth.

'I think it's better,' I reply. 'In fact, everything about this weekend so far has been better than I imagined it would be, and we've only just arrived. You?'

'Hmm. Let me think.' He frowns, as if concentrating hard. 'I was expecting some walking, the odd pint, maybe some light making out and a visit to Laura. Yeah, I think it's exceeded my expectations by a country mile or two.'

'If you'd prefer to backtrack, we could stick to light making out for the rest of the weekend.'

'Umm, no thanks. I like things just as they are if that's all right with you.'

'Yeah, I reckon I can put up with that,' I grin widely and take another sip of champagne.

We're interrupted by the sound of his phone ringing in the other room.

'Do you mind if I go and check that?' he asks. 'It's probably Lizzie. She often calls to tell me about her day before she has her tea.'

'Sure. I'm quite happy here with my bath and champagne,' I tell him.

I'm not actively eavesdropping as he answers the call, but it's hard not to listen when there aren't any other sounds to distract me. I'm surprised to discover that Jamie is talking in fluent French. He's still chatting away when I pull the plug and dry myself off, so I pad into the bedroom and get dressed.

'How was she?' I ask when he finally hangs up the phone.

'Good. Sorry it went on for so long. She wanted to tell me all about the celebration assembly they had at school today, where she was called up and given the star of the week prize for being so attentive and well-behaved in class.'

'I couldn't help noticing that you were talking to her in French.'

'Simone is keen that she grow up bilingual, so she only speaks French at home to counterbalance the fact that she speaks English everywhere else.'

'I didn't know you were so fluent.'

'I couldn't speak more than a couple of words before I met Simone. But her English wasn't great when we first started going out, so I kind of helped her with that, and she taught me French in return.'

Talking to him about Simone has pricked my curiosity and, although I don't really want to think about his other partners, I feel curious about them, because they're part of his story and I want to know everything about him.

'Jamie,' I begin, 'while we're on the subject of your previous relationships, who else do I need to know about?'

'What do you mean?'

'Well, I know you went out with Sarah and Simone, obviously. I also know that you had a few hook-ups, such as Elodie and me. Is there anyone else?'

'Who told you about Elodie?' he asks. He doesn't look embarrassed, merely curious.

'Laura, who do you think?'

'I'm very fond of Elodie and we're good friends, but she is one of the most bizarre women I've ever known. She literally came up to me in school one day and said, "I want you to go to bed with me. No strings attached, I just want to find out what you're like because I'm not sure Mitchell is the right fit in the sex department".'

'And they say romance is dead,' I laugh.

'Yeah. It wasn't the most satisfying encounter. I felt a bit like a performing monkey, actually.'

'Why did you do it then?'

'Let's think. I was a teenaged boy and an attractive girl offered herself to me on a plate. What else was I going to do?'

'Fair enough. So is there anyone else? Any other groupies or people you sold cars to?'

'I did go out with Emma Williamson for a while, but we never went to bed.'

'I don't remember her.'

'You wouldn't. She joined in the sixth form. All the boys were obsessed with her because she was beautiful but kept herself to herself. She was a mystery, you know? Anyway, I managed to persuade her to go out with me, and the very first time I kissed her, she turned to me and said, "You need to understand that I'm completely frigid, so don't get your hopes up".'

'She sounds like a bundle of joy.'

'Yeah. We weren't together for long.'

'Do you know what happened to her?'

'I do, as a matter of fact. Last I heard, she was living in Canada with her pastor husband and seven children, so she seems to have got over her standoffishness. Anyway, that's me. What about you?'

I blush, suddenly embarrassed. I should have thought of this before embarking on my mini inquisition.

'Umm,' I mumble.

'Go on. I'm not going to get all insecure, I promise.'

'It's not that, it's just that I've only actually been to bed with one person.'

It takes him a moment before the penny drops.

'Are you saying...?' he asks.

'Yup.'

'But how?'

'Well, you were the first; you know that because I've told you that before. After that experience, I wasn't really in the mood for boys for a while, and then I was rather busy with the business. I've been on dates, but there haven't been any relationships.'

'I don't know whether to apologise again or tell you how lucky I feel to be here with you now.'

'You can tell me how lucky you feel. And you can cook me steak.'

'*Oui, Chef!*' He grins at me and any discomfort I feel from our conversation vanishes, like fog burned off by the sun.

26

'I think you two were meant to be together,' Laura observes as I'm sitting on her sofa cuddling baby Isaac the following afternoon. Jamie is outside talking cars with Kevin, who seems to want to know every single party trick the Range Rover has up its sleeve.

'What makes you say that?'

'Just watching you. There are some couples you look at and you not only wonder how they ever got together in the first place, but also how on earth they're still together when they barely have a civil word to say to one another. Kevin has some friends like that; whenever they come round, all they seem to do is complain about each other or snipe at each other. It's exhausting.'

'We're not like that.'

'No, you aren't, thank goodness. The next category are the couples who seem largely indifferent to each other, but are basically too lazy to split up and go through the rigmarole of trying to find other people they might be happier with.'

'You could be describing my sister Molly there,' I laugh. 'I think they probably feel more strongly about each other than they let on, though. I certainly hope so.'

'And finally, there are the couples who are patently nuts about each other. That's the two of you, by the way.'

'I'm glad you think so, but that's normal when a relationship is new, isn't it? We might hate each other in a year or two for all you know.'

'I think that's unlikely. You'll be finishing each other's sentences and we won't be able to tell where one of you ends and the other begins. I have a nose for these things. Thinking of which, did I tell you I had a call from Elodie the other day?'

'No. How is she settling into married life?'

'Not great, from what I understand. She said the honeymoon was amazing—'

'Where did they go?' I interrupt.

'The Maldives. Such a cliché.'

'Why do you say that?'

'Because that's where we went for our honeymoon, and where we discovered everyone else in the world seems to go for their honeymoons as well. The only people who weren't honeymooners seemed to be smug older couples who were celebrating their children growing up and leaving home.'

'Oh. I'll make a mental note to avoid the Maldives for my honeymoon then.'

'Are you thinking about marriage already?' Her eyes light up.

'No, of course not! I was talking figuratively. Anyway, I interrupted you. Carry on.'

'What was I saying? Oh yes, Elodie. They had an amazing time on the honeymoon – to be fair, it's hard not to have an amazing time in the Maldives, cliché or no cliché – but I think the reality of life has hit them with a bit of a bang since they got back, and she's suddenly realised she's actually supposed to stay married to Daniel for the rest of her life.'

'But she loves him, right?'

'Oh yes, but is that enough? Look at Kevin and me. I love him to bits, and I know he loves me too, but having Isaac has been like an earthquake hitting our marriage. When it was just the two of us, it was easy, and we basically did whatever we wanted. Now, I'm a slave to Isaac's needs, my body doesn't feel like it's my own any more, and poor Kevin has had his world completely turned upside down as well. It's a lot of pressure, and if your marriage isn't that strong to start with, it could be enough to break it. So, if you're someone like Elodie, who seems hard wired to wonder what the grass on the other side of the fence is like, the reality of having just one man for the rest of your life is probably a difficult pill to swallow.'

'She shouldn't have married him if she had doubts.'

'She didn't, not at the time she said "I do" anyway. Don't worry about her; she'll find her way through. Tell me more about you. Are you having all the yummy sex you were hoping for this weekend?'

'I am,' I blush. 'It's even better than I was hoping for, if I'm honest.' My mind drifts back to this morning, where we acted out Jamie's shower fantasy. I had thought he just wanted to try sex in the shower, but it turned out that the shower was only the warm-up act. I shiver with delight as I remember our soapy hands caressing each other, before he gently dried me with a towel, kissing me all over as he went. By the time he carried me into the bedroom for the main event, I was pretty much tipping over the edge already.

'Are you still with me? You look like you drifted off there for a moment.' Laura's voice brings me back to reality.

'Sorry, I got distracted.'

'I noticed. If the expression on your face was anything to go by, it was a pretty steamy distraction.'

'There was steam involved, yes,' I giggle.

'So where do you go from here? Have you told him you love him yet?'

'No.'

'Why not? You both look pretty loved up to me.'

'Loved up, yes. "In love" is harder to answer. His life is complicated, and I still don't quite know how I'm going to fit into it long term.'

'Because of the daughter?'

'Partly, but this is all new for me, so I'm not quite sure what happens next and where we go from here. Do you know what I mean?'

'I think so. Have you met the daughter?'

'No. Jamie has told his ex about me, and he's promised to introduce me to Lizzie when the time is right, but I don't know when that will be. He's told me that Simone has some attachment issues where Lizzie is concerned. She also seems to message Jamie quite a lot.'

'Really? What about?'

'Lizzie, I think. I hope that's all she's messaging him about, anyway. Between you and me, she sounds like a bit of a control freak.'

'Hm. If you ask me, she needs to back off now that you're on the scene. How do you feel about being a stepmother?'

'Hang on, talk about jumping ahead!'

'I'm just following this to its logical conclusion. If you and Jamie were to get married...'

'It's impossible to say without meeting Lizzie. I'd like to think we'd get on, but she might hate me.'

'Or you might hate her. What about children of your own?'

'What about them?'

'Do you want them? Does Jamie want more children?'

'I don't know! Oh, God. You're making me feel like I've rushed into this. I don't know nearly enough about him.'

'No, you do. I'm sorry, I didn't mean to upset you. These are all things to talk about later when your relationship develops. For now, just enjoy what you have, yeah?'

* * *

'Are you OK?' Jamie asks as we're driving back to the cottage. 'You've barely said a word since we left Laura's.'

'Sorry. I've just been thinking about something she said, that's all.'

'Is it something you can share?'

'I don't know. It's a bit crazy and you might not like it.'

'You can't say something like that and then not tell me what it is!' he exclaims.

'OK. What relationship do you see Lizzie and I having?'

He looks baffled. 'What do you mean?'

'She's a big part of your life, and I don't really know that much about her or how all of this is going to work. I'm worried I'm always going to be a third wheel where she's concerned.'

There's a long silence. Jamie stares out of the windscreen at the road ahead and, just as I'm starting to think I've overstepped the mark, he surprises me.

'I think I understand why you feel like that,' he says slowly. 'I haven't given it a lot of thought, I'll admit, but I'm sure you two will get on great, if that helps.'

It doesn't, but I can't quite put my finger on why.

'Let me ask the question a different way,' I say eventually. 'Simone has issues about being separated from Lizzie, but you hope that you'll be able to have Lizzie to stay at some point, right?'

'Yes.'

'Do you think you being with me makes that more or less likely to happen?'

'I haven't really considered it.'

'Neither had I until just now. But if Simone is having difficulty trusting the father of her child to take adequate care of her, she's going to have even more difficulty trusting the father of her child and a complete stranger, don't you think?'

'Are you going to be there when she comes, then?'

'I think what I'm trying to say is that, if I'm going to be part of your life, and I very much want to be, we need to think about this stuff some more. Does that make sense?'

'Yes it does. In an ideal world, I'd have Lizzie round for the afternoon and you could come and meet her.'

'In an ideal world, you'd probably still be with the mother of your child,' I murmur.

'You don't think I still hold a candle for Simone, do you? Because I can assure you that you're miles off there.'

'Of course I don't, but it's not like she's an ordinary ex that you can cut yourself off from and move on. You made a child together, which means she's always going to be a part of your life, and I get that completely. But, if I'm honest, she's also an unknown quantity.' I trail off as my earlier thought hits me again. 'What happens if Lizzie takes one look at me and decides she hates me?' I ask.

'She won't.'

'But what if she does?'

'Why would she? The only person I can think of that she hates is the child catcher in *Chitty Chitty Bang Bang*, and you don't look or sound like him at all. Say, "there are children here, I can smell them" in your best child catcher voice, just in case.'

'I'm being serious. There are lots of reasons why she might not like me. She might see me as competition for your affection, or the woman who stole you away from her mum.'

'Hm. You know I said I'd told Simone about you, right at the beginning?'

'Yes. You said she needed time to get used to the idea of me, or something like that.'

'Simone told Lizzie that her daddy had a new *amie spéciale* – special friend – and do you know what she said to me the next time I saw her?'

'What?'

'She said she was happy for me because I wouldn't be lonely any more. I asked her what she meant and she said, "Well, Mummy has me to keep her company, but you don't have anybody. Everybody should have someone".'

'That's lovely.'

'Isn't it? So, I think she's predisposed to like you and you can stop worrying.'

Another thought comes into my head. 'What if Simone takes against me and refuses to let you see Lizzie?'

He sighs. 'She won't hate you either and, even if she did, she wouldn't be able to stop me seeing Lizzie unless she could prove you posed some sort of threat to her. I think she'll be more worried about the possibility of you not liking her.'

We both try to steer the conversation onto more light-hearted topics for the rest of the journey, but it feels a little bit forced. When we get back to the cottage, Jamie makes his excuses and disappears up the garden for his daily chat with Lizzie. I pick up my book and try to read, but I can't concentrate, so I watch him out of the window. He's sitting on a garden chair looking totally relaxed, and I feel desperately sad all of a sudden. His current demeanour couldn't be more different from the slightly strained atmosphere in the car, and it just makes me feel even more nervous about his family setup and how I might or might not fit into it. Silent tears begin to run down my cheeks.

'All done,' Jamie announces as he bounds back into the house. 'Are you OK?' His face falls and, before I have a chance to say anything, he's gathered me into his arms.

'I'm sorry,' I murmur into his chest. 'I'm being irrational, I know.'

He gently releases me and moves back just far enough so that his eyes can lock onto mine.

'I don't think you are at all. This is my fault; I should have known this would be difficult for you and acted sooner. I have a suggestion, if you're willing to hear it?'

'Go on.'

'How would you feel about meeting Lizzie on Monday? We could call in after she gets home from school if you like.'

I'm so surprised that it takes me a moment or two to gather my thoughts.

'Will Simone be there?' I ask.

'Yes but, as you said, she's always going to be the mother of my child, so you probably ought to meet her as well if you're up to it.'

'I thought you said things would have to be serious between us before I met Lizzie.'

'Jess,' he says solemnly. 'I am deadly serious about you.'

As I look into his eyes, I know he's being completely sincere, and I can feel the bubble of happiness building up inside me again, pushing the worry away.

'Do you know what?' I tell him. 'I'm pretty deadly serious about you too, actually.'

'So are you up for it? Meeting Lizzie and Simone, I mean.'

'Are you sure it's a good idea?'

'Jess, you can't have it both ways,' he laughs. 'If you were serious about wanting to be part of all of my life, then you need to meet them.'

'I know that! It just seems awfully sudden, that's all. However, I don't think there's ever going to be a perfect time, is there. I do want to meet Lizzie, and I know I have to meet Simone in order to do that. You'll need to check it's OK with them, though.'

He looks a little guilty. 'I haven't said anything to Lizzie, in case you said no, but I might have already floated the possibility with Simone on the call just now.'

'What did she say?'

'She's exactly as I predicted she would be: nervous and worried that you won't like her. But she'd like to meet you, and Lizzie will be super excited, I know. Can I call her back and say you'll come?'

'Yes, let's do it. I won't pretend I'm not a bit anxious about it, but that will be the same whether we do it on Monday or in six months' time, I guess.'

He gets his phone out of his pocket and dials a number. I hear a woman's voice answer.

'*C'est moi*,' Jamie says. '*Tu peux dire à Lizzie que Jess va venir.*'

There's a lot of conversation from the other end, and Jamie gives fairly short answers on the whole. Eventually he says '*Oui. A Lundi!*' and hangs up.

'I think we can assume Lizzie is pleased,' he tells me, 'but I have a question for you.'

'Oh yes?'

He pauses and studies me for a moment before a smile breaks out on his face. 'You know how you said you were deadly serious about me? I'm not convinced,' he tells me.

'Oh, aren't you?' I'm smiling now too.

'No. I think you're going to have to show me how serious you are.'

'And what did you have in mind?' I whisper as our lips meet.

'I don't know yet,' he replies as we sink onto the sofa together, 'but I'm sure something will come up.'

27

The rest of the weekend was as perfect as I had hoped and I'm looking forward to calling Alice later and telling her that her predictions of doom were unfounded. First, however, I have to face the ordeal of meeting Simone and Lizzie, and my heart is in my mouth as Jamie turns into the residential estate where they live.

'Here we are,' he tells me as he pulls up outside a perfectly ordinary looking, end of terrace property. I study it from inside the car, hoping to gain as many clues about its occupants as I can, but it's not giving much away. The front garden is paved over, with a small hatchback parked on it. The house looks like it might have been built as council accommodation originally, but the modern glazed door and windows clearly indicate that it's privately owned now.

'We bought this when Simone was pregnant,' Jamie explains to me, following my gaze. 'When we split up, it seemed unfair to expect her to find somewhere new to live on top of everything else, so I moved out and she's been here ever since.'

'Doesn't that feel odd, being a visitor in your old home?' I ask.

'No. She's changed quite a lot of things since I left, so it doesn't feel that familiar any more. Are you ready?'

'Not really.'

'It'll be fine. Come on.' He opens his door and climbs out.

'Are you expecting me to come round and open your door for you, like a chauffeur?' he laughs, when he notices that I haven't moved.

'No, sorry. I was just summoning my courage.'

'Remember what I told you on the way here: they're just as keen to make a good impression as you are.'

'I hope you're right,' I tell him as I unfasten my seat belt and climb down.

'I am. If anyone here should be nervous, it's me. I've got a lot riding on this, remember.'

'That doesn't help,' I tell him as I follow him to the front door. I briefly consider making a run for it as he rings the bell, but my mutinous legs refuse to move. After a couple of seconds, the door is flung open, and I come face to face with Simone for the first time.

'Jamie,' she smiles, leaning forward and kissing him on both cheeks. Her accent is still strong, so it sounds more like 'Jemmie'.

'Simone, this is Jess. Jess, Simone,' Jamie says, taking hold of my hand and encouraging me forwards.

'I am very happy to meet you,' Simone says to me. 'Please come in.' She steps aside and I follow Jamie into the house.

The first thing that strikes me is how tidy it is. As Jamie leads me into the front room, I can see that everything is precisely placed. Even the pictures on the mantelpiece are completely symmetrical.

'Où est Lizzie?' Jamie enquires as we sit down. Jamie and I are on the larger of the two sofas, while Simone settles herself on a compact two-seater.

'Dans sa chambre. Elle se change pour la quatrième fois. Elle ne sait pas quelle tenue choisir pour rencontrer Jess,' Simone tells him with a smile. 'She is very excited to meet you and cannot decide what to wear,' she explains to me, before going back out into the hallway and calling up the stairs. '*Lizzie! Ton père et Jess sont ici.*'

'Would you like a cup of tea or coffee perhaps?' Simone asks. 'I have also cold drinks if you prefer.'

'Tea would be lovely, if it's not too much trouble,' I tell her, getting back to my feet. 'Would you like a hand?'

'*Non, merci.* Lizzie will be down shortly, and she will want to know everything about you, I am sure.'

I perch back on the sofa as Simone disappears into the kitchen. Jamie obviously senses that I'm still nervous as he reaches for my hand and gives it a squeeze. 'You're doing fine,' he murmurs. 'Honest.'

There's a thumping from the stairs and then Lizzie appears in the doorway. She's dressed in blue denim dungaree shorts, with a pink T-shirt underneath and pink trainers. Her eyes are wide as she studies me. In one hand, she's holding a piece of paper, and the other has one of those plastic wallets full of colouring pens. She looks absolutely adorable.

'Lizzie, sweetheart, this is Jess,' Jamie tells her.

'*En Français, Papa!*' she admonishes him, before fixing her eyes on me once again.

'It's more polite to talk in English when we have English guests, don't you think?' he replies, before lowering his voice conspiratorially. 'Even your mother is speaking English to Jess, so I reckon we're allowed, don't you?'

Lizzie tilts her head to one side, considering, before climbing up onto the sofa next to her father and continuing to stare at me.

'*Veux-tu quelque chose à boire, Lizzie?*' Simone's voice calls from the kitchen.

'*Jus de pomme s'il te plait, Maman,*' Lizzie calls back. She turns to Jamie and whispers something in his ear. Jamie smiles widely and turns to me.

'She's a little shy, but she wanted me to know that she thinks you're very beautiful,' he tells me.

'You can tell her I think she's very beautiful too,' I reply.

Jamie turns back to Lizzie and starts to whisper in her ear, but Lizzie just giggles and pushes him away. 'I can hear what she's saying, Daddy!' she exclaims.

'Here we are,' Simone announces as she comes back into the room bearing a tray. 'I have a glass of apple juice for you, Lizzie, and tea for the rest of us. I also have Jaffa cakes.'

'Why are they called cakes when they're biscuit shaped?' Lizzie asks, helping herself to one and taking a big bite. This is something I know about, so I seize on the opportunity to hopefully bond with her a little.

'If I tell you, will you promise to keep it secret?' I ask her.

'Jess is a chef, so she knows everything there is to know about food,' Jamie explains to her and her eyes widen again.

'Not everything,' I qualify, 'but I do happen to know about this. It goes back to 1991, when the world was still black and white and ruled by dinosaurs. The government made a rule that biscuits were luxury items and should therefore be taxed, whereas cakes were a staple food and should not be taxed. Does that make sense so far?'

'Does that mean that people had to pay more for biscuits than cakes?' she asks carefully.

'That's exactly it.'

'That's a silly rule,' she declares, her earlier shyness seemingly forgotten. 'Biscuits are boring but cakes are yummy. Especially chocolate cake.'

'Is that your favourite?'

'Yes, but I can only have it on special occasions because Mummy says my teeth will all fall out if I have it too often.'

'She sounds like a very wise woman, your mother.' I lift my eyes to Simone, hoping to get her approval, but she's watching me intently in a way that makes me feel uncomfortable and causes me to lose my thread.

'Tell me more about the biscuits,' Lizzie prompts.

'Oh yes. Well, it is a silly rule, but that's what the government decided to do. McVitie's, who are the people that make Jaffa cakes, didn't want to pay the tax, because they'd been sold as cakes since 1927, which is so long ago that nobody knows what the world was like then. The government disagreed, and said they were biscuits because of their size and shape, along with the fact they were covered in chocolate. The case went to court, and do you know how it was decided?'

'No.'

'McVitie's were clever. They argued that cakes go hard when they go stale, but biscuits go all soft and soggy. A Jaffa cake was left to go stale, and it went hard. Therefore, they argued, it's a cake. The government lost the case.'

'Is that true?' Jamie asks, evidently as absorbed in the story as Lizzie.

'Absolutely. It was a landmark trial, and Jaffa cakes have been taxed as cakes ever since.'

'Are you going to tell Papa and Jess about your drawing?' Simone asks Lizzie, deftly moving the plate out of her reach before she can grab another Jaffa cake.

'*Oui, Maman.* I wanted to do a picture of you both as a present, but I didn't know what you looked like, Jess. So I've drawn Daddy, but I need you to sit still for me so I can draw you next to him.' She shows me the picture and, although it's a little crude, I can clearly recognise that the person on the paper is Jamie.

'Say please,' Simone reminds her.

'Please?'

'I'd be delighted,' I tell her. 'How do you want me?' I try out various silly poses and she giggles. I steal the occasional glance at

Simone, to try to gauge how well she thinks I'm doing with her daughter, but her face is a mask.

'Just sit normally,' Lizzie instructs, getting the pens out of the wallet. 'Daddy, you're in the way. You'll have to move.'

'Well, excuse me!' he laughs, trying and failing to sound affronted. 'I'll go and sit outside, shall I?'

'Don't be silly. You can go and sit over there, with Mummy.'

Jamie gets up and moves to the other sofa as instructed, while Lizzie stares intently at me and begins to draw. I can't help noticing how Simone's leg rests casually against his as they sit and my discomfort increases as I observe how familiar they are with each other. She's watching Lizzie, but I can't help noticing that, while her expression when she periodically shifts her gaze to me is still unreadable, she keeps glancing at Jamie and smiling at him. There's definitely something off here. There's an intimacy in the way they look at each other that makes me feel like an outsider, and my anxiety ramps up a notch.

'You have to smile,' Lizzie tells me. 'I can't draw you if you're frowning.'

'Sorry,' I say, switching my attention back to her and pasting on my best impression of a smile. I'm conscious that Jamie and Simone are now having a whispered conversation, but it's all in French so although I can hear the words, the meaning drifts past me.

'*Comment s'est passée la fête d'anniversaire de Maisie?*' I can just about make out him asking her. I know *anniversaire* is birthday but the rest is a mystery, so I concentrate on looking at Lizzie, as I don't want her to think I'm not engaging with her.

'*C'était super! Un magicien faisait toutes sortes de tours et il a ensuite fabriqué des animaux avec des ballons pour tout le monde. Lizzie le veut maintenant pour sa fête.*'

'Your mum tells me you had a good time at Maisie's birthday

party,' Jamie says to Lizzie. 'A magician and balloon animals, I gather.'

'He was brilliant, Daddy,' she enthuses, momentarily pausing her work to turn to him. 'He did real magic. I don't remember it all, but he did this one thing where he had a pound coin. He showed it all to us, and then he closed his hand and it was gone!'

'Where did it go?'

'He magicked it into Nathan's ear. Nathan says he couldn't feel it and it was obviously all fake, but how did it get there if it wasn't magic? Can I have him for my birthday? Pleeease?'

'I'll talk to your mother and we'll see. I'm not promising anything, OK?'

Lizzie sighs theatrically and turns back to her drawing.

'*L'avez-vous déposée là-bas avant de partir comme convenu?*' Jamie asks Simone. I have no idea what that means, but it seems to have riled her, because her tone has an edge to it when she replies.

'*J'ai essayé, mais la mère de Maisie m'a invitée à rester, et je ne voulais pas être impolie.*'

'Would you excuse us for a moment, ladies?' Jamie says to Lizzie and me. He's trying to sound relaxed, but the tightness of his jaw indicates that something is definitely up.

'*Viens dans la cuisine,*' he says to Simone, and she follows him into the kitchen, shutting the door behind them.

I try very hard to focus on keeping my pose and smiling, but I'm acutely aware of a muted argument taking place on the other side of the kitchen door. I glance at Lizzie, but she doesn't seem to be taking any notice. I strain my ears to see if I can make anything out, even though I have little chance of understanding it.

'I've finished. Would you like to see?' Lizzie asks as she carefully puts her pens back into the plastic wallet.

'I'd love to,' I tell her as she turns the page so I can see it. She's drawn me standing next to Jamie and, once again, I can clearly recognise enough of my features to know it's me. I'm just about to compliment her on capturing my likeness so well when we both hear Simone's raised voice from the kitchen.

'*Qu'est-ce que j'étais censée faire? Je n'aime même pas cette femme. Putain de merde, Jamie!*'

I may not know much French, but I know enough to realise that she's said she doesn't like me, and anyone who has looked up rude French words at secondary school would recognise the word *putain* and know it means 'prostitute' as well as *merde* meaning 'shit'. Given that she can't be talking about herself or her daughter, and that Jamie is also an unlikely candidate, that means those words can only be in reference to me as well. So much for her being anxious to make a good impression. This is even worse than I feared.

'I love it!' I say as enthusiastically as I can. The row in the kitchen seems to have blown over as quickly as it started as everything has fallen silent again, but the damage is done. Simone obviously hates me, and all my fears about being an unwelcome third wheel in their family dynamic have been proved to be correct. I can feel the tears pricking at the back of my eyes.

'Excuse me for a moment,' I say to Lizzie, who seems totally unperturbed by the whole episode. 'I'll be right back.'

Without waiting for a reply, I get up from the sofa and head for the kitchen. As I walk through the door and see Jamie and Simone pressed together with their arms wrapped tightly around each other, everything falls into place. Jamie may have described me as the icing on the cake of his life, but that's all I'll ever be, and that's not enough. If I'm only ever going to be the sideshow to the main act, Simone and Lizzie, what the hell am I doing? I need to get away. I can't play happy families and pretend everything is all right while my heart is breaking.

28

They break the embrace as soon as they see me, but it's too late.

'Are you OK? Do you need something?' Simone asks, her tone completely neutral, as if nothing is remotely amiss. At least Jamie has the grace to look a little uncomfortable. I can feel myself shutting down; all I want to do is get out of here as quickly as possible and keep it together until I'm in the safety of my own home.

'I just came to tell you that I'm off,' I say to them.

Jamie looks completely confused.

'I don't belong here, I see that. I'm leaving now, and I don't want you to follow me, do you understand? I need time alone.'

'Jess, wait!' Jamie calls, but I'm already closing the kitchen door. Lizzie is still sitting on the sofa, holding her drawing and I realise that, whoever her parents are, she doesn't deserve to be caught in the fallout. The argument appears to have started in the kitchen again, so I think I have a couple of moments to at least end things nicely with her.

'I'm really sorry, but I've got to go. It was lovely to meet you,' I tell her as warmly as I can manage.

'Will you come again?' she asks.

'I don't know. We'll have to see.'

'I hope you do. You're nice, and you make Daddy happy.' She holds out the drawing for me to take, and I give her a grateful smile as I fold it and put it in my bag before turning on my heel and slipping out of the front door.

As soon as I'm outside, I start to run. Thankfully, I've dressed down and I'm wearing a pair of trainers rather than heels, but it still doesn't take long before I'm gasping for breath. I know Jamie is going to follow me despite me telling him not to, so I need to get out of sight as quickly as I can. I don't have anything to say to him. I scan the road ahead furiously as I run, and my eyes land on the perfect hidey hole in a small parade of shops.

I've never been inside a betting shop before, but it's perfect. You can't see in from the outside, and it's the last place that Jamie would think of to look for me. I watch through the glass in the door and it's not long before the familiar shape of the Range Rover cruises past. I sigh with relief as it continues down the road, before I realise that my overnight bag is still inside. Sod it, it's just clothes and toiletries that can be replaced. I need to focus on me.

'Are you all right, love?' a voice behind me asks, and I turn to see a young man wearing a uniform with the name of the betting shop on it.

'Yes, absolutely,' I bluster as I glance round. There are half a dozen customers in the shop, and they're all looking at me.

'Were you looking to place a bet?' the man continues.

In addition to the silent TV screens showing various events, mainly horse races, there are posters on the wall advertising the odds for different events, and my eyes land on one.

'Yes.' I tell the man, trying to sound as If I know what I'm doing. 'I'd like to place a bet on that.' I point at the poster.

'You only get those odds if you predict the score correctly,' the man advises me.

'That's fine,' I reply. I just need to style this out for long enough to catch my breath, ensure Jamie is far away, and call a taxi to take me home.

'Over there,' the man tells me, pointing at a counter that looks rather like the ones you find in a bank, with the cashier protected by thick glass. She's an older woman, and she looks utterly bored.

'Help you?' she mutters.

'Yes, I'd like to put ten pounds on the Manchester United versus Chelsea game please.'

'Odds are four to six for a Man United win, seven to two for a Chelsea win, or three to one for a draw. If you want to get the odds on the poster, you have to predict the score correctly.'

'Fine. I predict Chelsea will win by two goals to one,' I tell her, trying to sound confident.

'Fat chance,' one of the other punters scoffs.

'What would you predict then, if you're such an expert?' I challenge him. The longer I find reason to stay in here, the more likely it is that Jamie will give up looking for me and I'll be able to make good my escape.

'Man United, one nil,' he replies, turning his attention back to one of the horse races.

'I'll go with him,' I tell the cashier, pushing across a ten-pound note. The cashier enters the details and hands me a slip.

'Bring that with you if you win,' she says brusquely. 'No slip, no payout.'

My phone starts ringing in my bag, earning me an irritated look from the other punters, so I hurriedly fish it out and decline the call. It was Jamie; of course it was. I switch it to silent and turn to the man who first spoke to me.

'Do you have the number of any local taxi firms?' I ask him. He points to a corkboard by the door, which has a load of business cards pinned to it, several of them advertising taxi firms. I select one

and dial, just as Jamie's Range Rover passes the door again, heading
in the other direction this time. The dispatcher tells me he has a car
in the area and it will be with me in a couple of minutes. I daren't
wait outside in case Jamie comes past again, so I hover by the door
until I see the cab pull up, and then make a dash for it.

* * *

By the time I get home, I have five missed calls from Jamie and two
voicemails, but I'm not ready to listen to them. The relief of getting
back to my flat combines with the shock of what happened earlier
and I collapse onto the sofa, letting the tears flow freely. My phone
vibrates periodically with more calls and messages, so I shut it in a
drawer where I can't hear it.

After a while, the tears start to subside, and I reflect on what I've
learned. Simone is obviously still in love with Jamie, of that I have
no doubt. If the way she took so violently against me isn't enough
on its own, the way she was looking at him, and the closeness of
that embrace fill in the rest of the blanks perfectly. They're obviously still a tight-knit family unit too, even if Jamie doesn't live
there. Simone has him wrapped around her little finger, and she's
not going to let that go for an interloper like me. The part that
doesn't add up is him. Unless he's a pathologically good liar, I still
can't believe he was telling me anything other than what he
thought was the truth when he explained their relationship to me.
It doesn't make any difference, though; I'm never going to be able to
compete for his attention with the mother of his child, and I don't
want to. I reach into my bag for a tissue, and my hand lands on the
folded drawing. I pull it out and study it, which only sets me off
again. I may only have met her briefly, but Lizzie is such a sweetie
and I hate the fact that I won't see her again when she obviously
had such high hopes for Jamie and me.

Eventually, I feel calm enough to do what I know needs to be done. I pour myself a large glass of wine and retrieve my phone from the drawer. There are now nine calls and four voicemail messages, which I delete without listening to them. I need a clear head for what I'm about to do, and listening to his explanations is just going to muddy the waters.

He answers on the first ring. 'Thank God,' he breathes. 'I've been so worried. Where are you? What happened?'

'I'm at home,' I tell him flatly.

'Why?' He actually sounds mildly irritated and my anger levels ramp up several notches.

'Because you're full of shit, Jamie. You said things were definitely, one hundred per cent over between you and Simone, but that's not true. She's never going to make room in your life for me, is she? Not properly, anyway. She might let me have the crumbs, but I need more than that, can't you see? Also, she's still in love with you.'

'What on earth gave you that impression?' he asks incredulously.

'Oh, just the little things. The way she was with you, the way she tore into me when you were in the kitchen, obviously thinking I wouldn't understand, the way I found you. Need I go on?'

'You've got it all wrong,' he says urgently. 'I can tell you're upset, but if you'd just let me explain—'

'I don't want to hear it. You need to talk to Simone because I'm done. Goodbye, Jamie.'

I disconnect the call before he can say anything else. The tears are falling again, and this time they're accompanied by ugly sobs. Before long, I'm curled on the sofa, an abject picture of snotty, shuddering misery.

29

I'm sitting in the dark, staring vacantly at a sitcom on the TV when the intercom buzzes. I've had a shower and I'm dressed in a soft hoodie and a pair of loose-fitting tracksuit bottoms and, although I've stopped crying for now, my face is puffy and blotchy. It's nearly nine at night, but I haven't eaten anything as my appetite has completely deserted me, understandably. The caller is bound to be Jamie, and he's the last person I want to see, so I shuffle over and lift the handset to tell him to go away. When I glance at the screen, however, I'm momentarily taken aback because the face I see is not Jamie's, but Simone's.

'What?' I ask coldly.

'Can I talk to you? Please?'

'Why?'

'Because Jamie told me what you said to him, and I think *tu as compris de travers*. What is the English phrase? Something about holding the wrong end of the log? Also, I have your bag.'

'Are you seriously suggesting I've got the wrong end of the stick?' I ask, unable to keep the incredulity out of my voice.

'Please, let me tell you some things that I think you might find helpful. If you still feel the same afterwards then fine, but I hope you will not.'

'I don't think there's anything you could say to make me change my mind. I don't even know why you're bothering, given what you said about me this afternoon.'

'I didn't say anything about you.' Even on the tiny screen, I can see the confusion on her face. She's a good actor, I'll give her that, but I'm not going to let her off the hook.

'You said you didn't like me. You called me a shitty prostitute.'

Her face goes blank for a minute, but her next reaction catches me completely by surprise. She laughs gently.

'I wasn't talking about you, I promise,' she assures me.

'Oh, come on. I may not know a lot of French, but I understand more than you obviously thought I would. I clearly heard the words *n'aime pas cette femme*, *putain*, and *merde*. Are you seriously telling me that they weren't directed at me?'

'I will tell you everything,' she replies. 'Can we do it face to face, though?'

There's no way I'm letting her into my flat, but I'm curious enough not to hang up. 'Fine. I'll come down,' I tell her.

The night air is cool and I notice she's shivering slightly when I open the door and step outside. My momentary pang of sympathy vanishes when I remember that she's turned up very much uninvited and unwelcome. So if she's uncomfortable as well, I'm perfectly happy with that. I'm less happy when she steps forward and takes my hands in hers.

'Jess,' she begins urgently, 'I know Jamie hurt you before, he told me what he did and I understand why you sometimes find it hard to trust him, but you should trust him when he tells you that there is nothing between him and me. You told him you think I am still in love with him, yes? I will be honest with you because I want us to be friends. The answer is *compliqué*.'

'I doubt that very much,' I reply sarcastically.

'*Ecoutez-moi bien* – listen to me,' she says, and I notice her grip on my hands has tightened to the point where I'd have to pull very hard to get away from her. 'I love him because he is a good man and he is Lizzie's father. I am not in love with him, though. I cannot give him the love he needs, which is why I am happy, really happy, that he has found that love with you. The way his face lights up and his voice softens when he talks about you; a man does not notice these things, but a woman does. He is in love with you, Jess, and I think you are in love with him also, *n'est-ce pas?*'

'I thought I was,' I tell her bitterly, 'but your antics this afternoon put paid to that.'

'I am going to tell you everything about Jamie and me, and then I hope you will understand. If not, then I will ask Jamie to leave you alone as you have said, OK? I meant it when I said I wanted us to be friends. I don't know you very well yet but you seem like a nice person.'

'You have a funny way of showing your approval of people if what I overheard is anything to go by,' I tell her.

She smiles. 'Let us start there then. You are right that prostitute is one translation of the word *putain*, but it is also a general swear word in French. *Putain de merde* is probably the equivalent of your English "fucking hell", and that's what I was saying. Nothing to do with you at all, honestly.'

'Really?' I ask dubiously.

'*Oui.* If you want to check, watch the TV series *Call my Agent*. I made Jamie watch it a while ago to help him with his French, and there is a lot of swearing in it, believe me. You will hear the word *putain* a lot, but they're not talking about prostitutes, I promise.'

'I'm not sure I'm up to watching French TV. I might recognise a few words, but that's all.'

'It has subtitles, although I didn't let Jamie use them when he watched it. The point is that we were not talking about you.'

'You also said you didn't like me. I'm pretty sure I got that bit right.'

'I said I didn't like Maisie's mother. Jamie and I were arguing because I was supposed to drop her at the party and leave her. It's part of me learning to let go of her a little; I think Jamie has told you about this?'

'Yes.'

'Maisie's mother invited me to stay at the party, and I didn't want to seem rude, so I did, even though I don't like her. Jamie was very cross, and that is what we were arguing about. That is what you heard.'

'Really?'

'*Oui.*'

'You said you were going to tell me everything about you and Jamie,' I prompt, eager to get away from my embarrassing misinterpretation now that Simone has explained it.

'I am. Did he tell you how we met?'

'He said you bought a car off him.'

'That is true, yes. I was working as an au pair for a family in Canterbury. Did he tell you why we split up?'

'He said you argued a lot when Lizzie was little, and it got to a point where you couldn't carry on.'

She smiles. 'He is a good man. He still tries to protect me. What he told you is true but there was more to it than that.'

I don't know what to say, so I just stare at her.

'He told you about Lizzie's birth, yes?'

'He said she was premature, and it was difficult.'

'English,' she says the word with disdain. 'Always making things sound less than they are. Lizzie was so premature that they told us it was unlikely she would survive, and I nearly died as well. That is more than just "difficult", *hein*?'

She waits for me to digest the information before continuing.

'Afterwards, the doctors told me they had had to give me an emergency operation, *une hystérectomie*, to save my life, and that I would not be able to have any more children.'

'I'm sorry, that must have been awful.'

'*Oui*. When they told me, I felt like I was no longer a woman, and I was obviously a bad mother as well because I couldn't protect my child and keep her safe inside me until the right time. When they took me down to see her, all I could see was this tiny thing and all these tubes. It was...' She shudders.

'I'm sorry.'

'It is OK. Lizzie, she got stronger, and I was so happy when we were allowed to take her home. But I couldn't leave her for even a minute because I was worried that something else would go wrong, that she would die if I wasn't watching her. I became more and more anxious. Even now...'

'Jamie said you had some issues.'

'*Oui*. I have been having therapy to try to help me with my anxiety and Maisie's birthday party was a test that I failed. I am improving, though. When Lizzie first started school, I would sit outside in the car for the whole day, just in case something went wrong and she needed me. After a week, the head teacher came out and told me that she was fine, she was making friends, and I needed to let her go. I cried all the way home, but now I can leave her at school and I even have a part-time job. Does this help you to understand how things are between Lizzie and me?'

'It does. Thank you.'

'So, I'm doing all of this for Lizzie, but I'm also feeling empty inside and I can't explain how I feel to Jamie. I can tell I'm hurting him, but I can't stop. The idea of sex, what is the point? All I could focus on was Lizzie. It was like Jamie no longer existed. I pushed him away and the more he tried to make things better, the angrier I got with him. It was such a relief when he moved out. You think I am a bad person now, *n'est-ce pas?*'

'No. I think you were depressed.'

'*Peut-être.* But Jamie, he is a good man. He is patient with me,' she smiles ruefully, 'most of the time at least.'

'So why are you so sure that you're not in love with him?'

'I will tell you something even Jamie does not know yet. I have met someone. Her name is Denise and, although it is very early, I have a good feeling.'

'Are you telling me you're gay now?' I ask, unable to hide my surprise.

She shrugs her shoulders. 'Gay, straight, these are just labels. Another thing you English seem to love. When I was in France, I dated both boys and girls. Nobody cared. Now that I am as I am,' she points at her midriff, 'dating men seems *inutile*, useless.'

'But you, Jamie and Lizzie are still a family, whatever happens. I felt like an intruder this afternoon.'

'Then that is my fault, and I am very sorry.'

'Be honest with me. How do you see this working?'

'We find our way, like everyone else. We all deserve to be happy. If I am happy with Denise, and you are happy with Jamie, then Lizzie will be very lucky, *non?*'

I can't think of anything more to say and silence descends as I digest everything she's told me. In a way, I'm coming to admire her. She's totally her own person and completely unapologetic for who she is. She must have run rings around poor Jamie.

'Does what I have told you make sense?' she asks after a while.

'It really does. I'm so sorry I flew off the handle earlier.' Simone looks puzzled and I realise that may be an idiom she hasn't learned yet.

'When someone gets upset and starts shouting, we say they have flown off the handle,' I explain.

'*Pourquoi?*'

'Do you know, I have no idea.'

'I would like us to be friends, you and I. Do you think that is possible?'

'I'd like that very much,' I reply, and I mean it.

'*Bon*. And what about Jamie? He is in love with you, and you need to tell him that you are in love with him. Why don't you put your bag inside and let me take you to him? You have much to talk about, *n'est-ce pas?* Come.'

'I can't go like this!' I exclaim.

'Pfft. He does not love you for how you look. He loves you for who you are. Also, I have left him looking after Lizzie.' She frowns for a moment and then smiles.

'What?' I ask her.

'Normally, I wouldn't be at all happy leaving Jamie on his own with Lizzie like that. But being here and talking with you, I haven't been anxious about her at all. Hm. Something to think about, *n'est-ce pas?*'

I decide to press my luck while she's buoyed up about her achievement. 'Simone,' I begin, 'have you seen the bedroom that Jamie has set up for Lizzie in his flat?'

'*Oui. C'est très jolie*. I hope very much that she will be able to stay there with him one day.'

'It would make him the happiest man alive, I think.'

'Then I will do my best, I promise. Thank you for understanding, Jess.'

'Thank you for sharing your story with me.'

'I think we both have homework, hm? I have to trust Jamie with Lizzie, and you have to trust him with all of your heart.'

'You have no idea how much I want that,' I tell her.

'Then we will do our homework together. Now come. Jamie is waiting.'

30

Any opportunity to plan what I'm going to say to Jamie is derailed by the death-defying ride to his flat. It may only be a ten-minute journey, but it feels like much longer as Simone happily carves up other motorists, making expressive gestures and using her horn liberally. She may be anxious where Lizzie is concerned, but she's a totally different creature behind the wheel. By the time we pull up outside his block, I'm a bundle of nerves and it has nothing to do with what I'm about to walk into.

Simone presses the button and the buzzer sounds almost immediately to let us in. Jamie is waiting at the door of his flat, chewing his bottom lip, and I realise for the first time how difficult this has been for him as well. Simone steps straight past him into the flat, leaving us alone and awkward.

'I'm so sorry,' I tell him. 'I thought...' My words dry up.

'I'm sorry too.'

This catches me by surprise. 'Why?' I ask.

'I made such a mess of everything, didn't I?'

'It wasn't you that stormed off,' I remind him.

'But it was me that made you storm off.'

'I misread the situation. I'm an idiot.'

'If anyone here is the idiot, it's me. Where did you go?'

'I hid in the betting shop to begin with. I had to place a bet.'

His lips turn up with the beginnings of a smile. 'What did you bet on?'

I fish the slip out of my purse and hand it to him.

'You're out of luck there, I'm afraid,' he says ruefully. 'Chelsea won two one.'

'How do you know?'

'I had the TV on to try to distract me, and the sports roundup program came on.'

'Jamie?' I ask anxiously.

'Yes?'

'Do you think we can fix this? I really am sorry. I know I've driven you mad with my trust issues, but I really want to put them behind me if you'll give me another chance.'

He smiles. 'I'd like nothing more.'

* * *

'Poor Simone, no wonder she has anxiety issues after what she went through,' I say to him some time later, after we've cried, talked and promised to both do better. Simone took a very sleepy Lizzie home a while ago, and Jamie and I are now cuddled up on his sofa.

'Now that you know the whole story, what did you make of them?'

'Simone's nice. She's just as you described her, actually. Lizzie is totally adorable, but then I hardly need to tell you that.'

He smiles. 'She was very taken with you too. She was already asking when you'd be coming round next while you were having your tête à tête with Simone. What did you do with the drawing?'

'It's at home. I'll stick it on the fridge.'

'Hm. I might have to ask her to do another for my fridge.' He smiles and I lean up to kiss him.

'So, you've met Simone and Lizzie,' he says a while later. 'Who do I have to persuade that I'm good enough for you?'

'Oh, nobody really. Just Alice, her husband Richard, their daughter Mia, my parents, my sister and her baby.'

'That doesn't sound like nobody to me. I'm starting to feel intimidated already. How many of them know about our first encounter?'

'Only Alice and Richard, but they're just pleased I'm happy so you don't need to worry about them. My parents are so delighted that I'm actually dating someone that they would probably adore you even if you had two heads.'

'Hm. That still leaves your sister and the baby.'

'She's fine. She'll be more interested in embarrassing me than interrogating you, and Henry doesn't speak yet, so as long as you can smile and gurgle at him, he'll love you.'

'And how long do I get to prepare for this examination?'

'When's your next Sunday off?'

'The weekend after next, the day after the track day.'

'That's when we'll do it then.'

He swallows exaggeratedly and widens his eyes in mock terror. I reach across and pat his thigh. 'They will all love you, I'm sure.'

'I hope so. Sorry to talk shop, but are you all set for the track day? Gerald will be on my case tomorrow.'

'Yes. I've had the package with the passes for me and Mike, along with directions on where to set up. The menu is all agreed and I'm under strict instructions only to serve people wearing green armbands with Jaguar Land-Rover on them. Anyone else is to be told politely to piss off, according to Gerald.'

'How did the discount negotiations go?'

'Swiftly. I told him he could have the same percentage as last time, or he could try to haggle for more and I'd charge him full price for his cheek. He loves me.'

'He certainly loves your food. I've heard him on the phone to a couple of our VIP customers, telling them about this amazing feast he's laid on.'

'We're having beef stew with dumplings, mashed potato and mixed vegetables; it's hardly the Ritz.'

'I don't know. A good beef stew is a thing of beauty and I can't even remember the last time I had a dumpling.'

'This will be a good beef stew, trust me.'

'What's for pudding?'

'Apple crumble and custard. Gerald's gone big on nursery food.'

'The customers will love it.'

'Is Ritchie Hart coming? I'm not sure it's the kind of food his girlfriend would approve of.'

'No. He has a chauffeur to drive him everywhere, so he's not at all interested in the off-road abilities of his car. Plus, he'd be a sitting duck for the paparazzi at a place like Brands Hatch. Do you want something to eat? All this talk of food is making me hungry.'

I realise that I'm actually starving too. 'I could rustle up a fish finger sandwich, if you happen to have the ingredients.'

He smiles. 'That sounds perfect.'

* * *

I may have been able to reassure Jamie that Alice and my family would all love him, but that doesn't stop me waking early on the Sunday morning that he's going to meet them all with a nervous flutter in the pit of my stomach. Very slowly, so as not to wake him, I roll over so we're facing each other. We haven't spent every night together since our bust-up, but I've become familiar enough with waking up next to him that I definitely feel his absence on the mornings when he's not there. His face is completely at peace, and it's all I can do to stop myself leaning in and waking him up with a kiss. His breathing is deep and even; he doesn't snore, but every so often he makes a gentle whiffling sound. I love watching him sleep.

'You're doing it again,' he murmurs quietly after a while.

'What?'

'Staring at me.'

'You're in my bed. It's allowed.'

'OK.'

'What do you think about, when you're staring at me like that?' he asks, a few minutes later. I don't know how he knows I'm staring at him, because his eyes are definitely still closed.

'Lots of things. I think about how happy you make me, or I ponder things you've said and conversations we've had. Sometimes I think very filthy thoughts and sometimes I think how amazing it is that we've ended up here from such an unpromising start.'

'Sounds tiring.' His eyes are still closed, but his mouth turns up in a gentle smile. 'The filthy thoughts sound fun though, I'd like to hear more about them.'

'I bet you would.'

He opens his eyes and looks into mine. Neither of us moves for what feels like an age.

'I love you, Jessica Thomas,' he says.

I'm not sure what I was expecting to happen when this moment came but I've been both looking forward to it and terrified of it at the same time. It's such a big thing to say to someone for the first time, isn't it? I've always thought it should feel like we were in a black and white movie, probably with me on a train that's just pulling out of the station, while he runs along the platform to keep up, shouting his declaration over the whistle of the steam engine and the swelling string music. A sleepy declaration in bed on a

Sunday morning is actually much better, although I can't put my finger on why.

'I love you too, Jamie Ferguson,' I tell him without hesitation as I snuggle into his arms and kiss him. As if on autopilot, his hands snake their way under my top, triggering a series of events that keep us in bed for a while longer.

* * *

'Hi, Jess. You must be Jamie. It's a pleasure to meet you at last,' Richard says as he opens the front door shortly after midday and ushers us inside.

'No golf today, Richard?' I ask him as we shed our coats in the hallway.

'Banned,' he tells us in a conspiratorial whisper. 'To quote my darling wife, "Jess bringing a boyfriend for lunch is way more important than dressing like a prat and knocking a little ball around".'

'I can hear you,' Alice tells him as she strides into the hallway. 'Welcome, Jamie. Jess, can I borrow you for a minute?' She grabs my hand and practically hauls me into her study, leaving Richard and a baffled-looking Jamie in the hallway.

'What's up?' I ask her as she closes the door.

'Is Jamie religious at all? I need to know.'

'Not that I know of, why?'

'I got myself in a panic this morning because we're having pork and I suddenly thought, what if Jamie is Jewish or something? You'd think I'd ask about dietary requirements automatically, given what we do for a living, but I completely forgot. I'm so sorry, Jess.'

'I'm pretty sure he's not Jewish or Muslim.'

'Only pretty sure?' She doesn't look reassured.

'I've seen his willy.'

'What's that got to do with – oh!' She laughs as she realises what I'm implying.

'Also, I can report that he happily troughed a bacon sandwich for breakfast.'

'Why didn't you just tell me that then, instead of going on about his willy?'

'To teach you a lesson. Don't you think I'd have warned you in advance if there was anything he didn't eat? You need to trust me.'

'Ha. Says the woman with a list of trust issues as long as my arm.'

'That's not fair. I had one trust issue, which was entirely justified and which I'm working on, thank you very much.'

'Fine. One whopping great trust issue which means you finally have your first boyfriend at the almost geriatric age of twenty-eight.'

'Yeah, well, said boyfriend is probably developing some trust issues of his own, wondering why you kidnapped me the moment we walked through the door. Shall we go back out, or is there anything else you need to know?'

'Nothing else, especially nothing anatomical. Thank you.'

'All OK?' Jamie whispers to me once I join him on one of the sofas in the sitting room. Normally I'd just perch on a stool in the kitchen, but it seems Alice is rolling out the red-carpet treatment for him.

'Yes. Alice just wanted to know whether you were circumcised.'

'What?' He sounds horrified.

I giggle. 'It's pork for lunch. She got herself in a tizzy because she realised she hadn't asked whether you ate it or not.'

Like Alice, it takes him a moment for the penny to drop. 'Ah, right.'

'Do you mind if I ask you a work-related question?' Richard says to Jamie as he hands us each a glass of sparkling water. 'I know you're off duty so I'll keep it brief.'

'Of course. What's up?'

'I was very taken with the Jaguar you lent Jess back in the summer. She took me for a ride in it; what a machine!'

'Did she let you have a go?' Jamie asks.

'Of course not!' I exclaim. 'I'd have had to sell my flat to pay for it if he'd had an accident.'

'The thing is,' Richard continues. 'I was wondering whether you ever got any second-hand ones in.'

'Interesting you should say that,' Jamie smiles. He may be off duty but he can't resist the whiff of a deal. 'The exact one Jess drove will be coming onto the forecourt next week. It was a demonstrator, so it's hardly got any miles on it, but we're offering it for a substantial saving on the list price. Is it something you'd be interested in?'

'It might be. I need to talk to my wife.'

'That's fine. No pressure, but it's bound to attract quite a bit of interest so you might want to move quickly if you're keen.'

'No time to waste then.' Richard practically runs in the direction of the kitchen and, although we can't make out the actual words, we can hear the burble of what sounds like a very animated conversation.

'You are a bad man,' I say to Jamie after a few minutes of listening to the enthusiasm in Richard's voice and the obvious reluctance in Alice's. 'I'm not going to introduce you to my friends if you're just going to use them as targets for your sales patter. What if she says no? He'll be crushed.'

'He started it,' he retorts. 'All I did was give him the facts.'

'Yes, but you couldn't help subtly turning up the heat, could you? It's probably in some sales person's manual somewhere: "You might want to move quickly, these are in high demand", or whatever it was you said.'

'It's true!'

'Yeah yeah.'

Our good-natured bickering is interrupted by Alice, who enters the room and closes the door softly behind her.

'Richard is practically salivating with desire in the kitchen and it's nothing to do with me,' she tells Jamie, not entirely approvingly. 'How much is this car?'

She flinches slightly when Jamie tells her the price, but I'm surprised to see that she doesn't immediately storm off to the kitchen to set Richard straight.

'Is that your best price?' she asks, fixing Jamie with a steely glare.

'I'm sure we could find a little bit of wiggle room, but there's not a huge margin in it.'

She sighs. 'Fine.'

'Are you saying you're going to let him buy it?' I ask, surprised.

'Yes. It's a ridiculous amount of money, but it will make him very happy and he assures me that we can just about afford it. I think he deserves a treat after all I've put him through with the business over the last ten years, don't you?'

'That's quite a treat,' I remark.

'Mm. I'm going to keep him dangling a little longer, just in case I can wrangle some new earrings or a handbag into the deal, so don't say anything just yet, OK?'

31

'I think Alice did rather better than the earrings or handbag, didn't she?' Jamie observes as we set off in the direction of my parents' house. 'You two are both fearsome hagglers, I'll give you that.'

The negotiations over lunch were good-natured and very entertaining to watch. Alice started off by demanding a two-week all-inclusive holiday in the Caribbean, flying in business class. Her argument was that, if they could afford the Jaguar for him, they could afford a holiday rather more exciting than a villa in France for her and Mia. Richard countered by saying that an upgrade to one part of their life didn't necessarily mean they could afford to upgrade everything, at which point Mia waded in with a point about collective benefit versus servicing one member of the family's midlife crisis, earning herself a high five from Alice.

In the end, they settled on one week flying premium economy, and Richard barely made it to the end of lunch before getting up from the table and disappearing into the study. By the time we left, he'd booked a departure to St Lucia on Boxing Day and paid a holding deposit to stop the dealership selling the Jaguar to anyone else before he got a chance to look at it, which he's going to do on Tuesday.

'Was Alice right when she called him a fool for paying a deposit upfront? Will your sales guys smell blood?'

'No. Lots of people pay deposits, particularly on cars like that. I meant what I said about there being a lot of interest, so we won't have any trouble selling it if he decides it's not for him.'

'I don't think he'll do that, do you?'

'No. Unless it breaks down on the test drive, which is pretty unlikely, I think he'll buy it. I'll make sure he gets it for a good price, don't worry.'

'I did wonder if Alice was going to demand to come too, as the voice of reason,' I tell him with a smile.

'I'd pay good money to watch that. Perhaps we should invite you two into the dealership one day as a training exercise for the sales staff.'

'Who was the guy that sold me my car?'

'Ian.'

'He loves me.'

'That's because I told him to give you the lowest price upfront, as you're aware. If I'd known what you were like back then, I'd have given him very different instructions and sold tickets to the show. Anyway, did I do OK? Did they like me, do you think?'

'Oh yes. Maybe try not to sell them anything else for a while, though.'

'And what about your family?'

'You're quite safe there. None of them can afford your stuff.'

'That's not what I meant. Talk me through them again. Your parents are Rosie and Jim, but you say they don't live on a canal boat like the puppets on the children's TV show.'

'And they won't thank you for making the joke either. I've lost count of the number of people who think they're the first to make the connection. It gets old really fast.'

'Any other taboo subjects?'

'Not really. My parents are fairly prudish, so no sex stuff.'

'Because I'm always banging on to people I've just met about sex,' he counters.

'I'm just telling you what you need to know. Molly is a school teacher, as is her husband, Paul. He probably won't be there. If you start Molly on anything to do with her work, she'll happily talk at you for hours. Mum will practically force feed you cake and Dad will probably fall asleep.'

I'm amused to see Jamie looking a little out of his comfort zone for the second time today as we park behind Molly's car on the road outside my parents' house.

'You'll be fine,' I reassure him. 'You've got the tough gig behind you. This will be a walk in the park.'

I'm still fishing in my bag for the key when the front door is flung open to reveal my mother, who has evidently dressed up for the occasion. Instead of her usual slacks and blouse, she's wearing a knee-length dress.

'There you are!' she exclaims as if she's been waiting all day for us, forcing me to double-check my watch.

'It's half-past three, Mum, which is when I said we would be arriving.'

'Of course it is. Come in, Jamie.'

'Thank you, Mrs Thomas,' Jamie replies as she practically shoos him into the house.

'Call me Rosie, please,' she twitters, and I swear I spot her batting her eyelashes at him.

'Come on in, Jess,' I mutter under my breath as I follow them, catching a whiff of my mother's perfume as I do.

'Jamie, this is Jessica's father, Jim,' my mother is explaining as I walk into the sitting room and notice that Dad has also been given a gentle makeover. Instead of his usual baggy blue jeans and a jumper, he's wearing smart black corduroys and a shirt.

'Pleased to meet you,' Dad says, hauling himself out of his chair, 'and congratulations on managing to catch my daughter's eye. We thought she would be single forever, didn't we, love?'

I turn to Molly, all prepared to share a conspiratorial eye roll, only to discover that Paul is with her.

'Hello, Paul. To what do we owe the pleasure of your company today?' I ask him.

'Wild horses wouldn't have kept me away,' he replies with a smile. 'When Molly told me that you were bringing your boyfriend to tea, I knew I had to be here for the occasion. What kind of super-powers would a man need, I wondered, in order to melt your frozen heart? Only one way to find out.'

I lower my voice so my mother can't hear. 'Paul?' I ask.

'Yes?'

'Fuck off.'

He laughs loudly, causing my mother to look at him sharply.

'What's so funny?' she asks.

'Paul is winding Jess up and she's swearing at him,' Molly informs her, delighted to dob me in as always.

'Don't swear, Jessica. It's coarse.'

'Yeah, stop fucking swearing, you dirty fishwife,' Molly whispers to me, causing me to snort with laughter.

'You'll have to get used to this, I'm afraid,' my father tells Jamie. 'They're always whispering and giggling. It's like they have some kind of secret language. I tune them out; it's for the best.'

It takes a bit of shuffling around and fetching of chairs from other rooms but eventually we all manage to sit down. Paul and Molly are on the sofa, with me perched on the arm, and Jamie is sitting next to me on one of the kitchen chairs. It's at this point that I realise someone is missing.

'Where's Henry?' I ask Molly.

'Paul's parents have got him for the afternoon. I thought it would be too stressful trying to manage him in a crowded room and give interrogating Jamie the focus it requires.'

'There will be no interrogation,' I tell her firmly.

'Spoilsport.' She leans forward to address Jamie. 'So, Jamie. Did you know my sister had a massive crush on you when you were at school? She used to practice signing with your surname and everything.'

'She has mentioned that she was attracted to me, yes,' he replies carefully. I think he's spotted that Molly is determined to make as much mischief as she can and is trying to avoid being drawn into a trap.

'Have some cake, you two. It's coffee and walnut.' It would seem that Mum is also trying to deflect Molly, and I shoot her a grateful look.

'Thank you, Rosie, that would be lovely,' Jamie replies.

'How's the sex?' Molly whispers to me while Mum and Jamie are occupied with the cake.

'Very nice. How's yours?' I reply.

'Good. I think I'll keep him.' She nods her head in the direction of Paul.

'What?' Paul asks, thinking her movement constitutes him being invited into the conversation.

'Nothing. I was just telling Jess how well you're looking after me.'

'I do my best,' he replies.

'I'm sure you do,' I tell him, causing Molly to giggle.

'Are we showing Jamie some embarrassing childhood pictures

of Jess from the family album?' she continues after a minute or so. 'There are some crackers, I can tell you,' she tells Jamie.

'Stop needling your sister, Molly,' Mum tells her.

'Aww, come on. I'm pretty sure you couldn't get the family albums out fast enough when I brought Paul home for the first time. There's that cute one of Jess in the paddling pool when she was three, for starters, or the one of her on the beach in Fuerteventura.'

'The one in the paddling pool is certainly not appropriate, Molly, as you well know.' Mum is looking irritated now. 'I'm sure there will be plenty of time for Jamie to look at the family albums another day.'

'Is it because Jess is naked in the paddling pool? I don't want to pop your balloon, Mum, but I rather suspect Jamie has already seen Jess naked, don't you?'

'Change the subject, Molly,' my father warns her firmly as poor Jamie flushes beetroot red.

'Fine. But, just so you know, I'm not doing anything she didn't do to me, OK?' She turns and grins at me. 'No hard feelings?'

'Absolutely none, but I will get you back, rest assured.' I smile sweetly at her while Mum apologises profusely to Jamie for our behaviour.

* * *

'That was quite an experience. Is your sister always like that?' Jamie asks once we're safely back in the car.

'You'll get used to her. She's competitive and she'll never miss an opportunity to get one over on me. To be fair, I did kind of deserve it.'

'Why?'

'You know the family album thing? When she brought Paul

home for the first time, I didn't even ask permission, I just brought it in and started showing him the most embarrassing pictures of her that I could find until Dad snatched it off me and tore me off a strip. I think she's been nursing that little grudge ever since. I got away lightly, really. I'm sorry if she embarrassed you, though.'

'Don't get me wrong, I liked her; I just think I'd be very careful what I told her.'

'The funny thing is that she's actually fiercely protective of me in lots of ways. Do you remember Suzanne Rees?'

'The psycho girl? Didn't she murder someone's cat and leave it on their doorstep because she wasn't invited to their birthday?'

'That was never proved, although I'm sure she did it. Anyway, I somehow made it onto her radar in year seven, and she decided to make my life hell.'

'Really?'

'Yeah, until Molly found out what she was doing. I don't know what she threatened her with, but she was suddenly sweetness and light to me.'

'Hm. I'd better make sure not to upset you then.'

'You better had!' I laugh. 'To be fair, most of her protective instincts are directed at Henry these days.'

'I couldn't get much of a read on her husband, Paul,' he observes after digesting what I've told him for a couple of minutes.

'I'm not sure how much there is to read there. He's a nice enough guy and they seem very happy together, but I think she probably runs rings round him.'

'I liked your parents.'

'My mother was particularly taken with you. How many slices of cake did you eat?'

'Two. What with Alice's lunch and your mother's cake, I don't think I'm going to need anything to eat this evening.'

'Really?' I try to sound disappointed. 'I thought I'd rustle up a seven-course tasting menu.'

'Ha ha. Today was fun though, thank you.'

'No, thank you for coming. I know it was a lot for you to deal with.'

'Hey, don't worry about me. I sold a car so I'm happy.'

'That you did,' I laugh. 'Luckily for you, I still love you, despite your predatory sales techniques.'

'And I still love you, despite your terrifying sister,' he retorts.

32

ONE YEAR LATER

'Hurry up or we'll miss the train!' Jamie calls up the stairs. 'What on earth is she doing up there?'

'*Elle est au toilette, Jamie. Attends quelques instants.*' Simone tells him as Denise hands over Lizzie's overnight bag.

'She is a very excited little girl,' Simone says to me. 'I don't think she slept more than a couple of hours last night.'

'How are you feeling?' I ask her.

'Like I am going to be sick.'

'We will take good care of her, I promise, and it's only two nights. You've done two nights before.'

'I know, but you're taking her out of the country. This is a big thing for me.'

'We'll phone you regularly so you can speak to her and we'll keep a close eye on her, especially in the park tomorrow.'

In the end, Lizzie never did stay in the room Jamie had prepared for her in his flat, but that was only because we moved into our new house nine months ago. Simone finally declared herself ready to let Lizzie stay the night a little over six months ago and she's been a regular visitor since. I am sympathetic to

Simone; our trip to Disneyland is seriously upping the ante for her.

Lizzie comes pounding down the stairs and practically hurls herself into Jamie's arms.

'Are you ready then?' he asks her gently.

'Yes. I can't wait to get there,' she replies.

'You might have to be a bit patient,' I tell her. 'Once we get through the Channel Tunnel, it's still over three hours of driving before we reach Paris.'

I can see her doing the maths in her head. 'That still means we'll be there just after lunchtime, so we'll be able to go into the park this afternoon.'

'Let's just hope the traffic gods are on our side,' I say to Simone and Denise. 'I don't think she'll be able to contain her disappointment if we get held up. Give your *maman* a hug, Lizzie, and then we'd better hit the road.'

Simone wraps her arms so tightly around her daughter that I briefly wonder if Lizzie is able to breathe, and I can't help noticing the wetness in Simone's eyes as she releases her.

'Have fun, Lizzie, and stay safe.'

'I'll be fine, *Maman*! I'll see you when we get back.' She clambers happily into the back of my car while Jamie adds her bag to our luggage in the boot.

'We've got drinks and snacks to keep her hydrated on the journey,' Jamie reassures a still fretting Simone.

'Don't let her go to the *toilette* on her own if you stop somewhere. You'll go with her, won't you, Jess?'

'I will. We won't let her out of our sight, I promise.'

Simone's face is a picture of misery as we pull away from the house and I'm very grateful that Denise is with her and Lizzie is too busy babbling about all the things she wants to do when we get there to turn and look out of the window.

When we get to the terminal and drive onto the train, she falls unexpectedly silent.

'Are you OK?' I ask her.

'Yes. I've never been on a train that you drive into before. Does it go underwater?'

'Kind of. We're going to go through a tunnel that's underneath the seabed.'

'Will we get wet?'

'I hope not!'

'And when we come out of the tunnel, we'll be in France?'

'Yup. You'll see, because we have to drive on the other side of the road and all the signs will be in French. Have you been to France before?'

'I've never been outside England before. *Maman* had to get me a passport specially. You have got my passport, haven't you?'

'Yes, your dad showed it to the official, do you remember?'

'Oh yes.' She falls silent again. When the train silently starts moving and the safety announcements begin, I can see her eyes widen.

'She's having the adventure of a lifetime,' I murmur to Jamie.

'If she's blown away by the train, imagine what she'll be like when we get there,' he replies.

In the end, it's nearly five o'clock by the time we've checked in to the hotel at Disneyland Paris, found something to eat and made our way to the park, but our timing couldn't have been better as we hit Main Street just as one of the parades is beginning. Lizzie is absolutely transfixed, and I take a picture of her on my phone and send it to Simone. We agree to leave the rides for our full day tomorrow, and concentrate on exploring the park and working out where everything is. Lizzie shouts with excitement every time she spots one of the Disney characters, and we manage to get pictures of her with most of them. The only dodgy moment comes when we go into the dragon's lair underneath Sleeping Beauty's castle and the dragon roars at her. For a moment, I wonder if she's going to burst into tears, but she merely tightens her grip on my hand and whispers, 'I think I'd like to go now.'

She brightens considerably as we walk through the main gate of the castle, but now Jamie is looking anxious.

'What's the matter?' I ask him quietly.

'Nothing, why?'

'You look like someone you know has just died.'

'No I don't! Why don't we climb up to the next floor? Apparently, there are some amazing views over the park from the balcony and we probably want to see them before it gets dark.'

We climb the stairs to the second level, which has a gallery with stained-glass windows depicting Sleeping Beauty's story in typical Disney style. Lizzie makes a big fuss of translating the French inscriptions for me but Jamie still seems a little disconnected. By the time we make our way out onto the balcony, he's looking like he might actually throw up.

'Something's definitely up with you. Spill,' I order him.

'I need to ask you something,' he whispers as Lizzie gazes in wonder at the view.

'Go on.'

'Will you marry me?'

'*What?*' I practically screech, causing Lizzie to jump and another tourist to look at us in concern.

'What's going on?' Lizzie asks.

'Your dad was just gave me a surprise, that's all,' I reassure her.

'Disneyland is the best place for surprises,' she replies, before turning back to look out at the park some more.

'Repeat what you just said,' I whisper to Jamie. 'I'm not sure I can have heard you right.'

'I asked if you would marry me,' he repeats.

'I did hear you right then,' I whisper back. 'Bloody hell, Jamie. You could have given me some warning at least!'

'How was I supposed to do that? "Hey, Jess, just to let you know, I might propose in the Disney castle"? Bit of a giveaway, don't you think?'

'Is that why you've been acting weird ever since we came in here? Was this your plan?'

He blushes. 'Yeah. I thought it would be romantic.'

'Hm. Proposing over a candlelit dinner in a fancy restaurant, that's romantic. Proposing in a tourist attraction while I'm clasping your daughter's hand?'

'It's the balcony of Sleeping Beauty's castle in the Magic Kingdom. That's got to be a solid nine out of ten on the romance scale,' he protests, just as an adolescent boy passes us and farts loudly.

'Well, that is truly magical,' I reply, bursting into hysterical giggles. Poor Jamie just looks crestfallen and my heart goes out to him.

'It was a lovely idea, really,' I tell him once my laughter has subsided.

'You haven't given me an answer, though. I assume you're trying to let me down gently. It's OK—'

'Oh do shut up!' I exclaim. 'Of course I'll marry you.'

'You can't get married!' Lizzie exclaims, a look of horror on her face.

'Why not?'

'Because you haven't done it properly. Daddy has to go down on one knee and he has to give you a beautiful ring. Everyone knows that.'

'I haven't brought a ring,' Jamie tells her. 'I thought Jess and I could choose one together when we got back to England if she said yes.'

'Then you have to have a sweetie ring.'

'A what?'

'Come on.' She leads us down and out of the castle to the candy palace on Main Street. After some searching, she finds what she's looking for, which turns out to be jelly sweets in the shape of rings.

'Buy those and give one to Jess,' she orders.

'Yes, ma'am!' Jamie laughs. Once he's paid and we're back out on the street, he opens the package and hands me one of the rings.

'No, Daddy! On one knee!'

'It will be your fault if I get trampled,' he complains, but obeys, sinking to one knee. A few other tourists notice and stop to watch.

'Jess, would you do me the great honour of consenting to be my wife?' he asks, making Lizzie giggle at his sudden formality.

'Nothing would make me happier,' I tell him.

'Please accept this gummy ring, which my daughter has chosen to mark our betrothal.' He gently pushes the ring onto my finger, and the small crowd that has now gathered bursts into spontaneous applause as I bend to kiss him before helping him back to his feet.

'Is that better?' he asks Lizzie once the other tourists have decided this particular sideshow is over and moved on.

'Much. Well done, Daddy.' She leans over to me and whispers conspiratorially, 'If you change your mind, you can just eat the ring.'

Any reply I might have had is drowned out by the announcement of the Disney Illuminations, and we hurry to secure our spot for the display. The narration is a little cheesy for me, but there's no doubting the quality of the light and firework display. Every so often, Jamie and I catch each other's eyes and grin stupidly.

'Did you really practise signing your name "Jessica Ferguson"?' he murmurs in my ear at one point.

'Why?'

'Just checking you're prepared, that's all.'

'Patriarchal bastard!' I hiss, keeping my voice down so Lizzie can't hear. 'Who says I'm taking your surname?'

'Hey, no pressure from me, I'm a modern man. I'd just hate all that practice to go to waste.'

I glance down at the sweetie ring on my finger and grin. This is one sweetie I definitely won't be eating, I decide as I think back to my sheets and sheets of teenage doodles. Jessica Ferguson. I like the sound of that. I like it a lot.

ACKNOWLEDGMENTS

Thank you so much for reading this book. As always, I need to say a massive thank you to the Boldwood team, who do so much to turn my scrappy manuscripts into a finished book. Due to a few changes in the team structure, I've been lucky enough to have two editors work on this story. Tara, as always, thank you for your patience and good humour. I wish you all the best in your future endeavours. Thank you also to Rachel, who has had to pick this up mid-edit. Not an easy task, but I've really valued your input and the story is definitely better for it. Thank you also to Emily for your copy editing, and Shirley for proofreading. Of course, getting the story as good as it can be is just the beginning, and I want to say thank you also to Amanda, Nia, Jenna and all the team for the incredible work you do connecting my books with readers.

As always, I've had to rely on friends where my knowledge is lacking. Thank you Richard, for your insight into the inner workings of a car dealership. Xavier, thank you for your help with the French and thank you also to Lisa for answering the Disney related questions. Mandy and Robyn, thank you both for your alpha and beta reading, especially Robyn who has had to fit it in around looking after her baby girl. Thank you as always to my family for being so supportive, and to Bertie for giving me that all important dog walk space to plot.

ABOUT THE AUTHOR

Phoebe MacLeod is the author of several popular romantic comedies. She lives in Kent with her partner, grown up children and disobedient dog. Her love for her home county is apparent in her books, which have either been set in Kent or have a Kentish connection.

Sign up to Phoebe MacLeod's mailing list here for news, competitions and updates on future books.

Follow Phoebe on social media:

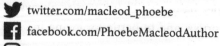

twitter.com/macleod_phoebe
facebook.com/PhoebeMacleodAuthor
instagram.com/phoebemacleod21

ALSO BY PHOEBE MACLEOD

Someone Else's Honeymoon

Not The Man I Thought He Was

Fred and Breakfast

Let's Not Be Friends

An (Un)Romantic Comedy

Love at First Site

Never Ever Getting Back Together

Boldwœd

Boldwood Books is an award-winning fiction publishing company seeking out the best stories from around the world.

Find out more at www.boldwoodbooks.com

Join our reader community for brilliant books, competitions and offers!

Follow us
@BoldwoodBooks
@TheBoldBookClub

Sign up to our weekly deals newsletter

https://bit.ly/BoldwoodBNewsletter